Best Wishes to

Hannah Newell

2018

Carroll Williams

# THOUGHT VOYAGERS

## The Journey Begins

**A Science Fiction Novel**

**by**

**Carroll Williams**

# Thought Voyagers

## The Journey Begins

### A Science Fiction Novel



For information contact Carroll Williams
Email: authorcarrollwilliams@gmail.com

Available for Kindle and E-Readers at Amazon.com
Available in print from Amazon.com

ISBN-13: 978-1512056792

ISBN-10: 1512056790

# DEDICATION

*This book is dedicated to my wife*
*Mary Lee Carter Williams*
*who has been my travel companion*
*on the Highways and Byways of Life*
*for the better part of seven decades*
*and who still shares with me*
*the excitement of the journey.*
*June 20, 2015*

## Acknowledgements

**Whitney V. Shoup**, my best friend from high school days read my short story entitled ***A Chip on His Shoulder*** and encouraged me to expand the theme into a full-length novel. My good friend and neighbor **John Lambert** listened to my idea for this novel over coffee and encouraged me to start writing. I want to recognize my friends at **Conway Creative Writers** who patiently listened to each chapter and offered ideas for improvement. My good friend and colleague **Masina Lane** of Quitman, Georgia performed invaluable editing services while reading an early draft. For this I am extremely grateful. I would also like to recognize my many friends and fellow writers at **Scribblers of Brevard**, a writer's club on the Space Coast of Florida. I fondly remember their encouragement and friendship. Last but not least I want to thank my wife **Mary Lee Williams** for listening to my ideas as they occurred to me. **Thanks to all of you. I really appreciate your contributions.**

# TABLE OF CONTENTS

# Introduction

This story is essentially about the human brain and human thought. For the first million or so years people expressed thoughts in words spoken to a listener. Around forty-thousand years ago thoughts were recorded in cave paintings. About five thousand years ago cuneiform symbols were pressed into clay tablets in Mesopotamia, and in Egypt inks and dyes recorded human thought on papyrus. For the first time in human history, writing gave rise to a powerful elite. Kings, Pharaohs, and Priests possessed recorded information and used it to wield enormous power over their people.

Knowledge spread among the ruling classes of the world. Knowledge percolated downward to common people in hand-copied manuscripts. Reading and writing spread very slowly until Johannes Gutenberg introduced movable type printing in 1439. His invention brought about a knowledge revolution.

For countless centuries human thoughts were shared entirely in some form of writing or printing. Letter writing was the standard means of communication. Letters were sent across miles and across the oceans taking weeks and sometimes months to reach their destination.

Sharing thoughts and images electronically over vast distances is a relatively new phenomenon and has only been possible for an incredibly short span of human existence. It was just 171 years ago that the very first primitive electric communication took place between Washington and Baltimore by way of audible clicks on Mr. Morse's invention, the telegraph.

The telegraph was totally revolutionary but was limited in many ways. It depended upon wires strung across the miles. An operator used Morse code, a system of clicks representing letters and numbers. While hearing the clicks, an operator receiving a message wrote down a translation and sent it by courier to the person for whom it was intended.

In 1876 Alexander Graham Bell invented the telephone giving rise to direct voice communication over a wire. It was up to others including Guglielmo Marconi, an Italian inventor, to introduce the world to wireless electronic communication. Marconi showed the world in 1897 that we can send messages through the air. A rapid series of discoveries and inventions including radio, television, radar, microwaves, and satellites brought the world to where we are now with instant long-distance communication of human thought racing through the air and into space beyond.

Today we use video conferencing to speak face-to-face with friends half way around the world. I connect my smart phone to a fifty-inch plasma television and see my friend displayed in front of me larger than life. Our thoughts and images fly up to a satellite in space and bounce around the world in a microsecond.

The Internet connects the world in a way undreamed of only a few decades ago. Think of the Internet as a globe girdling system of nerves connecting every human who cares to log on. It is now possible to share our innermost thoughts with almost anyone in the entire world. Some thought sharing is voluntary and hopefully we may be able to keep it that way. Digital recording technology makes possible the storage and retrieval of human thought in almost unimaginable quantities. Modern technology makes possible sharing our thoughts across the galaxy and across the centuries.

How many of our private thoughts are we willing to share in order to enjoy the positive attributes of modern electronic technology? One wonders just what limits exist in the collection, retention, and utilization of human thought public or private. I'm sure we will find out soon enough. Today we live in a world rapidly developing practical applications from ideas which only existed in the brains of science fiction writers in the not-very-distant past.

This story begins with the premise that today's technology can and likely will evolve into amazing reality in the not-so-distant future. Technical applications which exist today include all sorts of detection and tracking devices. This story starts with a fictional company, GMH Technology, manufacturing and selling a line of RFID chips for business and industry. RFID stands for Radio Frequency Identification. The RFID chip isn't new technology by any means, but only in the past few decades has it come into wide use.

Today's RFID chips are used by manufacturing firms

and retail stores all across the globe. These inexpensive little electronic chips are placed in merchandise packaging, on load pallets, and even on trucks and on cargo containers. A short range combination radio transmitter and receiver is placed in a location a tagged item must pass through.

An RFID chip is queried and responds with data that says things like, *"Here I am, I'm a 70 inch plasma TV and I'm headed out the door. If the customer didn't pay for me, then you better catch me if you can."* Well not quite that simple perhaps, but it amounts to the same thing and it cuts down on losses to stores, warehouses, and factories. Another version of an RFID chip is inserted into the shoulder of the family pet to help recover dogs and cats if they go astray.

Current robotics research and development is proceeding apace in a number of universities and labs. In Sweden doctors recently bolted an artificial robotic arm directly to the bone in the stump of a man's severed arm and fused his nerves directly into the artificial limb's electronic circuits. At Johns Hopkins Applied Physics Lab a man whose arms were missing at the shoulders is now controlling a set of robotic arms with his brain waves. For all practical purposes these men and others in similar circumstances are Cyborgs, part human, part machine. They control machines with their thoughts.

Medical practice today seems light years ahead of where it was even twenty years ago. Today many thousands of people are kept alive and functioning because they either wear or have implanted devices which were not even thought of until recent decades.

In this story, the company's fortunes and the fate of the world change rapidly as the CEO and owner, Gordon Michael Hollister, hires three brilliant young scientists to head his Research and Development efforts. Nothing will remain even remotely the same when 'the whiz kids' as Gordon calls them, come to work at GMH Technology. This team of brilliant young scientists along with the owner's two adventurous and brilliant children push the frontier of what is possible into realms we can only imagine.

So let the journey begin.

## DISCLAIMER

Any resemblance to persons living or dead is purely coincidental. Some locations are real, and others are fictitious. All action attributed to any location is purely fictional.

# CHAPTER 1

## A SEISMIC SHIFT

Gordon Michael Hollister will attend a staff meeting today which will bring about a seismic change, not only in his life and the lives of his family, but quite possibly in the lives of everyone living on planet earth. When he hired Chun Li, Oren Lunsford, and David Goldstein, to lead the Research and Development team at GMH Technology, Gordon had no idea it would lead to applications beyond his wildest imagination. He doesn't realize it now, but soon a genie will be out of the bottle and there will be no putting it back.

Gordon Hollister is a fifty year old entrepreneur who founded GMH Technology using the proceeds from his father's life insurance policy. It was the only asset left from the estate of his father who lost almost everything in a series of bad stock transactions. Gordon is determined to give his wife Patricia and their kids Mike Jr. and Maria a better life financially than he experienced while growing up. He was fortunate to be able to graduate with a business degree from a well-respected university after serving in the U.S. Air Force for four years as an electronic technician.

Chun Li, the head of Research and Development is a thirty-two year old Chinese woman with a graduate degree in applied physics and bio-medicine. She grew up in San Francisco and is the daughter of a Chinese-American mother and a father from the People's Republic of China. Chun Li majored in bio-medical research, and attended graduate school at a prestigious university where she developed thought-controlled electrically driven robotic prostheses for amputees. Chun Li recently returned from a year-long fellowship at CNRI, the Chinese Neurological Research Institute near Guangzhou, China.

Oren Lunsford is a twenty-eight year old young man from Utah with a doctoral degree in computer chip design. In graduate school, Oren developed methods for the miniaturization of central processors and related chips. He pioneered in data compression and in new ways to manufacture integrated and complex digital processors.

David Goldstein is a fun-loving thirty-two year old who grew up surfing the waves along South Florida's beaches. David earned his bachelor's degree in molecular engineering and his doctorate in chemistry and applied nano technology. David is currently investigating ways to literally grow microprocessors and nano machines from chemical soup in the laboratory.

These three brilliant young scientists are team players. Working together they added hundreds of new patents to the company's long list of intellectual property. When he considers their contributions to the company, Gordon Hollister realizes that the sum of the whole is far greater than the individual parts. He affectionately dubbed these three young people 'the whiz kids.'

Since coming to GMH Technology, these three brilliant young minds have been responsible for expanding the company's product line exponentially. GMH Technology previously manufactured and sold several lines of RFID chips for tracking inventory from manufacturing to final retail sales and for finding lost pets. For years these chips supplied the firm's primary income stream, but Gordon Hollister realized that the older product line was getting crowded and profit margins were growing thin as many other firms entered the field. This is why the company's new line of monitoring and tracking chips so appealed to him when his 'whiz kids' introduced him to their way of thinking about new products.

Led by his R&D team GMH Technology became the sole supplier in the field of personal identification chips. These are chips which are very small, so small that they are inserted through a needle into a person's body with virtually no pain. Each chip holds an enormous amount of data.

Digital information is stored in data sectors within the chip. A personal ID chip may hold a person's birth certificate, driver's license, passport, voter registration, educational records, employment history, bank account, credit cards, insurance policies, and total medical history. Information in each sector may only be accessed and updated on a need-to-know basis by a government agency or private entity with a legal data scanner and a legal right to do so.

Congress passed and the president signed a law requiring

that every American citizen be equipped with a personal ID chip within the next decade. It is for the safety and security of not only the individual, but also for the nation. The United Nations adopted a resolution urging all nations to employ the personal ID chip as a way of controlling population movements and suppressing violent extremism around the globe. The UN urged member nations to comply with the resolution within a decade.

In addition to dominating the emerging personal ID chip market, GMH Technology holds a virtual monopoly in special medical monitoring chips and devices. The firm has a line of applications which measure and monitor everything from a patient's vital signs to the patient's exact location. If a patient's situation becomes critical and requires medical intervention, GMH Technology's Mark 3 chip summons immediate assistance. It is no longer necessary for a patient to call for help. The patient's own body makes the call from an implanted device and delivers all relevant medical information to responding personnel through a discrete cell phone application.

Gordon's own mother received a GMH Mark 3 chip implant after suffering a series of mini-strokes. Later her life was spared when the system worked as designed. The chip sensed a dangerous spike in blood pressure while she lay asleep. It not only called emergency responders, but led them to her exact location and gave them a complete list of symptoms before they arrived. David and Oren included among other things in the design of the Mark 3 chip, a GPS feature which shows the patient's location down to one meter, or about three feet. Rapid intervention stabilized his mother's blood pressure and may have prevented premature death or disability from a potential cerebral hemorrhage, or bleeding of the brain.

Gordon remembered how his maternal grandmother died at age fifty-nine when she suffered a cerebral hemorrhage following a high blood pressure spike. Gordon thought, *how different from the past. How far we've come in saving people's lives and preserving their health into what once was considered old age.*

The conference room at GMH Technology is situated directly behind Gordon's office. It is equipped with a large coffee maker and a fully stocked cupboard with snacks, a refrigerator and a microwave. Gordon believes it is important to fuel the minds and bodies of creative people. This morning's meeting was called for nine o'clock.

Chun Li, Oren Lunsford, and David Goldstein entered right on time. As they came through the door they were noisily arguing about how to add a host of new features to the Mark 3 medical chip.

Chun Li opened the meeting. "Mr. Hollister, we are using a modified Mark 3 chip as a test vehicle to prove a theory of universal language and comprehension. Brain waves appear to be universal in humans and animals. We are able to read and decode brain waves from both animals and humans using the same computer algorithm. During my year in China I discovered that brain waves can be detected throughout the body, not just from electrodes attached to the skin as we did in the development of thought-controlled prostheses back in graduate school. What we've done in the lab here is to add brain wave detection to the otherwise long list of capabilities already in the Mark 3 medical chip."

Gordon looked at the group quizzically, "How have you proven this theory?"

Oren spoke up, "We designed a new version of the Mark 3 chip with ultra-sensitivity to brain waves. It reads the thoughts of an animal or human, codes those thoughts into digital format and passes those thoughts through our algorithm and displays output in the form of text on a cell phone. We developed an encrypted cell phone app which performs all of the steps."

Chun Li interjected, "We believe that human speech is an artificial development and that language is actually universal. Different sounds and gestures represent exactly the same thoughts among all peoples or animals. We believe that all ideas are born in the brain in the form of feelings, or emotions produced by various stimuli. These emotions are translated in the brains of humans and animals into a form of shared audible sounds or words. These sounds are recognized within an ethnic or tribal group among humans. Among animals common sounds are recognized by members of a species, a pack or family group. We have already detected brain waves from our own feelings and emotions in our lab tests. We are able to translate animal and human brain waves into understandable speech patterns and present them in almost any human language and send the results to our cell phone app in the form of text."

David spoke up, "Oren and I wrote a computer algorithm which translates captured thoughts into virtually any human language known. We took turns testing it in the lab. We taped a modified Mark 3 chip to our necks and took turns reading each other's thoughts. We achieved ninety-nine percent accuracy in detection and ninety-eight percent accuracy in translation. Since Chun Li often thinks in Chinese, she volunteered to test the system's translation accuracy into English."

Chun Li spoke up, "For today's field trial we are using Oren's chocolate Lab named Murphy. He is a very well trained dog. The vet inserted into his shoulder a modified Mark 3 chip which is even smaller than the current line of pet chips we produce. What do you think?"

Gordon was always astonished at developments flowing from his group of young scientists. "When do you want to begin?"

Chun Li smiled, "This afternoon at 1 p.m. sir."

Gordon gave the group a knowing look. "Go to it then. Let me know if I can do anything to expedite your work."

After lunch Gordon got a call from Chun Li.

"Sir we are ready to test the new modified Mark 3 chip

in the field behind the parking lot. If you would like to observe Murphy going through some field tests we'll begin in about ten minutes."

Gordon walked out through the parking lot and about fifty yards further to a patch of grass. The area is fenced on three sides and hidden from the street on the fourth side by the main building housing GMH Technology.

Oren Lunsford was playfully teasing his dog Murphy. David stood by with his modified cell phone in hand to receive any signals from Murphy's newly implanted modified Mark 3 medical chip. If any decipherable signals are picked up they will be transmitted from the modified medical chip directly to David's cell phone. They will also be picked up by the company's wireless network and relayed to a cloud server and preserved for posterity. Translated text output will appear on the cell phone screen for immediate viewing.

Gordon stood by and watched as three brilliant young people began what would ultimately produce a major shift in our understanding of human and animal brain activity.

David looked down at his cell phone. "It's working.....it's working. Murphy is excited. He says, "throw the ball...throw the ball....throw the ball."

Oren tossed a yellow tennis ball about fifty feet from the group. Murphy dashed out and retrieved it.

David excitedly read Murphy's translated text from the cell phone, "I'll get it....I'll get it.........I'll get it...........I got it....... I got it...... I got it."

Murphy dashed back to Oren and dropped the ball at his feet and continued his thought transmission, "Throw it again....throw it again....throw it again."

Murphy stood panting beside Oren who let him catch his breath for a moment.

Oren teased Murphy by pretending to throw the ball and holding onto it instead. Murphy's text transmission came through unequivocally.

"Throw the ball, don't hold onto it. Quit being a jerk and throw the ball. Throw the ball and stop teasing me. O.K. you do that one more time and I'll quit playing." Murphy lowered his head onto is front paws. His thoughts continued flowing. "Go ahead.....throw the ball. There....I'll get it.....I'll get it."

Oren and Murphy played throw and retrieve for the next ten minutes. The group enjoyed the fresh air, the camaraderie and the companionship of a truly intelligent four-footed fellow traveler on planet earth.

Gordon suggested that they wrap up the test and return to the conference room to discuss what they experienced this afternoon.

Back inside Gordon looked around at the three and spoke with almost an air of disbelief in what had just transpired.

"O.K. guys, are you sure you're not just pulling my leg a bit with a talking dog trick?"

David laid his modified cell phone on the table in front of Gordon and said, "Take a look at what Murphy is thinking right now."

Murphy lay motionless at Oren's feet, eyes half closed with a look of contentment. The dog's thoughts flowed continuously as text on the screen. "Where is she? Where is that other Lab I met at the dog park? She was one of the finest females I ever encountered, and what an encounter it was. I hope we go back to the same park soon. I miss her, oh I miss her."

Suddenly Murphy sat bolt upright and barked. Murphy's text continued to flow on screen. "There's another dog out there, I know it, I know it. I marked my territory in the parking lot, but there is another dog out there right now challenging my territory. Let me out....let me out....Let me out." With that Murphy lunged toward the door and gave a low growl followed by two quick barks.

Oren said, "Well, let's see if Murphy is right." He pointed to the wall-mounted security monitor facing the group. There in the parking lot was Gordon's Secretary Margaret getting into her car. She was accompanied by Scout, her German shepherd, a dog which was a frequent visitor to the plant. Scout violated Murphy's territory by marking a lamp post at the end of the walkway.

Murphy growled toward the door as his text flow continued. "Scout I'll never forgive you for this. If I get outside you're toast."

Gordon was totally amazed at this turn of events. He no longer had any doubts about what he just witnessed. He looked at the group and spoke slowly and deliberately.

"I have to confess I am always amazed at you three. What you come up with. What you have shown is possible today. I hope you all grasp the significance and the scope of what happened here this afternoon. The knowledge which we now possess can be harnessed for good or evil depending upon who applies it and for what purpose."

Gordon paused, studied their faces, and continued, "Please, don't discuss these developments with anyone outside of this group. Let's spend some time trying to understand the implications of your discovery. I can't tell you how proud I am of each of you. The way you constantly come up with new and brilliant ideas. Now, have a great evening and I'll see you in the morning."

On his way home Gordon thought, did *I really see history made this afternoon with a dog communicating thought to humans in the form of deciphered text? This could usher in a whole new level of understanding the thought process. Where do we go from here?*

## CHAPTER 2

## BEST LAID PLANS

Gordon watched his kids noisily exit the townhouse and head off to class at their local high school. It seems like just yesterday they were in kindergarten. His son Mike is a junior and his daughter Maria is a sophomore. Gordon is so deeply involved in the day-to-day operations of GMH Technology, the company he founded on a shoestring a decade earlier, that he pays little attention to his family. He suddenly feels guilty that he isn't around to attend his kids' school events.

Gordon turned to his wife Patricia and asked, "How are the kids doing in school? I'm afraid I've been too immersed in the company to know what's going on in their young lives."

Patricia smiled across the breakfast table and responded, "Well, I'm glad you asked. It's a relief to know you care. If you find the time we all need to do some things together and get you away from the rat race for a while."

Gordon thought to himself, *I have to get to know my kids before they grow up and leave home. I really need to spend more time with the family.* He downed his second cup of coffee, kissed his wife and made his way to the carport.

This morning was no different than any other in South Florida's humid climate. Gordon picked up the garden hose which lay beside his white Mercedes and sprayed the windshield and windows of his car. The brisk stream of water washed away the heavy nightly dew clinging to every square inch of the car including the head lights and tail lights.

On the drive in to work this morning Gordon began thinking about how he could spend more time with his kids. *Perhaps he could get the kids to come to the plant and spend time in the lab with the R&D Team of Chun Li, Oren Lunsford, and David Goldstein.* His kids could learn a lot from these three brilliant people, and in the process they could learn some responsibility and even earn a paycheck. *What the heck*, he thought, *if it works out I'll get to see more of my kids, and they will learn more than they ever imagined they could in high school.*

At the morning conference Gordon brought up the idea to Chun Li, Oren, and David. They were eager to meet the kids and get to know them. Until this morning the only views they ever had of Gordon's family were a few small photos on a shelf above his desk in his office.

Oren Lunsford asked, "What level of science and math have your kids completed?"

Gordon confessed, "I'm sorry to say that I have been so busy with work here at the plant that I have no idea, but I will find out and let you know."

Chun Li smiled, "Mr. Hollister, we will take care to advance your children as far as they are capable in math, science, and information technology. Trust us, we will be good teachers."

Gordon's secretary Margaret Wilson stepped into the conference room. "Mr. Hollister I hate to disturb you but there is a Mr. Harold Cunningham here to see you. He is in the outer office. Will you have time to see him?"

Gordon stood up and adjourned the morning conference. "Well I'll see you all tomorrow at nine. Hope all is going well with your modifications to the Mark 3 medical chip."

As Gordon stepped into the outer office a tall slender man stood up and extended his hand to greet him. "Good morning Mr. Hollister, I am Harold Cunningham from the Internal Revenue Service. I am here to initiate a total audit of your firm."

Gordon shook his hand. "We were audited not more than two years ago. What brings this about?"

"Mr. Hollister, your firm has generated an enormous amount of revenue since your last audit. The service simply wants to make sure that GMH Technology is abiding by the current tax code. So many firms have failed to keep up with the ever-changing requirements of the IRS code."

Gordon assured him, "Mr. Cunningham, your people will have the full cooperation of our staff. My secretary will introduce you to the people in the accounting department. And yes, I agree, it is virtually impossible for any firm doing business in this country to keep up with the, as you put it, ever-changing tax code. If you bureaucrats had to earn a living in the private sector you might come to appreciate just how difficult your tax code can be to navigate. Sir, I hope this hasn't anything to do with my political affiliation and past political contributions."

Harold Cunningham narrowed his gaze and looked over the frames of his glasses, "Mr. Hollister, the IRS never considers political alignment when we decide who will be audited. You seem to have a negative attitude toward your nation's taxing authority. I hope you won't make this audit more difficult than it has to be for our people. I wouldn't like to think you are hostile to the IRS. That can sometimes cause unintended consequences if you understand me sir."

Gordon quickly ended the conversation. "Mr. Cunningham, you will have our full cooperation and we will complete our work in a timely manner. Count on it." With that he excused himself and returned to his office.

*The nerve of that guy threatening me that way. Well, what else would you expect from the IRS,* he thought? *Must forget it and get on with more productive endeavors.* Little did he realize that anything but productivity was about to dominate almost all activity at GMH Technology while the IRS audit was in progress.

At dinner that evening, Gordon opened the conversation with his family. "Mike and Maria I've been thinking you two have some school activities coming up soon. Why don't you tell me about them?"

Mike spoke up, "Dad I'm playing basketball against our

arch rival next Friday evening. Would you like to come to the game?"

Without hesitation, Gordon responded, "Son I'd love to see you play. I'll be there."

He turned to Maria, "Sis don't you have a band concert sometime soon?"

Maria looked at her dad incredulously. "What have you done with my real dad? Surely this isn't my dad asking about our concert."

Gordon's wife Patricia chimed in, "Honey tell your dad about your concert and invite him to attend. He is making an effort to connect with all of us, so help him out here."

Maria grinned, "O.K. if you really want to know, our band is playing at the opening of a new shopping mall on Saturday. We're performing some jazz and some traditional band pieces like marches and stuff."

Gordon smiled at his daughter, "It will be great for me to hear you play. I played in a high school band. I was a snare drummer. I couldn't carry a tune so the rhythm of drums were my natural outlet when it came to music. Count on me. I will be at the mall when you play. I'm looking forward to it."

"Before I forget it," Gordon continued, "I have an offer to make to both of you. How would the two of you like to work as paid interns in our Research and Development Lab at the plant during your school break and maybe after school hours if your schedules permit. How about it? You don't have to decide right now, but please be thinking about it. O.K?"

Mike looked at his dad across the table. "I'd like to do something like that, I need to get some work experience before I send out college applications next school year. I'm not the brightest bulb in the pack, but I'll try to measure up if you will have me."

"Don't sell yourself short Mike. If you work in close proximity with my R&D staff I'm sure some pretty good things will happen." He continued, "And Maria, you will no doubt benefit by associating with the folks in the lab as well."

Maria responded, "Dad, I'd really like that. I mean getting to come to the plant and be where we could have lunch together and see each other occasionally. That would be really neat."

After supper, Maria and Mike went to their rooms to make video calls to their friends. Gordon and his wife Patricia went to the kitchen and began loading the dishwasher. Patricia hugged Gordon and said, "Thanks hon, I really appreciate you making an effort to get better acquainted with the kids. They won't be home much longer. Mike only has one more year before leaving for college, and Maria only has two more years in high school."

Gordon gave her a hug and a smile. "Well it is about time I found out what the kids are up to. I hardly ever know what they are doing lately. I can't remember the last time I did anything with them."

The following Friday evening, Mike's high school basketball team crushed their arch rivals in a stinging defeat with a final score of 76 to 42. Mike scored 18 points unassisted to become the team's MVP, the most valuable player. On Saturday afternoon, Maria and her fellow band musicians wowed an overflow crowd of shoppers at the opening of a new mall and were treated to several rounds of enthusiastic applause.

Following Maria's band concert, the family explored the new mall. They stopped in front of an electronics store. Mike spoke up, "Dad, Maria and I would like to take a look the newest cell phones. How about it?"

Gordon hesitated for a moment, "Well, why not? Let's find out what's available. How long have you kids had your current cell phones?"

Maria responded, "Dad, you got them for us four years ago. There are tons of things the new phones can do that ours can't. Maybe it's time to get new ones. How about it dad?"

Gordon didn't resist. He turned to his wife and suggested, "Hon, why don't you spend some time in your favorite clothing store while the three of us get involved in some high tech talk here at this place. You never seem to be thrilled with tech talk nearly as much as we are." He grinned.

Patricia smiled back, "OK, but don't be all day in there. We have to pick out a place to eat later. I'll see you all in about an hour in the food court in front of the coffee shop."

Gordon smiled and motioned Mike and Maria toward the

electronics store. "Let's go you two, while I'm in a generous mood."

It didn't take long for two teenagers to choose the highest priced new phones with the greatest number of features. They chose the Sino Dragon SP-7 smart phone. Sino Dragon is a relatively new cell phone maker located in Guangzhou, a major industrial city in the People's Republic of China. The most appealing features of the new phone are its 128 gigabytes of built-in memory and its expansion slot for a micro SD chip. The slot for the SD chip really caught Mike's attention. He could imagine all sorts of apps he could download and use if he added more memory. What neither he nor Maria could imagine this afternoon was that these two phones would soon be involved in some very serious business.

To celebrate this very special week-end Gordon took his family to dine at a five star restaurant at the top of one of the city's tallest office buildings. *The view of the city and the countryside beyond is impressive,* he thought, *but the view of three smiling, happy people around this dinner table is the most impressive view of all.* Yes, he was beginning to reconnect with the most important people in his life. Technology right now was the farthest thing from his mind. *Business can wait,* he thought.

When the school year ended, Gordon took Mike and Maria to the plant to begin their internship. He began the morning conference as usual at nine a.m. He started by introducing Mike and Maria to Chun Li, Oren Lunsford, and David Goldstein. These five seemed to hit it off right away. They quickly got into a free-wheeling conversation about computer chip design, organic chemistry, and radio propagation using microwaves. When the meeting adjourned, two very excited youngsters went off to the R&D lab to begin work with three of the brightest scientific minds in the universe.

Gordon Hollister thought, *how could this not be the best thing that ever happened for my kids? What could possibly go wrong?*

## CHAPTER 3

## A CHIP FOR THEIR THOUGHTS

During the summer Mike Hollister spent several weeks working in the lab with David Goldstein on a project to create a totally new outer shell for the rapidly changing Mark 3 medical chip. The chip was only a fraction of the size of a grain of rice, but until recently it suffered a major short coming. When implanted in a patient the outer shell slowly deteriorated and it had to be replaced periodically if it was to serve its purpose, that of monitoring vital signs, tracking the patient's location, and protecting the patient from life-threatening conditions.

The inner electronics of the chip were designed by Oren Lunsford who continuously increased the capacity of the chip until it performed prodigious data analysis. Total data storage within the chip grew to rival the capacity of main frame computers from just a few years earlier. The chip is divided into sectors with each sector containing information available only to specific users on a need-to-know basis. Electrical power consumption was reduced to a miniscule level. Power was obtained in one of three ways depending upon the chip's environment. It could generate its own power from light, from vibration, or it could scavenge power directly from its host.

Chun Li took Maria Hollister as a protégé teaching her about brain waves and how they are detected and how the computer algorithm at GMH Tech translates them into readable text through the encrypted cell phone app or application which is exclusively the property of the company. Maria and Mike were astounded to learn that an experimental version of the Mark 3 medical chip could actually read thoughts from animals and humans. Chun Li cautioned both Maria and Mike not to reveal what they learn at GMH Tech to anyone beyond the R&D staff.

The siblings were treated to more than one demonstration of thought capture from Oren's dog Murphy. In a round of human trials, Maria and Mike took turns reading text flowing from each other's thoughts. With a chip taped to their neck or temple, they were totally awed by the possibilities of reading another's innermost thoughts. During the trials, Mike managed to install a surreptitious copy of the encrypted cell phone app into both his and his sister's Sino Dragon cell phones, *for future reference,* he reasoned.

During the weeks Mike and Maria worked in R&D the team accumulated a large stockpile of chips in various stages of development. The newest version of the chip was renamed the CR3 for cerebral reader version three. This differentiated it from the Mark 3 which was only intended for medical monitoring.

Late one afternoon after Chun Li and the other R&D staff left the lab, Maria and Mike gave in to temptation. They gathered up several dozen of the CR3 chips, folded them into a tissue and put them in a pocket of Maria's jeans. *Nobody will miss a few of these*, they thought, *and besides they belong to our dad anyway.*

Mike encouraged his sister to pilfer the chips. He had a devious idea about how the two of them might use them to have some fun. Neither of these teenage kids realized at the time just how many unintended consequences they were about to set in motion.

Arriving home with their dad, Mike and Maria went to their rooms and changed clothes. They put on their swim suits and headed for the pool. The townhouses were situated in a series of rectangles, with each group of homes surrounding a pool and a club house. Maria and Mike loved swimming and snorkeling. They liked the camaraderie of meeting some of their friends at the clubhouse and in the pool.

This afternoon Beverly Talbot came over to talk with Maria. The girls clung to the side of the pool and watched the guys showing off their diving skills. Beverly lamented, "It won't be long until we are all back in school again. What would you think about having a party?"

Maria was quick to respond. "Awesome. We could invite some friends to the club house and have a blast."

Beverly was quick to add, "Just a few of our best friends, not any of the dorks who think they're so smart."

Maria agreed, "So O.K. who'll we invite? I have an idea, make a list of people you think we should invite and text it to me tonight."

"You got it," Beverly responded. "Your brother is

getting to be quite the athlete. Watch him dive from the high board."

Mike's friend Alex Gardner followed Mike off the high board. The boys made a constant circuit from the water to the board, and back again until the sun disappeared behind the club house. Mike quit this routine and strolled over to where the girls were visiting along the edge of the pool. "Time to go Sis, mom will have dinner on before we can shower and get dressed."

Maria showered and changed into some dry clothes. Suddenly she noticed that her jeans were not on the back of the chair where she left them earlier. "Mom, have you seen my jeans?"

"There in the wash sweetheart along with all the other clothes from your laundry hamper."

"Oh no!" She yelled, "You shouldn't have. There was something in the pocket that I need."

"Well," her mom responded, "You should search your pockets when you take off our things. How many times have I told you?"

Maria panicked. She remembered the CR3 chips folded inside the tissue. *What if the chips are destroyed?* She thought. She rushed to the laundry room hoping to get there before any damage was done. The jeans were in the dryer which had already run its course. She pulled them from the dryer expecting to find nothing useful in the pocket.

To her great surprise and relief, there in a much messed

up tangle of tissue were all of the CR3 chips completely intact. They showed no signs of damage. Maria turned them over and over in the palm of her hand and couldn't believe her good luck.

After dinner Maria took Mike to one side and told him about leaving the chips to possibly be destroyed or lost in the laundry. Mike was ecstatic when she showed him the undamaged chips. He told Maria how many hours he and David Goldstein worked to develop a more survivable outer shell for the chip. Perhaps this inadvertent trip through the laundry is proof that the chips in their possession are indeed the latest batch and impervious to destruction.

Mike smiled, "This is really good news Sis, you just don't know how good."

Maria trusted her older brother. She wasn't quite sure what he had in mind, but she was sure of one thing, she was about to find out. Like many of their other adventures she was sure she would probably enjoy it.

Maria got a text from Beverly Talbot with the names of friends she wanted to invite to their party. Beverly especially wanted to invite Raul Ramos, a guy she had her eye on. Maria didn't know Raul except seeing him around school, but since her best friend Beverly wanted him in the group, she agreed. Mike made some suggestions as well and the list was completed and text invitations sent.

After an hour of swimming, a loud and boisterous group of teenagers showered, dressed and entered the club house party room. Food and drinks were scattered about on tables throughout the room. Mike insisted on having fresh orange juice with lots of pulp, not for anyone's health, but for his own devious plan to introduce CR3 chips into as many party goers as possible. Maria inserted a tiny CR3 chip into a number of drinking straws. Mike's theory was that swallowing the pulp in the orange juice would make swallowing a tiny CR3 chip along with it virtually unnoticed.

Mike learned from Oren Lunsford during his time in the lab that each CR3 chip has a unique code which differentiates it from all others when its text is scanned by the cell phone app. As partiers partook of all the drinks and snacks, one by one they were swallowing a marvelous piece of technology. Mike and Maria assumed correctly that the chips would only remain in the human tract for a few hours at best. Lab tests had shown that the chips were capable of picking up brain waves from any location in the human body. So tonight this pair of scheming teenagers were about to learn a lot about science, but a lot more about people. Some things they really didn't want to know and would find difficult to handle.

Rhonda Barrett and Cassie Phelps were at the table with Maria and Beverly. Cassie looked across the room at a newcomer to the party. "Who invited Bobby Durand? He's such a dork. He isn't any fun to have around and he's always negative about stuff. What a downer!"

Beverly blurted out, "Don't look at me, I didn't invite the

dweeb. He's a crasher. Shall I throw him out?"

Maria offered, "Hey you guys. Don't be so hard on the guy. He can't help how he is. He's lonely and probably heard about the party and thought it was open to all the kids in the townhouses. Do you guys know anything about him? He doesn't have a dad that is he lives with his mom, and I've never seen his dad. His mom is from some foreign country and barely speaks any English."

Cassie spoke up, "Well I don't care what his problem is this was supposed to be our party. I can't stand that kid. I think I'll tell him to leave."

Mike spotted Bobby and walked over to meet him. "Hey Bobby, come on over here and join the guys. Here have an orange juice."

Bobby smiled and reached out and took the plastic cup from Mike's hand. "Thanks Mike. How have you been?"

Maria gasped, "Oh no, Mike don't….." She cut her comment short.

Cassie said, "Don't what? A minute ago you were all like telling us to be nice to the dork, and now you're all like don't hand him a drink. So what is it with you anyway?"

Maria didn't know what to say. She got up and hurried over to Mike's side. Bobby Durand had already moved away to talk with some other guys. "Mike, what were you thinking? Those straws were all for the people at the party. Bobby Durand wasn't invited."

"Cool it Sis. If our plan works, don't you think it will be fun to get inside the head of a nerd like Bobby Durand?"

She chuckled. "Well, maybe, but I thought we were going to keep it within our own group of friends. Anyway, in a few hours it will all be over when the chips pass out of everyone's system. I wonder what dad would think if he knew some really high tech stuff was going to be flushed down the sewer before long."

"Sis, dad would probably tear us up if he knew what we're doing with the results of one of his most expensive and most complex experimental projects. Man I hope he never finds out. There were so many CR3 chips at the lab that I didn't think a few dozen will be missed."

Cassie strolled over to where Mike and Maria were talking. "What is with you two, you're looking so serious. Loosen up, have a good time. Come on Mike, let's dance." She pulled Mike into the center of the room where several teenagers were dancing as if nobody was watching. Every couple did their own thing. The music didn't seem to matter.

Maria couldn't resist the temptation to look at her cell phone. She began by reading the output from the chip ingested by Raul Ramos. What she saw grabbed her attention. The text flow from Raul was all about Cassie Phelps and not about her friend Beverly Talbot. What Raul was thinking! Wow, Maria couldn't fathom that a boy would have thoughts like that. What would her friend Beverly think if she knew what Raul had in mind? Well, Beverly would never hear it from her. She couldn't even imagine how to explain what she had just read. *I'm glad I'm not Cassie Phelps,* she thought, *I hope Cassie doesn't do that stuff*."

The cell phone app for reading CR3 output differentiates individual chip signals. Maria began moving her finger over the screen to find other chips among the partiers. She stopped on one that was obviously picking up the thoughts of Bobby Durand. *Wow,* she thought, *that kid is so sad. What is it with him?*

The text stream from Bobby continued, "I hate Mr. Oglesby, god how I hate what he does to me. Maybe it's my own fault. He's been doing this stuff to me since eighth grade. Maybe I should just kill myself and get it over with. Then that pervert wouldn't have me to........" He didn't finish the thought.

Maria recognized the name. Under her breath she gasped, "Mr. Oglesby is the boy's gym teacher."

Beverly was seated beside Maria now. She said, "Of course Mr. Oglesby is the boys gym teacher. What on earth are you muttering about?"

Shocked that she had been overheard, Maria put her phone in her pocket and turned to face Beverly. "Oh, nothing. Nothing at all." She thought, *quit before someone gets suspicious.*

On the way back to their townhouse, Maria grabbed Mike by the elbow and held on. "Mike, have you looked at any of the CR3 text output tonight?"

Mike shrugged, "No Sis, not yet. Cassie wouldn't leave me alone long enough to take a look. Why?"

"Mike, I think we have a problem."

"What kind of problem Sis?"

"Well for starters, we shouldn't have done this. I already know more about two people than I ever wanted to know. Bobby Durand wants to kill himself and Raul Ramos wants to rape Cassie Phelps."

"Whoa! Slow down Sis, you're hyper. What's all this about?"

Maria spent the next five minutes giving Mike a run down of what she saw in the text flow from the chips ingested by Raul and Bobby. He found it hard to believe that Bobby Durand was suicidal. He didn't find it hard to believe that Raul had strong sexual thoughts about the cheer leader and hottie Cassie Phelps. What horny lad couldn't see her as a potential sex partner? But suicide? Why would Bobby want to kill himself with girls like Cassie to look at and to dance with?

Maria continued, "Well forget about Cassie for a minute, and let's think about Bobby Durand. Do you think we should tell somebody what we know?"

"Sis, how would we be able to do that? You think we can just call up somebody and say we've been reading the brain waves of a friend and we think they may want to hurt themselves? They would tell us we're nuts."

“Well, Mike, we can’t let Bobby know how we found out what he’s thinking, but we can’t let him actually kill himself either.”

“You’re right Sis, we gotta do something, but what?”

Maria thought for a moment, “Bobby hates the gym teacher at school, Mr. Oglesby. He says, that is he was thinking, something about what Mr. Oglesby has been doing to him since he was in the eighth grade. I can’t imagine what Mr. Oglesby could do to make someone want to die.”

“Well.....uh.....I’m glad you can’t imagine something like that, but I can, and I will try and find out more from Bobby. If it’s what I’m thinking it’s pretty bad stuff. When we get home, I’m going to look into some of the output from any other chips we planted tonight and see if there is anything else we probably shouldn’t know.”

He paused for a moment, “Maybe this wasn’t such a great idea after all.”

## CHAPTER 4

## BUSTED

As soon as Mike got to his room he took out his Sino Dragon cell phone and began scanning to see how many CR3 chips he could interrogate. *Wow*, he *thought, this is going take some time.* There were a total of twelve chips returning signals. He slid his finger over the list and selected one he thought might be Cassie's. The text came scrolling across the screen revealing the innermost thoughts of the girl he had been dancing with only an hour earlier. *Dang, the guys were right, girls do think about the same stuff we do.* He felt a little embarrassed knowing what Cassie had been thinking while they were dancing. *Well, unless I want to get totally involved with Cassie I better keep her at a distance. She could compromise my whole future. I just don't want to go that far with any girl for a while at least.*

Mike scanned a few more of the chips ingested by the girls at the party. They revealed a side of teenage girls he never imagined. Next he took a look at the output from a chip ingested by Raul Ramos. *What?* He thought, *Raul has a cousin involved with a drug cartel. Wow!* Raul's text flow revealed his thoughts were about someone named Diego Ramos. Over and over his thoughts expressed fear that if the Feds find out what his cousin does for a living he would wind up going to prison for a very long time. The family is close and Raul doesn't want anything bad to happen to any of them.

Mike couldn't stop thinking about Bobby Durand wanting to kill himself. *Man that must be awful*, he thought, *should I do something now or wait until tomorrow?* Mike remembered a school counselor making a presentation to his class about teen suicide. At the time he didn't think much about it because he never knew anyone who had committed suicide or even talked about it. But this was different. Fortunately or unfortunately he was now privy to the innermost thoughts of a teenager who might be on the verge of actually doing it.

Mike decided to take drastic action. He and Bobby Durand were not friends in the sense that they did things together. He wondered how he could approach Bobby and not seem too eager to get better acquainted with the kid everyone made fun of. Well, if Bobby's life is in the balance, it was time to act.

Mike opened his favorite social media website and sent an instant text message to Bobby inviting him to come over and talk about the opening of the school year which was only a few days away. Mike feigned interest in having Bobby help him understand Calculus, a subject Mike already knew quite well. Everyone knows that Bobby Durand is a math and science nerd and makes the best grades so it seemed natural to ask for his help. Bobby responded immediately. He seemed delighted to be asked by one of the more popular guys.

The boys sat out on the patio in a pair of hammocks facing each other and talked about Calculus at first and then about a host of other things. Mike kept Bobby talking until well after midnight. Bobby recounted how his dad Roy Durand had been a worker on an oil rig off the coast of Venezuela. How his dad met and married his mom in Costa Rica. He talked about a disastrous explosion and fire on the oil rig. How several workers including his dad were blown off the rig and their bodies never found. The boys fell asleep in the hammocks and didn't stir again until Maria came looking for Mike well after daylight. She was surprised to find Bobby Durand had spent the night.

After breakfast the boys went to a park to throw a football around for a while. When that activity ended, they sat down on a bench facing a small pond. Mike got up his nerve to open a sensitive conversation. He knew he would have to lie to Bobby to get him to talk about Mr. Oglesby.

"Hey man, you really talk in your sleep. Did you know that?"

Bobby looked surprised, "No.....actually nobody ever told me that before."

Mike continued, knowing all the while that he was lying, but he felt he had to get Bobby to open up, "Well last night I woke up a couple of times and you were really going at it. You were cussing and arguing with Mr. Oglesby the gym teacher. You weren't a happy camper man, you were totally teed off about something. Do you remember what you were dreaming?"

Bobby didn't know how to respond. He stammered and finally composed himself. "Man you have no idea, and I hope you never find out what that guy is like."

"Care to tell me about it?" Mike asked.

"There isn't anything to tell. He's rotten and that is all there is to it."

"Wow! What makes you say that?"

Bobby continued, "It's some crap that started in the eighth grade and he just won't quit bothering me. Every time I go to gym in sixth period he makes me stay after and clean up and put away equipment. Nothing else."

Mike knew better, but he needed to proceed with caution here. "Man you were talking like there is a lot more to it than that last night. You were ready to kill him. That's not a normal reaction to just working after hours in the gym."

Bobby looked away. "Mike, it's something that you wouldn't understand."

Mike looked him straight in the eye and said, "Try me. See if I understand. If it's what I'm thinking we need to put his sorry butt away for a long time in a place where bad stuff happens to guys like that."

Bobby began sobbing. "Mike, I don't know where to begin. Oglesby treats me like a sex toy. This has been going on for three years. I hate that pervert, but I just don't know what to do. Can you help me stop him?"

Mike looked directly at Bobby. "Bro, I think I know a

way. Trust me. I have some technical stuff we can use to nail Oglesby and stop his crap once and for all."

"Mike, nobody ever cared enough about me or any of my problems to even ask, let alone offer a way out. What have you got in mind?"

"Guy, we will put Oglesby out of business on the first day of classes. Here's how." Mike proceeded to lay out a plan. Bobby would wear a hidden spy camera which would take video and audio and upload the results to a cloud server. If Oglesby or anyone else found and seized the camera, the incriminating evidence would be safe and ready to use against him.

Bobby was surprised at the idea. "Mike, do you have a camera like that?"

"You bet, and I have some other tech stuff in my arsenal. We'll take Oglesby out. Count on it."

By this time Bobby was smiling contemplating the idea of Oglesby going away instead of himself. He frequently thought of leaving this life in a coffin, but had only hesitated because of how he thought it would impact his mother. She would never understand. *Now*, he thought, *Oglesby will be gone and not me.*

On the first day of classes, Bobby Durand and Mike Hollister came to school with a plan and with the means to carry it out. Bobby wore a hidden video camera which had a feature Mike hadn't told him about. It also carried a CR3 chip which was pressed against Bobby's bare chest. Now that would be the combination. Not only will the boys get video evidence, but Mike will be sure to know exactly where Bobby is every minute of the day and will be able to know everything he's thinking.

During fourth period, a number of Mike's friends began sending text messages to a phone number set up to receive tips, anonymous or otherwise, about dangers to the school. Tips were encouraged no matter what those may be about. Students were urged that if they 'see something, say something.' That slogan even appeared on banners throughout the building. So it was natural that the plotters would make good use of it. By the end of fifth period over eighty tips were received by school and law enforcement officials. The tips described an impending act of sexual violence about to be committed by a faculty member against a student. The crime was to take place in Oglesby's office just behind the boy's locker room at four o'clock that very afternoon.

As four o'clock approached, Bobby went as usual to the boys' locker room. There Mr. Oglesby greeted him. "Hi lad, step into my office. We need to get together. It's been too long for me, how about you?"

Bobby tried to stay cool. Slowly, without a word he entered the office just off the locker room. Herman Oglesby reached out and began to stroke Bobby's hair. "Bobby, you know this has always been a very special time for us. I hope you know how much I care for you."

Bobby cringed. He hoped Mike's plan worked before

Oglesby went too far. Just as Oglesby dropped his trousers the door opened with a crash against a nearby steel file cabinet. In rushed three cops, the school resource officer, two assistant principals and three male teachers.

Oglesby turned pale. He stammered, "Wha....wha...what is all this? Where did you guys come from? This isn't what it looks like! I swear it isn't!"

The first cop who entered responded, "Mr. Oglesby, you're under arrest for sexual molestation of a minor under your authority. You have the right to remain silent, you have the right to an attorney. If you cannot afford an attorney one will be provided for you. Anything you say can and will be used against you in a court of law. Do you understand that Mr. Oglesby?"

Another officer spun Herman Oglesby around and put the cuffs on him. The last Bobby saw of Herman Oglesby he was seated in the rear of a police vehicle outside the rear door of the school gym. Mike's plan really worked.

Bobby thought, *if I can just live a normal life like the other guys, well, at least now I really want to live and not do anything bad to myself or leave my mom. She's suffered enough without my dad.*

Gordon Hollister streamed the morning news on his tablet computer at the breakfast table. Breaking news: ***High School Gym Teacher Arrested.*** The story gave a few details: *Mr. Herman Oglesby, age 49 arrested on charges of sexually molesting a student for almost three years. The name of the* *student, a minor, is being withheld by authorities. No additional information is available at this time.*

Gordon turned to Mike, "Son did you know anything about this Gym Teacher, a Mr. Oglesby?"

Mike hesitated, "Well....Dad....yes actually I do know who he is. I saw him around school, but I never had a gym class with him."

Mike thought, *Dad if you only knew how deeply involved I am with this case you would probably skin me alive for using GMH Tech stuff this way. Man I hope you never find out for my sake and for Maria's sake as well.*

Bobby Durand met Mike in the hallway before first period class. He was agitated as he spoke: "Mike, the cops told me I might have to go to court and testify about Mr. Oglesby when his trial comes up. I don't want to have to tell everybody what he did. My friends and my mom don't know anything about this and I don't want them to find out."

Mike wasn't sure what to say, but he wanted to reassure Bobby that the nightmare was over for him. "You may not have to testify if other witnesses and the video we made convict the guy. So don't worry. Things may work out for the best. Wait and see. Be patient."

After school Mike spent some time in his room reviewing some of the text output collected from the CR3 chips ingested at the party. He opened the text flow from the chip inside Raul Ramos. Raul again was fretting about the possibility of his cousin going to prison on drug charges. *But wait, what's this?* Raul was evidently in a conversation while visiting with someone in the same jail with Herman Oglesby. His thoughts showed him to be concerned that the now former Gym Teacher would get off from the current charges. As the thought stream continued it became clear that whoever Raul was conversing with seemed to assure him that justice would be done and Oglesby would never be free again. Mike wondered what this might mean. He hadn't long to wait to find out.

The next morning a new headline appeared on the news stream on his dad's tablet computer. Gordon Hollister handed the tablet to his wife and exclaimed, "Well, look at this! That gym teacher from the local high school who was arrested.... died in jail last night."

Patricia Hollister read to a startled Mike and Maria, "The story goes on to explain that Herman Oglesby died of natural causes in his sleep sometime during the night. He was discovered by a jailer. The news says the county coroner will investigate, but it appears that his death was caused by a ruptured aneurysm."

Mike thought to himself, *Well Bobby can quit worrying, he won't have to go to court. Karma is a bitch. It bites. But I wonder if it really was by natural causes or by someone accelerating nature through physical force.*

Mike never expected any of the CR3 chips to remain inside anyone who ingested them at the party for any length of time. By the end of the fifth day there were fewer and fewer cerebral text streams emitted from people who swallowed the chips. However, the GPS feature was still very active and many of the chips were traced as they flowed into the municipal sewage disposal plant and into its settling ponds. One-by-one those chips ceased to function. One chip in particular seemed to have lodged at least for now in the tract of Raul Ramos.

Mike and Maria returned to work at GMH Technology at every opportunity. While there they became aware of an almost total paralysis in every department. Nothing was getting done. Everyone was occupied digging into file cabinets and printing spread sheets from office computers. Nobody was producing anything meaningful. The reason: Harold Cunningham from the IRS had his auditors and agents demanding the most bizarre kinds of paper work.

Mike and Maria discussed the problem with their dad at home. Gordon was frustrated by the auditor's constant presence, but felt he couldn't do anything about it. They were like locusts, they were poking into everyone's activities and demanding access where it seemed they had no business.

After dinner Mike and Maria went out onto the patio and sat in the hammocks facing each other. They decided enough is enough. Maria suggested, "Why don't we see if we can get Mr. Cunningham to swallow a CR3 chip and find out why he and his people are so aggressive?"

Mike, always ready for a challenge, quickly agreed but

asked, "How will we get one into him Sis?"

Maria responded, "I've eaten in the cafeteria near Mr. Cunningham several times. He likes Mexican food and often leaves his tray untended to go for a drink refill. If I can slip a chip into one of his burritos without him noticing it, he might just swallow it."

Mike grinned, "It's worth a try. Let's do it. No telling what we can learn from his thoughts."

Evidently Maria's scheme worked. Harold Cunningham wolfed down his burritos with gusto and with a CR3 tracking chip as a bonus. Mike was ready with his cell phone app to read out the text stream from Cunningham's thoughts.

*Wow! What's this?* Mike thought. *Cunningham is totally agitated about something. Oh wait. He's thinking about a conversation he had this morning with his wife Darlene. Seems like she told him if she ever catches him cheating, her brother Clyde, a lawyer, will help her take Harold for everything he owns or will ever own in two lifetimes. He's planning to stop and spend time with his mistress Vivian this evening. He's wondering how to lie to his wife about not coming home until late. He thinks he can't live without getting together with Vivian every day.*

*Well now,* Mike thought, *how shall we use this little nugget? The direct approach is probably as good as any.*

Mike stepped over to the table where Harold

Cunningham was just finishing lunch. He walked up directly behind the IRS agent and placed his hand gently on the man's shoulder. Harold turned and looked into Mike's face. "Young man, just what is it that you want?"

Mike smiled slyly and said, "Mr. Cunningham, perhaps it's time that Darlene meets Vivian. What do you think? How about it?"

The color drained instantly from Harold Cunningham's face. He gasped. "What did you say?"

"Mr. Cunningham I believe it is time that you introduce your mistress Vivian to your wife Darlene."

Harold Cunningham rose from the table trembling. He rushed from the cafeteria into the men's room and threw up. He thought, *how did this young punk find out about Vivian? God knows I kept it a secret from my wife and from everyone else as far as I know. How could he possibly know so much?*

When Harold emerged from the restroom Mike blocked his path. He spoke softly, "Mr. Cunningham I think the audit should come to an end. Wouldn't you agree?"

At home during dinner, Gordon Hollister announced to his family. "I don't know the reason for it, but the long nightmare audit which cost us so much productivity suddenly ended this afternoon. Mr. Cunningham didn't explain why, but he abruptly pulled all of his people out of the plant and told me that the IRS is completely satisfied that GMH Technology is clean and never had a tax problem. Isn't that great?"

Mike responded, “Dad, you just don’t know how great that is, you just don‘t know!”

# CHAPTER 5

# THE CARTEL

Mike Hollister didn't know just how to tell David Goldstein about the CR3 chip's recently tested durability. He and David had worked together for weeks to make the CR3 survivable under harsh conditions. How was he going to tell David that he and Maria put the CR3 through a home laundry, washer and dryer, and that the chip came through with no apparent defects? How could he possibly explain that he and his sister Maria fed a dozen or more CR3 chips to their teenage friends in order to literally get inside their friends heads? How could he admit to his brilliant mentor that the company escaped from the tentacles of a vicious IRS auditor because he and his sister Maria fed a CR3 chip to the chief inquisitor and blackmailed him to call off his goon squad?

Mike was still curious about the chip swallowed by Raul Ramos. It continued to furnish information long after most of the other chips had gone to an ignoble end in the local sewage disposal system. Perhaps it caught somewhere in Raul's digestive tract and anchored itself there. *Well,* he thought, *somehow he had to share this knowledge with David for the good of science.*

David Goldstein and Mike took a break from the lab and went out on the terrace to grab a snack. Mike broached the subject in a roundabout way. "David, what would you think if for some reason the CR3 chip needed to be used to gather information from a person, but the person might not be willing to have a chip inserted into their body? What if the chip could be introduced into a person, say a security risk person, or a foreign spy, or some criminal and we needed to get it into a person without them knowing it was there? How would you suggest going about it?"

David took a minute to think about this before responding. "Mike, it sounds like you have been reading spy novels or watching espionage flicks or something. If the CR3 or a chip of that sort were to be used for intelligence gathering perhaps it might be swallowed by a person without them knowing it. After all, it is much less than half the size of a rice grain and it might be slipped into food or a beverage the person would consume."

Mike quickly picked up on that thread, "That's a great idea, but what if the chip went through the person's digestive tract too quickly for any useful information to be gathered? What then?"

David responded, "Well, it would require an outer shell that not only would survive the environment, but would actually anchor itself innocuously enough in the person's tract and stay long enough to be useful. However, even if we were to develop such a chip, it would probably be obsolete before it was used. You might be interested to know that Chun Li, Oren and I are working on a totally new concept to capture and decode thought. Perhaps without chips. We haven't gotten very far with it yet. So in the meantime, perhaps you and I will work to perfect the outer shell of the CR3 and see what we can come up with."

Mike was relieved that David didn't appear to want to know why he pursued this line of thought. After all, David Goldstein was like many young scientists, interested in making the next great leap forward in technology without much concern for the ethics or the ramifications of such a leap. For this Mike was grateful. He could only imagine how his father might respond to his recent activities.

At home that evening Mike finished dinner with the family and went out onto the patio to sit in one of the hammocks. He enjoyed being alone for a awhile and he wanted to try again to review the thoughts streamed from the CR3 chip in Raul Ramos. Mike opened the proprietary app on his cell phone and began reading text.

It appeared that Raul was again visiting a person in the county jail. From the text Mike couldn't identify the person in the conversation, but he was sure they were talking about the death of Herman Oglesby. It appeared that several inmates learned of the charges against Oglesby and word spread within the jail population that the former high school gym teacher was a pedophile. That is a class of offender looked down upon by hard working kidnappers, armed robbers, drug pushers and car thieves. The text stream revealed that Oglesby was attacked in the exercise yard the afternoon before he died and received a severe beating which probably resulted in the ruptured aneurysm during the night.

*So,* Mike thought, *I was right. Oglesby's death was not totally from natural causes unless one considers a brutal beating an act of nature. A twisted nature to be sure, but an unfortunate part of human nature. Karma really does bite.*

Before the jail visit ended, Mike learned the identity of the inmate. He is Julio Ramos, a relative of Raul and he is being held as a suspected drug dealer. *Perhaps another cousin,* thought Mike. He wondered, *how many of Raul's cousins are narcotics traffickers?*

When Raul left the jail and got into his car, his thoughts turned away from his cousin. The text stream on Mike's cell phone continued. Raul was thinking about Cassie and the other girls around school. He even thought about Maria Hollister. Mike perked up when is sister's name came up on the screen. Raul was pondering how each girl might respond to 'roofies' or 'ecstasy' a couple of date rape drugs. Raul was thinking about the supply furnished by Julio and wonders how many girls he could be with using even what he has on hand, and he thought about how easy it is to get more when his current stash runs out.

Mike almost exploded. *That dirty bastard! He's thinking he will use those drugs to take advantage of some of the girls including my little sister? Well,* he thought, *I have to warn Maria and her friends not to ever find themselves alone with that guy and especially never to allow him near their food or drinks under any circumstances. That low life. Man how can a guy stoop so low?*

Mike suddenly realized that he and Maria are involved in something that is most likely not ethical, but what they were doing, at least so far, had done some good. He wondered, *would it always be doing a good thing to use high tech the way they recently used the CR3 chips? Could this technology be used for evil purposes?*

The next afternoon Chun Li, Oren Lunsford, and David Goldstein held a meeting of the R&D staff to announce a serendipitous discovery. Chun Li told the group, "The CR3 chip has a quirk not recognized earlier. When queried using an upgrade of the encrypted cell phone app the chip is capable of returning live streaming sounds emanating from the animal or human in which the chip is inserted. It can also pick up sounds from a person or animal in close proximity to the wearer. So not only does it capture the thought of the wearer, but also the speech which along with thoughts are then recorded for future reference."

Chun Li continued, "This is a game changer for using the chip to gather human thought. It now enables us to compare what people say with what they are thinking."

Mike and Maria shot each other a knowing glance. If they were to make use of this new feature, they would need to upgrade the encrypted cell phone app. Fortunately for the two schemers, they were able to stay later than the entire R&D staff and download the new app to both of their cell phones. *Well,* thought Mike, *this is a whole new ball game. I wonder where it will lead.*

Gordon Hollister's secretary Martha Wilson buzzed her boss on the video intercom. "Mr. Hollister, there is a Mr. Jack Reynolds here to see you. He says it is about your children Mike and Maria. Shall I send him in?"

"Yes, by all means Martha, send him in."

Jack Reynolds stepped into Gordon's office, closed the door and extended his hand. "Mr. Hollister, I'm Jack Reynolds from the Drug Enforcement Administration. Here is my card."

Gordon took the card and motioned the visitor to a chair directly in front of his desk. "What brings you here sir, and what does this have to do with my kids?"

Jack responded, "Sir, your children have done nothing wrong, so you can put aside any concerns there. I would like to talk with your son and daughter this afternoon if that is possible. We could all talk right here in your office with you present so that we are all on the same page."

Gordon agreed. He leaned forward and selected the R&D lab on the video intercom and buzzed. Mike answered from the lab. Gordon spoke, "Mike I would like you and Maria to come to my office. It is important. We need to talk."

Mike thought, *Oh no! Dad probably knows what we've been doing with the chips, but how on earth could he have found out?*

Mike and Maria entered their dad's office and were introduced to Mr. Jack Reynolds. Mr. Reynolds got right down to business. "Mike, you and Maria are acquaintances of a young man named Raul Ramos. He is a student at your high school. I am an investigator with the DEA, the Drug Enforcement Administration. If you agree to help us in an on-going investigation, your country will greatly appreciate your efforts. It doesn't require you to do anything dangerous, just to keep your eyes and ears tuned to any hint of drug activity carried on by young Raul Ramos. Would you be willing to do that?"

Mike was relieved that this meeting was not about their misuse of the company's technology. It wasn't a summons from his dad to confess to playing fast and loose with the results of millions of dollars spent on R&D. *So*, *OK,* he thought, *why not?* He responded, "Well, I suppose we can keep our eyes and ears open for the DEA, but we don't want to get into anything dangerous, as you said Mr. Reynolds. What about you Maria, are you in?"

Maria was equally relieved that the two of them were not getting busted by their dad for their recent adventures. Maria nodded in agreement, "Yes, I'm willing to help."

Mr. Reynolds gave each of them his card and called their attention to a phone number. "This is a discreet phone number. You can text or leave voice messages there 24/7 so please keep us informed if you learn anything at all concerning illegal activity. Sometimes even an innocuous bit of information can lead us to bigger things."

Mike and Maria assured him that they would do all they could to help stem the tide of illegal drugs. Mike remembered the thought stream from Raul Ramos about 'roofies' and 'ecstasy.' He remembered how furious it made him when he read the data stream. *Well, Raul, you and your family are going down if I have anything to do with it.*

That night Mike and Maria stayed up a bit late. They tried out the new feature of the encrypted cell phone app. For the first time using the CR3 chips they could actually hear a conversation in progress between Raul and his cousin Diego Ramos. Raul seems to be far more involved in moving drugs than anyone at school ever suspected. From the tenor of the discussion it appears that Diego is not only the head of the Ramos family, but he is also the head of a local branch of the Zetas, a notorious narcotics trafficking organization. The Zetas are a murderous bunch of thugs who brook no opposition. They kill wantonly and have no mercy for anyone who gets in their way.

Mike wondered, *what are we getting into? This might not be as safe as we originally thought. What the heck, either we're all in or not at all. So let's do it.*

Maria looked at Mike and asked, "What do you think? Did we make a mistake agreeing to help the DEA?"

Mike shot back, "No Sis, we need to help and you know

we have the tools to do it." He grinned. "We're sitting here listening to conversations and tracking the thoughts of a member of an important drug gang. I'm sad to say I know the kid and feel sorry for him, but he is part of a larger problem and we can't ignore his criminal behavior just because we know him."

Maria agreed. "But Mike, how will we tell Mr. Reynolds what we know without him guessing we know more than we should?"

"Leave it me Sis. I think we can relay information without Reynolds knowing how he got it. I know how to spoof a phone number. We can send text to Mr. Reynolds without him knowing where it comes from."

"Mike, how can you do that?"

"Sis, you don't think that the information technology class at the high school is totally about following the course syllabus do you?" He grinned. "Some of us learned more than what the teacher had in mind. We learned it from each other. One of the guys is the son of a telemarketer. He put me onto some software for phone spoofing. Telemarketers use it to fool people into thinking they are getting a legitimate call when in fact they aren't. It's easily available for download if you know where to go on the Internet."

Maria was never surprised that Mike would always come up with a way to do things using computers. Long ago she learned that her brother had a devious streak in him and right now she appreciated that streak more than ever.

Mike realized that the text stream coming through his cell phone contained information the DEA would find very useful. It appeared that Raul and is cousin Diego were expecting a very large shipment of cocaine and other illegal drugs. It was to arrive in a cargo container in the center of a number of legitimate products which would hide its presence and mask any detectable odors. The cargo container would arrive by truck at a terminal a few miles away within the next twenty-four hours. Raul was to make sure the container was the right one by checking its cargo manifest and matching it to the container itself. That was his role. He would not be directly involved with distribution to individual drug dealers.

Mike realized there was no time to lose. Using the spoofing software, he set up a phone connection to the secure line provided by Mr. Reynolds. He transferred an enormous volume of text directly from his cell phone. The text stream included not only the thoughts flowing directly from Raul's brain, but also all captured audio conversation converted into text.

The morning TV news reported a big drug bust. DEA agents along with state and local police seized eighty million dollars worth of cocaine and other popular street drugs from a cargo container at a local truck terminal. Nobody was arrested, but an investigation is ongoing.

Mike and Maria could hardly hold their composure. They went to the patio and opened the cell phone app to track the chip in Raul Ramos. He was with his cousin Diego who was in a rage. He was saying that they had never lost a shipment like that in the past. He couldn't understand how it could have been detected. The trucking company was in on the operation and there must have been a leak somewhere. If he finds out where the leak occurred he would plug it any way he could. There must be someone held accountable. They would pay with their lives if he ever finds out who it is.

Again, Mike opened a phone connection using the spoofing software and sent all of this directly to Mr. Reynolds. Jack Reynolds was astounded by the volume and the value of the information he received.

That afternoon after school Mike and Maria met with Mr. Reynolds. He asked them, "why did you send the data from what appeared to be a spoofed phone number?'

Mike responded, "Sir we didn't want to take a chance of being traced by someone not on your team."

"Well I don't blame you for taking precautions. We've had occasions when someone in our organization sold out to the cartel for a price. That's good thinking on your part." He continued, "But how in the name of sam hill were you able to get that much information? It's almost like you got inside the head of Raul Ramos."

Mike hesitated. "You have no idea sir! Just no idea!"

# CHAPTER 6

## THE BANQUET

Jack Reynolds, the DEA agent continued his conversation with Mike and Maria Hollister in their dad's office at GMH Technology. "You two supplied us with a vast amount of useful information. From it we were able to seize a record amount of street drugs and keep them out of the hands of the cartel. We also learned that Diego Ramos is planning a banquet for his entire organization on Saturday evening at his mansion. I wish I could be a fly on the wall so to speak at this soiree." He chuckled.

Mike wasn't sure what to make of Mr. Reynolds' last remark. He wondered, *Is Jack Reynolds beginning to suspect the two of us of having some sort of super powers to get inside the heads of cartel members? Of course,* he thought, *we actually do using the CR3 chips.* He tried not to smile.

Maria gave Mike a sideways glance. She also felt this might be a leading remark. She asked, "Mr. Reynolds, do you know who will cater the banquet? I have some friends who work part time for a local caterer down near the bay."

Jack Reynolds responded, "An outfit on the boulevard." He glanced at his cell phone. "Here it is, it's called *Royal Catering*. Why do you ask?"

"Sir, I know some girls from my high school who work

there and who might be recruited to do a favor." She stopped herself without saying anything more for fear she would tip their hand about how they use the CR3 chips planted in food and beverages.

Mr. Reynolds cautioned the two, "I wouldn't ask anyone to place themselves in danger. The Zetas are a murderous lot, and if they even suspect someone of spying on them in any way, the person will likely disappear without a trace. It happened to one of our best agents. The cartel takes no prisoners. So please, don't ask your friends to do anything which could endanger themselves."

Maria nodded. She said no more.

On the way home, Maria and Mike came up with a plan. They sat in Mike's car in the carport for an hour and laid it out in detail. First, Mike would get his hands on several dozen of the newest CR3 chips from the lab. Maria would persuade her friends Cassie Phelps and Alicia Byers who work at *Royal Catering* to let her into the kitchen where they would prepare the banquet for Diego Ramos' organization.

The next afternoon Mike waited until the R&D staff departed the lab. Left alone and trusted to clean up and put away equipment, he quickly gathered several dozen CR3 chips and hid them in a tissue. He was in luck. The total supply of chips in the lab was extensive. A few dozen would never be missed. These were the latest version he and David Goldstein generated though nano engineering. The new chip has an outer shell more likely to lodge in and remain innocently in the human digestive tract. The shell characteristics had been thoroughly tested before finished chips were created with the full range of electronic features.

Maria sent text messages to Cassie Phelps and Alicia Byers and invited them to swim with her the next afternoon at the townhouse pool and to stay over for dinner with the family. Cassie answered almost immediately. She never missed a chance to be near Mike Hollister. Alicia answered later in the evening.

Dinner with the family ended with the girls going out onto the patio and sitting in the hammocks. Conversation ran the gamut of boys, music, concerts, and last but not least Maria asked for a favor. She told her friends she wanted to visit *Royal Catering* where she knew they both worked after school and on Saturdays. Maria knew that the crucial day would be this very next Saturday.

Her friends agreed that next Saturday will be a good day to show Maria around the business. They were sure their boss wouldn't mind. He was always open to having people visit the establishment. Alicia told her, "If you are there you can help us out. We are a little shorthanded and we are preparing for a big banquet at the home of one of our best customers."

Cassie said, "How about it? Want to earn a buck or two helping us out?"

Maria couldn't believe her good fortune. "Of course.

I'll be glad to help."

When Saturday came, Maria, and Alicia, met at Cassie's townhouse and rode with her to work at the caterer's place in Cassie's Ford Mustang convertible. They put the top down to enjoy the great weather. Cassie parked the car in the alley behind the business. On-street parking was almost non-existent on the boulevard near the bay.

Cassie introduced Maria to Mr. Charlie Jacobs, the owner. He told the girls, "It's great you brought some extra help, we gotta hustle. The banquet we're prepping is a big affair. It's at a mansion on one of the bay islands. It's at the home of a guy named....let me look here on the invoice....it's at the home of a Mr. Diego Ramos."

Maria thought, "*Pay dirt. That's the one Mr. Reynolds wants to have under surveillance. Now to do my part, and get home before dinner time.*"

While everyone was busy cooking and packing up the meal, Maria was able to find a time when no one was watching her. She mixed over sixty CR3 chips into a variety of dishes. Many of the dishes either contained rice or items like refritos or guacamole dip. Hopefully there would be enough exposure that the entire cartel would ingest at least one or more CR3 chips. She hoped that Mike would be able to interrogate the chips during the evening and relay the text output to Mr. Reynolds.

They loaded the catering truck in the alley outside the rear door and were ready to deliver this very important meal.

Charlie announced, “OK ladies, let’s get this affair on the road. There is room for all of you in the truck, so no need to take your car Cassie.”

Maria did not expect to be involved in setting up at the Ramos mansion. The other two girls had not explained the days plan fully. What could she do but go along with it?

Charlie Jacobs pulled the catering van into a delivery driveway alongside one of the older and more elegant mansions on a man-made island in the bay. The home was built during the heyday of rum running and prohibition in the 1920’s. It was set well back from the street and the property backed up to a canal which leads to the Intracoastal Waterway.

Obviously Diego Ramos was among the more affluent folks in the neighborhood. A sixty-foot motor yacht was tied to his dock on the canal. Several smaller water craft including jet skis were scattered about on racks in his backyard near a huge swimming pool.

The girls helped Charlie Jacobs unload the food and beverages and set up serving tables in a large screened area just inside the mansion opposite the pool and patio. A crowd was already gathering in the dining room inside the mansion. People stood around with drinks in their hands. Diego Ramos entered the dining room, and as if on cue, everyone took seats around the table which Maria estimated to be twenty feet long.

The people at this banquet ranged in age from the late teens to what appeared to be octogenarians. There were men and women of all ages. The girls were not expected to serve the guests at the table. For that Diego Ramos had his own in-house servers. Maria and her friends were simply here to unload and keep the food warm and to make sure to re-supply the serving table from the catering truck if any item ran low.

As the evening wore on and the dinner was winding down, the girls began repacking the catering truck with empty containers for the trip back across the bay. It was getting late. In the dim light along the service driveway Maria found herself alone for a moment. Someone came up behind her. She heard footsteps along the concrete driveway, but thought it was one of her friends bringing out another load of empty pans. She didn't turn to see who it might be.

A pair of hands covered her eyes from behind. A male voice said, "Guess who!"

Maria whirled around and stared into the face of Raul Ramos. He was grinning. "Surprised you didn't I?"

She laughed a nervous laugh. "Yeah, and you almost got a surprise yourself. I almost gave you a knee in the groin."

Raul laughed out loud. "Oh so you're a feisty one are you? I like feisty. Maybe you and I should go out sometime. I could show you a great time."

Maria remembered what Mike told her about Raul's attitude toward the girls at the townhouse party. She would take no chances with this guy. She hadn't yet warned her friends about him. She couldn't think how to bring up the idea that she knew exactly what he was thinking. How could she possibly explain that she and her devious brother Mike had been literally rummaging around inside this guy's head?

*Well,* she thought, *I have to protect my sisters. This guy has some totally gross ideas of what he wants to do to young women.*

Maria and Raul made some small talk for a while and Maria excused herself and returned to the house where she felt a little more at ease. Inside there was more light and her friends were there as well as Charlie Jacobs.

Raul followed her inside and engaged the other two girls in conversation. Maria didn't have time or opportunity to talk privately with her friends. Raul poured a drink and offered it to Cassie Phelps. Cassie was busy and motioned him to set it down while she continued gathering up additional equipment to return to the catering truck. Raul evidently was satisfied that Cassie would imbibe what he offered. He didn't stay to watch. As Raul left the area to talk with other guests, Cassie reached for the drink. Maria pretended to slip on a slick spot and crashed into Cassie knocking the drink and the plastic cup onto the floor.

"Oh crap, look what you've done. You spilled my drink all over my feet. What a klutz Maria, what's wrong with you?"

Maria apologized profusely. "Here let me get you another one."

Maria knew from the text flow she and Mike read from Raul's earlier CR3 chip, that he harbored a desire to use 'roofies,' or date rape drugs, on young women. She couldn't stand by and watch that happen to a friend. She also knew from the text flow that Cassie liked the idea of sex, but she did not know nor care if Cassie was active in that way and she also thought that even if she were, Maria didn't consider it any of her business. Maria reasoned that consensual sex was not the same as forced sex using drugs. She felt she had to protect her friends from guys like Raul.

The crew arrived back at *Royal Catering* after midnight. The girls helped Charlie unload the van and then headed out in Cassie's Mustang. Cassie and Alicia wanted to go find some fun somewhere, but Maria wanted to get home. She had called home several times during the evening to tell Mike and her folks what was going on, but she never expected this gig to last so long.

Alicia said, "OK party pooper, we'll drop you off and then head out looking for some fun."

Maria wears a plastic mood ring which contains the same GPS tracking technology contained in the CR3 chip but without the thought reading characteristics. When Maria arrived home Mike was waiting up for her. He tracked her all evening from her mood ring and knew exactly where she was. Even so, he still worried about his sister's safety.

Maria seemed surprised that Mike was still awake. He was seated at the kitchen table when she came through the door from the carport. His Sino Dragon cell phone lay on the table in front of him tracking dozens of CR3 chips now residing in the inner most regions of a number people who were at the banquet just a few hours earlier.

Mike looked up, "Hi Sis, glad you're home. I was a bit concerned when I heard Raul Ramos harassing you. I was worried he might offer you a drink with something sinister in it, but I figured you'd not accept anything like that from him."

Maria recounted how she deliberately knocked over and spilled the drink Raul poured for Cassie. "You know Mike, that guy creeps me out."

"Yeah Sis, me too. Say, you did a number on the cartel this evening. I set up an automatic transfer sending all the CR3 data flow coming from the chips. It's going straight to Jack Reynolds secure phone line. I hope he doesn't get suspicious about how we gathered so much stuff in so little time."

It was not long until Mike's fears were realized. He and Maria were summoned to meet with their dad and Mr. Jack Reynolds.

Mr. Reynolds began, "Something doesn't make sense to me. I barely mentioned to you last time we met that there would be a banquet at the home of Diego Ramos. I cautioned you both not to get too involved. I only asked you to keep your eyes and ears open. It appears that you, or someone you know has literally opened the minds and hearts of five dozen people. I have received and processed a constant information flow which appears to be the thoughts and words of everyone in the cartel and then some by a factor of at least two or three."

He paused. Mike and Maria shifted nervously. Then Jack continued. "Would you care to explain to me and to your father just how you managed to get so many people to literally open up to the DEA?"

Maria couldn't keep it in. She blurted out, "Mike and I have been planting CR3 chips in people, getting them to swallow the chips by putting them in food and drinks. We started doing it at our pool party and it worked so well, we decided to keep doing it. We found out that Bobby Durand was molested by Mr. Oglesby and Mike got Oglesby arrested, and we found out that Raul Ramos wanted to rape Cassie Phelps, and we found out that some of the boys including Raul use date rape drugs to get sex when their girlfriends say no and we found out that.........." She stopped abruptly.

She didn't know if she should tell how she and Mike gave Mr. Cunningham of the IRS one of the chips in his food and then blackmailed him into halting the disruptive audit. She wasn't sure that a DEA agent could be trusted not to turn them in to the IRS for what they did.

Gordon Hollister looked at his two teenage children. Were they remorseful, or were they bragging? He wasn't quite sure but he was proud of them at any rate.

Jack Reynolds did not seem surprised that these kids used technology developed by their dad's firm to have some fun. He has kids of his own and he knows it is part of being a teenager to push limits. But he was concerned that Mike and Maria may have put themselves in some degree of danger if the cartel ever figures out what happened to expose their operations.

Gordon told Mike and Maria to return to the R&D lab and wait until he called them. In the meantime, he and Mr. Reynolds would discuss the situation.

Jack Reynolds proposed that the DEA offer a contract to GMH Technology to purchase CR3 chips and related software for surveillance. Gordon made a counter offer to lease but not to sell the intellectual property to the government and to include any upgrades during the life of the contract. Mr. Reynolds agreed to take it up with the DEA. He assured Gordon that he would expedite the process and have a contract ready to sign within a few days.

After dinner that evening Gordon Hollister asked Mike and Maria to step into his home office. They weren't sure what was coming, but they felt it was probably going to hurt.

Gordon began, "You two are very important to me and your mom. We love you both very much and we don't want any harm to come to either of you. What you did using the chips was not wise, and you know it. In many ways what you did was unethical and illegal. You are not a law enforcement agency and you had no legal authority to spy on anyone. You violated the privacy rights of the kids you spied on after your pool party. I'm not a lawyer, but I can guess that you violated constitutional guarantees against illegal search and seizure as well. I read the constitution in my history classes at the university. Privacy is part of the bedrock of our nation's heritage. Now, I realize that you did a good thing in exposing Mr. Oglesby for molesting your class mate. I know you meant well when you exposed the drug cartel, but kids, there is a limit to what any citizen should get involved with. You need to leave the heavy lifting to government agencies charged with enforcing the law. Is that clear?"

Mike and Maria sat silently absorbing their father's thoughts. They felt ashamed and proud of themselves at the same time. Maria offered, "Dad, do you remember how surprised you were when Mr. Cunningham suddenly ended the IRS audit?"

Gordon looked puzzled, "Don't tell me you had something to do with that. I probably shouldn't know even if you did."

Mike and Maria just smiled at their dad. He returned the smile and said, "Well enough of all this for now. We can talk more about this later if we need to. Off to bed with both of you."

At breakfast Gordon Hollister viewed the TV news. *Drug cartel rounded up in overnight raids. Forty three people arrested on charges of importing and distributing illegal drugs including heroin and cocaine. Warrants issued for seventeen additional suspects who are still sought by authorities.*

## CHAPTER 7

## SITUATION WELL IN HAND

Martha Wilson called her boss on the video intercom. "Mr. Hollister, there is a Mr. Myron Russell from the General Services Administration here to see you sir. Shall I send him in?"

Gordon Hollister welcomed his caller into his office. "What can I do for you Mr. Russell?"

Myron Russell handed Gordon his card. "Mr. Hollister I am here to present you with a government contract calling for the purchase of and use of proprietary hardware and software which your firm developed."

Gordon reached out and took a large envelope from Myron Russell. He sat back down and opened it pulling its contents onto his desk. "Mr. Russell, I was under the impression that Mr. Jack Reynolds would present us with a limited contract from the DEA. I expected to see a contract several months ago. Mr. Reynolds thought it would take a week at best. What took the government so long to make a decision?"

"Mr. Hollister, these things often take time. Several agencies are involved and the entire process is dependent upon available appropriations from Congress. Some appropriations are circumscribed by conditions written in various committees, so as you can see, the government moves at a different pace than the private sector."

Gordon looked over the documents spread before him. "This appears to be a contract cutting across all government agencies. Would you care to explain?"

"Of course, it is quite simple Mr. Hollister. To save money, the government often makes purchases for the benefit of any and all federal agencies which may find a new technology useful. I hope that doesn't get in the way of our doing business with GMH Technology."

Gordon chuckled, "Well, that is a switch. The government interested in saving money I mean. Don't get me wrong Mr. Russell, I like the idea of economy in government." He continued, "Who will we be delivering our product and services to if not directly to the DEA?"

"The GSA will coordinate all purchases and deliveries to the various agencies. We will want to know that this technology is secure against our nation's enemies, so we will be assigning some personnel to work directly in your company with your R&D staff and production departments. I assure you, they will not get in your way, but will be on hand to assist you in any way you find them useful. I am not a scientist Mr. Hollister, but I understand that your new technology is a scientific accomplishment of the highest order and it could be of the utmost importance to our national security."

Gordon responded, "You make it sound almost as if we had invented a nuclear weapon or something of that magnitude."

"Mr. Hollister, if I understand correctly this technology

could actually be more important in the long run than nuclear weapons, which by the way, some in government are hoping that your development may make nukes and other weapons of mass destruction totally unnecessary in the future. We could use a more peaceful world. Don't you agree?"

Gordon studied his visitor for a long moment. "Yes, I do agree. I have two kids. I hope we never see another war in this century or any time in the world's future. But the world has seen many technical developments which promised peace, but instead brought on destructive wars. We can only hope."

"Mr. Hollister, please have your legal department study the contract I handed you. If your people propose any changes, my office phone and fax numbers are in the folder. Please have them contact my staff. Well, I'll leave this with you for now. We hope you will agree to our contract proposal. Thank you for your time, Mr. Hollister."

Gordon accompanied his visitor to the outer office and shook his hand as they parted. "We'll get back to you as soon as possible Myron. Thanks for coming by."

Gordon paged his secretary and asked her send the contract packet to the head of the company's legal department. Martha Wilson stepped in and picked up the packet. "Right away sir."

"Thank you Martha. Please hold any calls for me until I return. I am going to visit the R&D staff. I shouldn't be long.

Gordon entered the lab and found his team of young

scientists in a heated debate about how to further develop the idea of detecting brain waves and to do so from a greater distance than using a chip inside a subject. When he walked up behind them, they didn't notice his presence.

"Well, this sounds serious. So what is the next great thing to emerge from this lab?" He smiled.

The three turned and greeted him. "Oh, hello Mr. Hollister, we didn't hear you come in."

"Well, that was obvious. What are you three plotting to do now that you have shown us you can capture and process human thought and speech and the subject doesn't even know you are doing it?"

Chun Li spoke. "Mr. Hollister we believe that it may be possible to detect and to process human thought waves from outside, not inside the body and doing so with nothing attached to the person. This would give us the ability to capture thoughts without the need to have a subject accept a chip to be inserted medically, or as we learned from Mike and Maria that some subjects actually ingested the chips."

Gordon paused for a moment. "I'm not sure I approve of their actions, but what was done is done."

"Mr. Hollister," Chun Li continued, "Don't be too hard on the kids, they provided us with, .... Shall we say, ....field trials we didn't expect to conduct. And the results they shared with us are a credit to any scientist." She added, "Maria and Mike have a great future in science. I'm sure they will go far."

Gordon grinned, "If I catch them doing anything else as bizarre as the antics they already pulled, they both may go far, but it won't be in the direction they are counting on." He laughed. He continued, "Well, the reason I came to see you is that we are considering a contract with the federal government to utilize your discoveries. This will mean some changes to a few things around the plant and the lab. For starters, the government will assign some people to secure our facilities and to secure our personnel against threats from bad actors who might want to steal our development or worse, threaten harm to our staff, including you three."

David Goldstein spoke up, "Mike is very well versed now in nano technology and related chemistry. While he is still in high school he already knows more than I did through much of my bachelor's degree studies at the university. If, as you say, bad actors have any thoughts about us, you need to know that Mike could be almost as vulnerable as we are."

Chun Li added, "And Maria is very advanced now for a high school student in her knowledge of brain wave research. As David said, Mike and Maria could become targets for bad actors if they find out what the kids have learned."

This gave Gordon pause. Until this moment, the thought hadn't occurred to him that his kids could become a high value target on the national security scene. He was aware that if the drug cartel ever learned of his son and daughter's involvement with their downfall, things could get ugly very quickly. Well, now he thought, he also must consider that his children, his flesh and blood, could be in the cross hairs of some very vicious people on the planet, people who don't exactly appreciate the United States.

After dinner in the evening Gordon and Patricia watched the local news. Mike and Maria were playing games on their cell phones out on the patio. Gordon hit the record button on the DVR. He turned to his wife, "Pat, I want the kids to hear this when they come inside. This could affect all of us in some way."

The news story detailed how a federal judge dismissed all charges against several members of the Zeta drug cartel. The judge lectured the federal prosecutor in the case and pointed out that he had produced no forensic or other evidence to connect those arrested with importing, possessing or distributing illegal drugs. The only evidence the prosecutor had presented was hearsay evidence lacking any credibility at best and worst of all, had been obtained without a search warrant.

When Mike and Maria came into the family room, Gordon motioned for them to sit down and listen to the story from the DVR. Maria turned to her dad and asked, "What does it mean, if they have the thoughts and listened to the audio of a bunch of criminals and they can't even charge them with a crime?"

Mike spoke up, "Sis, it sounds like the judge didn't accept what the prosecutor put before him because of what it was and the way it was collected. This can sometimes be a good thing or a bad thing. It is good if you're the one charged, and bad if the drug gang goes free and they find out who finked on 'em and got 'em arrested. And that would be you Sis, that would be you."

Patricia chimed in, "Mike don't tell your sister things like that. You know better than to tease her."

Mike responded, "Mom, I'm not teasing. If Raul Ramos ever finds out that Maria was the one who….." He stopped himself. He wasn't sure if his mother knew that he and Maria were in over their heads playing detective and using the latest technology from their father's company.

Gordon spoke up, "Alright you two, you have nothing to worry about, so go on to your rooms and make sure you have your homework finished before you hit the sack tonight." He gave each one a hug and sent them out of the family room.

Patricia turned to her husband. "OK, spill it. What should Mike and Maria be worried about?"

Gordon couldn't keep things away from his wife when he knew that she was an equal partner in both bringing these kids into the world and in raising them. During pillow talk that evening Gordon tried as gently as he knew how to break the news to Patricia that their children had not only become quite advanced in the science of brain wave detection, but that they had also played private detective. In so doing they busted a sexual predator at their school, and helped the DEA to arrest members of a vicious drug cartel.

A second bit of news which he hadn't yet shared with Mike and Maria but now shared with Patricia concerned the impending contract with the federal government and how it might also effect Mike and Maria. He filled her in on how much progress in science the kids made while working with the R&D team. He let his wife know that their children could become a target of espionage to learn what they knew about thought collection and transmission. Needless to say, Patricia was not happy when confronted with the totality of these developments.

"My God, Gordon, what if the Zeta cartel comes after our kids? What if they murder Maria for her role in helping the DEA? What if some foreign country wants to kidnap the kids and torture them to make them tell all they know about this new technology? Do you have any idea how much danger our family may face?"

Gordon did not sleep well. He pondered his wife's concerns. In the light of the morning, and over a cup of his favorite coffee, Gordon managed to conjure up a more positive attitude. *Well, so there are dangers in the world.* He thought, *Don't we all face dangers of all sorts every time we get out of bed? Of course we do, but we live our lives anyway and we live with a positive attitude without fear of what could happen, we just live our lives and try to make good things happen.*

Gordon's secretary stepped into his office and began to announce that there is an Ariana MacKenzie to see him. Before she finished her statement Ariana followed Martha into Gordon's office. The newcomer thrust out her hand. Gordon stood up and extended his hand in greeting. "Well, to what do we owe the pleasure of your visit Ms. MacKenzie?"

What was not yet known to Gordon or anyone at GMH Technology is that Ariana MacKenzie is a thirty-two year old graduate of the Naval Academy where she majored in Information Technology and applied it to weapons systems. She is a veteran of the War in Afghanistan having served there with the United States Marine Corps rising to the rank of Major in Intelligence Operations. She completed three tours of duty in the war zone. Ariana earned black belts in Judo and Tae Kwon Do. She is a weapons expert in fire arms and explosives. She is ambitious. She speaks several languages including Arabic, Farsi, German and Spanish.

"Mr. Hollister, allow me to introduce myself. I am Ariana MacKenzie. Mr. Myron Russell from GSA, General Services Administration told me I should report to you this morning to begin my duties as a member of the R&D Staff in the role of Chief of Security. Have you read my resume sir?"

Gordon didn't know quite what to say. He began, "Ms. MacKenzie, I have not had the privilege of reading your resume. It hasn't come to my attention. Perhaps it is in the material on my desk this morning. I usually get a ton of material delivered by my secretary each morning and I take some time before lunch to look through it."

"Please Mr. Hollister, call me Ari. That's what all my friends call me and that's what I prefer."

"Well....ah....Ari....if that's what you prefer. I am a bit surprised that you are here, as you say, reporting for duty. We have not yet signed our contract with GSA."

She interrupted him, "But you will be signing."

"Well....I suppose so, but our legal department hasn't yet accepted the GSA proposal or made a counter proposal."

"No need to worry sir. We have the situation well in hand. Your R&D Staff and Department will be secured starting this morning. My assistant, a Mr. Kurt Rinehart will arrive within the hour to begin an inventory of security requirements. I trust we will have your full cooperation sir."

Gordon began to wonder what he was getting into. He hadn't previously done business to any extent with federal authorities. He wondered, *Is this a portent of things to come?*

Gordon accompanied Ari to the R&D lab and made the introductions. As the five were beginning to get acquainted the door swung open and in walked a newcomer. Ari turned in his direction, "Please allow me to introduce my assistant, Mr. Kurt Rinehart. You will be seeing a lot of both of us from now on."

Gordon and the others were soon to learn all about Kurt Otto Rinehart from his resume. He is a thirty-four year old grandson of German immigrants who fled Nazi Germany in 1937 to settle in Santiago, Chile. He grew up speaking both German and Spanish and learned English while attending High

School in South Florida. He earned a degree in Electrical Engineering at the University of Miami with a minor in Information Technology. He is a former employee of a covert federal agency and has traveled extensively overseas in various assignments.

Kurt shook hands all around and stood by silently while Ari continued speaking. "Kurt and I will take a look around the entire plant and make an inventory of security issues which need to be addressed. We will concentrate first on the R&D Lab and its immediate vicinity. We trust we will have your help if we need it. We promise not to get in your way. If we can explain our role as we go along, just ask us and we will try to answer honestly anything you ask. Are there any questions?"

Gordon and the others stood by with blank expressions. Gordon served in the Air Force and recalled how military people speak and how they are prone to take charge of a situation. From Ari's demeanor Gordon instantly recognized a person with poise and a military bearing. They would soon learn much more about this young woman and her assistant.

Gordon hoped that for the sake of his family, the firm, and the country what Ari said earlier in his office would turn out to be true. *"We have the situation well in hand."*

# CHAPTER 8

## A GREAT LEAP FORWARD

Maria Hollister spent more and more time in the R&D Lab working alongside her mentor Chun Li. She learned that while Chun Li was at the China Neurological Research Institute during her year there, she pioneered in two-way communication with the human brain. Not only is it possible to detect and translate brain waves into readable text but it is also possible to translate information into data packets which can be uploaded into the human brain. The staff at CNRI had only performed a few experiments using electrodes connected directly to a person. Chun Li suggested that it might be possible to do the same thing by way of a CR3 chip with some modifications to the software and the encrypted cell phone application.

Chun Li and Maria talked it over with David and Oren and the four of them decided to try incorporating two-way communication using a modified CR3 chip. Oren and David modified the chip's internal circuitry and Oren wrote an upgrade version of the cell phone app and the chip's software.

Maria brought her tablet computer containing all of her high school text books in electronic form to the lab. Chun Li suggested they use this material to try and prove the new chip design. Maria selected her second year physics course for the trial run. For the test, she wore a modified CR3 chip taped to her temple. The chip was formatted into sectors with all of her private thoughts isolated to one sector. All new information would be kept in a separate sector so that she would not be embarrassed by the lab crew knowing how she felt about very personal ideas.

The trial run was a bit bumpy at first. Maria received several chapters but did not recall everything which was uploaded into her brain. After a few sessions, her recall became almost perfect. When the Physics text was completely uploaded, she felt like pushing limits. Next the crew used her advanced calculus text, followed by organic chemistry, World History, and World Literature. At the end of the trials, Maria and the R&D team were totally astonished at her ability to retain and recall everything. She passed all trial exams with scores of one hundred percent.

At the end of the third week at school Maria became bored with the pace of her classes. She was making one hundred percent on all in-class exams as well as homework assignments. This trend did not go unnoticed by some of her peers. Rhonda Barrett and Beverly Talbot questioned her new found ability. In the hallway at the end of the school day, Beverly demanded to know, "Girl how do you do it? You are suddenly some sort of genius and we know you don't even study, because we hang out with you."

Rhonda looked askance, "What did you do anyway, memorize all the text books?"

Maria thought, "I can't tell them about the modified chip at my dad's plant. What will I tell them?"

Beverly broke in, "I'll bet you found a way to cheat on the exams."

This stung Maria. She had always been honest and had never cheated even when she knew other students did. "You know, I can't explain it, maybe my mind has grown some since last school year."

Rhonda shot back, "It's gotta be something more than that. You just aren't the same Maria we've always known."

Maria thought, *if this new method of learning is going to pay off for me and for the R&D Team I'm going to find a way to take advantage of it. To heck with what anyone else thinks.*

Working with Chun Li, Maria added all the courses for her next and final year of high school. For one solid week, these two converted the entire senior year curriculum into data packets and uploaded them to Maria's brain. She was able to score one hundred percent on all practice exams. *Now,* she thought, *I am a year ahead of my brother Mike, but how do I go about proving this to my family and best of all to my teachers?*

Chun Li and the R&D Team were delighted with the results of these experiments. Needless to say, so was Maria. She made an appointment to talk with one of the counselors at the high school. She received encouragement from her counselor and arranged to take the end-of-year exams for both the junior and senior years.

The faculty testing Maria barely believed what they saw. Here was a young lady they had known through her ninth and tenth grade years. Her previous grades were good, but not perfect by any means. Now, suddenly she has completed the last two years of high school in just four weeks. Teachers and administrators investigated the testing procedure and found nothing amiss. *Well*, they thought, *sometimes students show a side we never knew existed.*

Patricia Hollister received a call from the high school principal. She requested a conference with both parents. *It is about your daughter Maria* she was told. Patricia was puzzled. Maria was the good kid in the family. Mike got into mischief sometimes and she and Gordon had to go to a parent conference about their son on occasion. *But not our daughter*, she thought. She couldn't imagine what this was all about.

After dinner that evening, Patricia took her husband aside and told him about the phone call. Gordon was just as puzzled as his wife.

Gordon and Patricia Hollister stepped into the outer office of the school principal and spoke to the secretary. The secretary called the principal and announced their visit.

Principal Harriet Lattimore stepped into the outer office and greeted the Hollisters. "Please come in, we have a lot to discuss."

Neither Gordon nor Patricia had any inkling of what was coming. Ms. Lattimore began by explaining the seemingly unreal phenomenon. “Maria has tested out of all remaining courses for high school graduation,” she told them.

Gordon and Patricia glanced at each other with a puzzled look.

Patricia spoke first, “Ms. Lattimore, are you sure you have the right Maria in mind? This just doesn’t sound like our daughter. Her grades up to now have been good but by no means outstanding. Surely there must be some mistake.”

Ms. Lattimore responded, “We all thought the same thing at first, but we’ve looked closely at the process by which Maria was able to complete these end-of-year exams in all courses, not only for her junior year, but for her senior year as well. It strikes me that your daughter may have been a latent genius all along and just didn’t reveal it until now.”

Gordon thought for a moment, “What do you propose that we do now? She is only sixteen and it appears that she is ready to leave high school.”

“Well, Mr. and Mrs. Hollister, if I were you I would be very proud to have a daughter like Maria. I would encourage her to go on to university as soon as possible. Her teachers and I have discussed this and we think she is mature enough to handle university courses.”

Gordon and Patricia tried to absorb all of this. Patricia asked, “Ms. Lattimore, will Maria receive a high school diploma as a result of these exams?”

“Absolutely, as soon as the school board approves the

issuance, one will be presented to your daughter."

At home that evening, Gordon and Patricia called the family together. Mike and Maria heard the news from their parents. Maria would be out of high school this week, and on her way to university.

Maria explained to her parents and her brother that she and Chun Li have advanced the use of the CR3 chip to include two-way transfer of brain waves. They believe that the technique will lead to a whole range of uses. Maria said that Ari and Kurt were fully aware of the development and that they are in contact with some people in Washington who are very interested in this new technology.

Mike expressed interest in advancing his own academic career by using this new method. Maria encouraged him to discuss his desire with the R&D team. "They are always ready for a challenge, and I don't see why my brother shouldn't challenge them totally and push the limits of his brain." She chuckled as she said it.

Gordon expressed pride in both of his children, "Maria is teasing you Mike. Your mom and I know you are both very smart, and with this new development you obviously can become a lot smarter than you have shown us in the past. So, Mike, if you want to advance, then talk with Chun Li tomorrow when you come in to work."

Gordon started the morning staff meeting in the conference room. "I received a briefing from Chun Li about a further development of the CR3 chip. Chun Li suggests we re-designate it as the CR4 since it includes a host of new features, not the least of these is its ability to allow feedback to the human brain via two-way communication. I was totally impressed by what Chun Li and my daughter Maria have shown to be possible using this new chip. My wife and I learned just yesterday that Maria is graduating from high school almost two full years early as a result of tests conducted right here in our lab. Again, I can't tell you how proud I am of all of you."

Gordon's secretary Mrs. Wilson stepped into the conference room. "Mr. Hollister, there's a gentleman waiting to see you when you adjourn your meeting."

"Thank you Mrs. Wilson. I'll be in my office in a few minutes, and you can send him in."

When Gordon received his visitor he wasn't prepared for what he was about to be asked to do. Douglas Winslow introduced himself and began, "Mr. Hollister, I am a member of the president's White House Staff. When he was elected the president promised to close the Guantanamo Bay detention facility. We've just learned about a new technology your company developed. It seems it is capable of planting thoughts into someone's brain. That capability could enable the president to carry out his campaign promise to close Gitmo before his term expires next year."

Gordon Hollister was too busy to follow the politics of the administration and he was taken aback by this proposal.

"Just how do you propose to do that Mr. Winslow?"

"The detainees at Gitmo are generally of two types. One type is the dedicated terrorist who will never under any circumstances be amenable to rehabilitation. That type will always return to the fight against the United States and its allies no matter what. The second type is a person who is amenable to rehabilitation and can be pointed in the direction of peaceful behavior and resettled into a country which will welcome him. We propose to use your discovery to....well as some would say....brain wash the second type and turn them into peaceful people."

Gordon sat silent for a moment. He was thinking, *just yesterday I learned that my own daughter has....perhaps been brain washed as this man puts it, but with a positive outcome. Maybe what Mr. Winslow proposes could also bring about a positive outcome, not only for some jihadi rotting away in Gitmo to be rehabilitated, but if it works, perhaps it could be positive for the world at large.*

"Mr. Winslow, how did the administration hear about our development so quickly? I only learned of its full extent yesterday."

"The government has two people working in your firm Mr. Hollister, Ariana MacKenzie and Kurt Rinehart. They keep their superiors in DC fully apprised of developments here."

Gordon responded, "Well, we haven't yet signed a contract to do business with the government."

Winslow smiled. "But you will sign. Of that much we are certain."

*Now where had he heard that before?* Gordon wondered, oh yes. *From Ari herself the first day she arrived at GMH Tech.*

"Well Mr. Winslow, since you put it that way, I suppose you and the administration will insist on a contract. I'll meet with my legal staff and see what the delay has been. I'll see if I can expedite the process. I must say, I am intrigued at the suggestion that we may be able to turn bad actors into good people."

Winslow stood up, "We will need to have some time to train our people to use the technology. When can we begin?"

Gordon responded, "When do you want to begin?"

"Tomorrow morning if that is alright."

"It's a little soon, but I will let my people know someone is coming and I'm sure they will adjust their schedules."

"Thank you Mr. Hollister, I'll be in touch from time to time. You have my card, and your secretary knows how to contact my office. By the way, Ariana MacKenzie will be in charge of the project and will see to the transfer of necessary equipment and personnel to Gitmo. Thank you for your time."

When Winslow left, Gordon paused for a moment. He remembered an old saying in the Air Force, *Hurry up and wait. Well* he thought, *things haven't changed much when you're dealing with the federal government. Jack Reynolds promised a contract with DEA within a week at most, and instead Myron*

*Russell shows up many months later with a government wide contract from GSA.*

Gordon met immediately with his legal staff and signed the GSA contract to do business with the federal government. To do business with any and all agencies of the government, civilian, military, and now it seems political branches as well. He hoped something good would come from this new business source. Perhaps a new revenue stream.

At eight o'clock the next morning a Mr. Frank Fletcher entered the R&D lab in the company of Ariana MacKenzie and Kurt Rinehart. Mr. Fletcher seemed to be in charge. He introduced himself all around and got right down to business.

"I'm from *The Agency*, this is a euphemism for a covert section of the federal government. You will always refer to us as *The Agency*, no other designation is necessary. The reason I'm here is to give you our requirements for a modification you will make in the CR4 chip."

Fletcher seemed to know a great deal about this new chip, much more than anyone might be expected to know who only arrived this morning. He continued, "We will be using the feed-back feature to good advantage in an upcoming program, but we have two additional requirements for that and for future programs of similar nature. First, we must be able to trigger excruciating attacks of tri-geminal neuralgia in both sides of the face. This will act much like a shock collar on an animal only its effect will be thousands of times worse. The second requirement is that we be able to shut down the autonomic nerve system to bring on death when necessary. Can you incorporate these requirements?"

Chun Li looked stunned. Oren and David stared at this newcomer in disbelief.

Chun Li spoke, "Mr. Fletcher, what you are asking us to do is to torture and or kill a person who has the modified chip. We are scientists, but we are also human beings and we have serious reservations about your requested changes."

Fletcher shot back, "Reservations or not, you are under contract with *The Agency* and we have certain requirements which must be met."

David Goldstein responded, "Mr. Fletcher, with all due respect, my grandparents were tortured and murdered by the Nazis at Dachau. I personally have an aversion to carrying out what you are asking. Isn't there some alternative to these features?"

Fletcher gave David a cold stare. "Son, the world is awash with terrorism right now. Civilized nations are forced to fight back with everything available. The CR4 chip with these modifications may well be one of the best ways to fight these murderous thugs. While I appreciate your feelings about the loss of your grandparents we are trying to prevent just such atrocities as those carried out by the Nazis at places like Auschwitz Buchenwald, Bergen-Belsen, and Dachau and all of the other six dozen Nazi extermination camps spread across Europe during the holocaust. If we lose this fight, there will be new place names added to the long roster of those infamous places. Names like Mosul, Tikrit, Fallujah, Haditha, and countless others where ISIS kidnaps, rapes, tortures, and carries out mass murder. We can't afford to lose the fight with this new band of murderous barbarians."

David responded, "Well, I will have to do some deep soul searching before I put my talents to such a development."

Oren added, "I'm with David, I will have to think about this sir."

Ari spoke up, "Mr. Fletcher that is all we need to know at this time. We will keep you informed as to our decision. Thank you for coming."

As Frank Fletcher left the lab the R&D staff sat in stunned silence.

# CHAPTER 9

# THE GENIE ESCAPES

Chun Li, Oren Lunsford, and David Goldstein were already in the conference room when Gordon Hollister arrived. They were very quiet which was in bold contrast to their usual raucous discussions about new ideas for incorporation into the company's products.

Gordon sat down at the table, looked around and began the meeting. "Why is it that I get the impression that something is not quite right with my whiz kids this morning?"

At first no one spoke. Oren and David looked to their leader Chun Li hoping she could explain the situation to the company owner.

Chun Li began, "Mr. Hollister, we received a visit in the lab yesterday from a Mr. Frank Fletcher. He is from....what he euphemistically referred to as...... *The Agency*. It appears to be a covert federal program of some sort. What disturbs us is that Mr. Fletcher demands that we make two major modifications to the CR4 chip. He wants to use the chip to read out people's thoughts and upload new thoughts into those subjects, but he also wants to use the chip to torture and even kill subjects wearing the chip. The three of us find that abhorrent."

Gordon was taken aback by this revelation. He thought it would be a simple process dealing with federal authorities. He never dreamed that his firm would be asked to create a death-dealing product. No not asked, demanded to make a deadly device.

"Did Mr. Fletcher explain why *The Agency* has such requirements?"

Oren responded, "Mr. Hollister, it sounded like the government wants to harness our chip in the never-ending war on terrorists around the world."

"Well, what do the three of you think about that idea?" Gordon asked.

David responded, "We discussed it among ourselves when Mr. Fletcher left the lab and our consensus is that we will not make the modifications he demands. It is against our consciences."

"I hear you, but I don't quite know what to say at this point. I will get in touch with Frank Fletcher and see if I can learn more about these requirements. Don't worry about it for now. I encourage all of you to continue improving the capabilities of all of the company's products just as you always have. Leave this problem to me for now. I'll let you know what I work out with the feds."

Mike Hollister came to work in the R&D lab at every opportunity. Chun Li agreed to accelerate his academic career just as she had done for Maria. Mike absorbed his entire senior year curriculum in just two sessions.

Principal Harriet Lattimore was more than a little amazed at this young man, the sibling of her most recent student prodigy. Ms. Lattimore called Mike's parents with the same message about their son she had very recently delivered to them concerning Maria. The faculty and staff again examined the testing process and all agreed everything was above board. There was no cheating going on. But, they seemed to ask, how could a student who previously showed no outward signs of genius suddenly develop so rapidly? It would remain a mystery for a while, but not for much longer. What they could not foresee was that chaos would soon reign in the academic world.

Mike and Maria received their high school diplomas in a special ceremony in the school auditorium. The student body was in total disbelief. What, they wondered, could possibly be a logical explanation for this phenomenon? After all, Mike and Maria were ordinary students, not known for outstanding academic performance. Suspicion reigned. Were their parents bribing the faculty? Was money and influence used to get these two their diplomas so far ahead of their peers? Speculation was rampant. Conspiracy theories gained traction on campus. Even a few teachers who did not know the Hollister siblings were suspicious of the administration and gave voice to doubts further advancing talk of conspiracy and possible bribes.

Mike was able to enroll along with Maria in the university. The siblings began their college careers on an equal footing. However, Maria, always wanting to try and one up her older brother decided to try the CR4 system again to see if she could advance beyond her freshman year.

Maria and Chun Li set up the experiment using the entire four year list of courses leading to the Bachelor of Science degree in Bio-Medical Engineering. Chun Li spent several days converting all course material from e-book format into data packets to be uploaded into Maria's brain. She warned Maria that this much data had never before been uploaded in lab tests, and that it might be a bit risky to do it all in one session.

Maria insisted on doing it in one session so that she could get on with her life. Secretly she thought, just wait until Mike finds out. She had always been in some sort of competition with her older brother. Even when they were very young, Maria not only competed with Mike on the playground, but always wanted to be first in any endeavor they were a part of. *Now*, she thought, *this will be the big one.*

Chun Li insisted on secrecy from the other members of the R&D lab team. The transfer process was carried out in a small room beside Chun Li's office. When the upload began, all seemed to go well. In the second hour, things started to become complicated. Maria felt flushed and just a little nauseas but did not complain. By the third hour Maria started to sweat profusely. Chun Li was unaware that anything was amiss. She took a break to go for a snack and a cup of tea. Well into the third hour of uploading to her brain, Maria passed out and fell forward striking her head on the edge of a table. Chun Li was not in the room and did not witness the event. When she returned from her break Chun Li stopped the upload and called out for help.

Ari and Kurt rushed into the room. They picked Maria up from the floor and placed her in the chair from which she had fallen. She had a bad gash on her forehead where she struck the table. Maria was unconscious and very warm. There was a small trickle of blood down her nose from the wound on her forehead. Chun Li called 9-1-1 immediately and then called Gordon Hollister on the video intercom.

Gordon rode in the ambulance to the local hospital with his daughter and Chun Li. Patricia Hollister met them at the emergency room. Maria's temperature was dropping slowly, but at its highest point it had reached 103 degrees Fahrenheit. Gordon and Patricia were puzzled by this turn of events. Maria had been in seemingly perfect health when she left home that morning.

The ER doctor recommended that Maria be admitted for observation. All lab tests came back negative, but the doctor expressed concern about the sudden onset of Maria's condition whatever it might turn out to be.

Patricia and Gordon sat up all night beside their daughter. Mike joined them around nine p.m. that evening. He talked in low tones with his parents about his sister. He said that in spite of all their sibling rivalry he really does love the kid and doesn't want anything bad to ever happen to her.

The next morning a staff physician accompanied by three other people in white lab coats came by to examine Maria. By this time she was semi-conscious and babbling about some things Gordon and Patricia could not quite fathom. The medical staff in the room looked askance at one another. One of them spoke, "This girl is talking about a lot of the things we learned in medical school."

He turned to Gordon and Patricia, "Is your daughter a medical student?"

Patricia responded, "Certainly not. She is barely out of high school. She is however, beginning her first year in the university. I believe she is majoring in Bio-Medical Engineering."

One of the medical staff spoke up, "Well, from the sound of her ramblings she has a good grip on the subject already."

Gordon and Patricia looked at each other. Gordon motioned to Chun Li to follow the parents out into the hallway. Gordon inquired, "What can you tell us about this? Have you and Maria been using the CR4 system chip to accelerate her knowledge again?"

Chun Li had grown to love Maria like a little sister. She knew she had to share the truth with the young lady's parents.

"Yes, Maria insisted and I went along with it. We were attempting to upload the entire four year curriculum leading to the Bachelor of Science in Bio-Medical Engineering. It is all my fault. I should have known better than to try and upload the entire four years in one session as Maria insisted on doing."

Chun Li began to sob. "If anything bad comes of this I will never forgive myself."

Patricia put her arm around Chun Li's shoulder and told her, "It certainly isn't your fault. Our daughter always has been overly ambitious and unfortunately is always competing with her brother over almost anything you can name."

In midafternoon a staff psychologist came to the room and examined Maria. When he completed his interview he asked Gordon and Patricia to follow him to a private room for a conference. He told the parents, "The medical staff can find nothing wrong with your daughter. She doesn't have a treatable illness. We believe that she is under a great deal of stress right now. It would appear that she has a lot on her mind."

Gordon thought, *Doctor, you have no idea how much my daughter has on her mind. If I told you, you would never believe it.*

Maria was released and went home with her parents. After dinner Mike and Maria went out onto the patio and sat facing each other in opposite hammocks. Mike told Maria, "I've got some bad news Sis. Ari and Kurt have told the R&D staff and they told dad that for security reasons our access to the lab will be sharply curtailed in the future. They said that the developments at the lab are just too sensitive to allow us unlimited access."

Maria frowned. "But what will we do to continue learning about brain wave and chip development if we can't go to the lab like we used to?"

"Don't fret little Sis, I've made sure that if this ever

happened we can carry on our work here at home."

"Mike, what on earth are you saying?"

"I feared this day would come so I collected dozens of CR3 and CR4 chips, and I downloaded all of the latest software from the server in the lab into both of our Sino Dragon phones. I've got everything we need to continue our involvement without going to the lab. I have the latest computer algorithms for two-way communication, I have the translation software, and the entire design for the whole dang system. And do you want to know what else I did?" He grinned.

Maria was never quite sure she wanted to know what Mike was up to in case the two of them got caught in some nefarious scheme. "OK Mike, what else did you do?"

Mike paused.....he grinned at his sister for a long moment as if to keep her guessing. Then he offered, "I managed to get a CR4 chip into all three of our R&D staff. When we all got together in the cafeteria for lunch, I offered to prepare our burritos. I slipped all three of them a chip in their food and from what I can see on my phone app it worked like a charm. Later I even slipped a chip into Ari and Kurt as well. This could come in handy sometime. I am keeping up with their whereabouts and everything they are doing. I am able to read their innermost thoughts. This should give us a leg up when it comes to knowing what is going on in the lab and beyond."

Maria gasped, "Mike! Holy crap, what if dad finds out?"

Mike just kept on grinning. “Well, let’s hope that never happens.”

Patricia stepped out onto the patio. “OK you two, it is past ten o’clock and time for you both to get ready for bed. Maria you’ve had a rough day. I don’t think you need to sit out here in the evening dampness and possibly catch cold. So off to your rooms with the both of you.”

Patricia hugged her kids as they went inside. The parents sat for a while in the family room. Patricia spoke, “Gordon, what do you think will happen to our kids if this pace of academic acceleration continues? I mean, it seems that every time we turn around one of our kids has vaulted over another great hurdle in their educational path. Where will this all lead?”

Gordon wasn’t sure how to respond. He just smiled at his wife, gave her a hug, kissed her and said goodnight.

The next week at the university, Maria approached her academic adviser, Dr. Emily Landis. She wasn’t sure how to proceed. She asked rather timidly, “Dr. Landis, what would you think if a student wanted to test out of the courses in their major?”

Her adviser didn’t hesitate. Dr. Landis responded with a friendly smile, “That is something we do all the time. Which course would you like to test out of?”

Maria sat for a moment, not sure how to respond. Finally she found her voice, “All of them.”

Her advisor had never faced this prospect before. “Are

you telling me that you are ready to complete all of your requirements for your Bachelor of Science in Bio-Medical Engineering? Is that what you are saying?"

Maria responded, "Pretty much that is it. I feel ready. I....I uh....have been preparing for this...and I think I am ready."

Dr. Landis studied this young lady's expression for a long moment. "Well, it has never been done before, but I suppose there is always a first time for everything under the sun. It will need to be approved by the Board of Regents, the President, the Academic Dean, and the Faculty Senate, but let me see what I can do."

That was all Maria could expect for now. When she got home that evening she felt confident that things were going her way. She thought, *if this works the way I hope it does I will be ahead of my dear brother for sure. At least for now.*

She fell asleep filled with ideas about what she could do with a Bachelor's degree at the age of sixteen. Perhaps she might be able to earn enough to afford to begin taking flying lessons. It was a fantasy she held since kindergarten. *Maybe now,* she thought, *she could give wings to her fantasies.*

# CHAPTER 10

# GITMO

Gordon Hollister's Secretary Martha Wilson buzzed on the video intercom and announced, "Mr. Hollister there are two gentlemen from Washington here to see you. Do you have time to meet with them?"

"Please send them in Mrs. Wilson. I'll make time to see them."

Douglas Winslow and Frank Fletcher entered. Gordon motioned them to be seated. "What brings you gentlemen to South Florida?

Douglas Winslow opened the conversation. "Mr. Hollister, the last time I was here I made it abundantly clear to you that the President desires to empty the detention center at Guantanamo Bay in Cuba of all detainees remaining there following our military actions in the Middle East and Afghanistan. Mr. Fletcher here informs me that your R&D staff is unwilling to cooperate with his people to modify one of your products to meet our requirements. What can you tell me about that?"

Gordon knew this conversation would come up sooner or later. *Well*, he thought, *now is as good a time as any to dispose of this issue.* "Mr. Winslow, my R&D team is one of the finest in the world of science. They conveyed to me their objection to incorporating features to torture or to kill a human being. I'm sure you understand. I cannot and I will not pressure these fine people to go against their deeply held convictions."

Frank Fletcher broke in, "Mr. Hollister, I'm sure you are aware of the requirements stated very clearly in the contract you signed for your firm. It empowers *The Agency*, if need be, to take possession of any product or process we deem in the interest of national security and to manufacture it in our own facilities. It allows *The Agency* to make any and all modifications to your products we deem necessary for the exigencies of the current situation, the war against terrorists."

He continued, "If your staff will not make the desired modifications we will be forced to take over and do whatever is necessary."

Gordon was not pleased with this prospect, but he realized he was up against an intransigent bureaucracy. One against which firms like his own seldom prevail.

"Mr. Fletcher, I will do what I can to cooperate with *The Agency*, but I will not countenance any overt or covert threats." Gordon knew he was bluffing, but it sounded good just to say it and hear his own words while watching the faces of these two bureaucratic bullies.

Fletcher continued, "Mr. Hollister I will expect your R&D people to turn over to my people everything we need in the way of design characteristics and processes used in the creation, testing, and production of the CR4 chip and all of its supporting software and hardware."

Gordon agreed. What else could he do? "Mr. Fletcher

we will deliver what you need within the week. I assure you."

Fletcher responded, "Thank you Mr. Hollister that is all we want. Ariana MacKenzie will be in charge of transferring the technology to our lab in Maryland. We trust we will have a good working relationship with your firm as we go forward with meeting the nation's security needs."

The two visitors stood up to leave. Douglas Winslow said, "Mr. Hollister, allow me to thank you as well on behalf of the President's national security team. We truly appreciate your cooperation."

When they were gone, Gordon thought, *Cooperation or coercion? More of the latter as I see it.*

The next morning Miles Burwell and Dennis Cottrell called upon Gordon at his office. They identified themselves as employees of *The Agency*. They said they had come to take possession of all relevant material related to the development and deployment of the CR4 chip.

Gordon introduced these two gentlemen to the R&D staff. They were quick to learn and very methodical in their approach. It turned out that Miles Burwell is a reverse engineer in all things electronic. He is an expert at identifying and replicating all parts of the most complex and miniature of computer circuits down to the tiniest detail. Miles earned an advanced degree in nano and chemical engineering. Dennis Cottrell is a software engineer with vast experience hacking into and copying almost any software or firmware program.

Ari was not surprised at the arrival of these two. She worked alongside Miles and Dennis in the lab and encouraged Chun Li, Oren, and David to brief them on all aspects of the CR4 system. At the end of a week, Ari, Kurt, Miles and Dennis departed. They were on their way to a well-secured site in Maryland to begin modifications to the CR4.

Mike and Maria Hollister followed these events. They monitored the CR4 chips they fed Ari, Kurt, and the R&D team and were privy to the entire transfer of technology to federal control. They also tracked the whereabouts of Ari as she, Kurt, Miles and Dennis traveled to the site in Maryland. Every time Ari or Kurt were in close proximity to anyone in the Maryland lab it was as if Maria and Mike were standing at their elbow. So clear was the data flow from conversations and Ari's thoughts that nothing escaped their attention.

A month went by and then a second month. Finally Maria and Mike learned the results of the modifications. The feedback feature of the CR4 chip could now be used to trigger a massive electrical shock to both sides of the face of anyone who had the chip on or in their system. The way it worked, the chip stimulated the brain stem which in turn sent a terrible shock to the trigeminal nerves on both sides of the face. It was almost like getting tazed with fifty-thousand volts on both jaws at once. Maria was aware of the trigeminal nerves and how they could be used to torture a person. She had completed all of the requirements for a four year degree in bio-medical engineering.

What disturbed Maria and Mike even more was a feature the federal lab incorporated into the CR4 chip which can take over the hypothalamus and shut down the autonomic nerve system bringing almost instant death to a person. Maria and Chun Li had often discussed the responsibility of a scientist to work to enhance life, not to destroy life. Maria scanned Ari's CR4 output and learned from her thoughts that she had no qualms about using science to hurt or kill humans if necessary.

Another major modification made in the federal lab was how the CR4 communicates with a tracking cell phone. No longer would a regular cell phone be the only means to track thoughts and convey feedback, now the newly modified CR4 had a second and more important method for tracking. It could be accessed by a satellite phone. This feature vastly extended the range for two-way communication. Mike and Maria followed this development closely and would one day copy it and make good use of it.

Watching Ari's thoughts through the text flowing on her Sino Dragon cell phone, Maria learned a lot about the lady. It seems Ari harbors strong animosity for all terrorists, especially those in the Middle East and Afghanistan. Ari remembered how some of her fellow Marines in Helmand Province in Afghanistan were blown to bits by roadside IED's, improvised explosive devices, set by the Taliban. She often ran scenes through her mind that deeply disturbed Maria and Mike as they viewed the text. Perhaps they thought, we've lived a relatively sheltered life. *Maybe,* they thought, *we should try to understand how deeply mortal combat effects some of our military veterans.*

With all modifications to the CR4 made and tested, Ariana MacKenzie made arrangements for herself and Kurt Rinehart to travel directly from a nearby naval air station in Maryland to the naval station at Guantanamo Bay, Cuba.

Riding as passengers aboard a U.S. Navy Boeing P-8 maritime patrol aircraft, a military version of the popular Boeing 737 passenger liner, Ari and Kurt landed at Gitmo early in the morning. They exited the aircraft into the humid tropical air and carried their bags to a waiting van. The two were billeted in a BOQ, or bachelor officer's quarters, near the airfield. Ari's bag contained all that was needed to put into place a system which the White House staff was counting on to fulfill the President's promise to empty the detention center at Gitmo.

The federal lab in Maryland designated the latest version of the CR4 chip as the CR4M, or militarized version of this unique technology. Ironically the government requires a top secret clearance to know about and to work with the CR4M system. What they don't know is that two teenagers in South Florida are totally acquainted with the new chip and have its entire design on their personal computer hard drives as well as in the memory of their Sino Dragon cell phones.

Ari and Kurt showered and changed clothes. They caught a ride with a Jeep driver to an officer's mess in time for the noon meal. At exactly 13:30 hours they reported in to Major Leslie Stratton USMC at her office. The Major gave them a briefing and introduced them to two people with whom they were to work for the next several days.

"Ms. MacKenzie and Mr. Rinehart I want you to meet Captain Brett Wilcox who is my adjutant, and Sgt. Glenn Shelton who will be your liaison within the detention facility. Sgt. Shelton will, along with Cpl. Edmund Harris assist you in everything that you do on this post. Any questions?"

The Major continued, "The two of you hold top secret clearances as do all the people in my command who are involved with the CR4M. It is imperative that we keep the system out of the hands of anyone without this level of security clearance. The purpose of this project is to render each and every detainee fit for expedited release. We are under orders from the CIC, the Commander in Chief, to repatriate all detainees to a selected country willing to accept them. In order to carry out this mission, we will install the CR4M chip in each detainee. We will do this by having them ingest the chip without their knowledge. With the chip in place, our interrogators will be able to identify detainees who are cooperative. Those will be the ones whose thoughts match their words. We will be able to track them after release through the satellite phone system. If any show signs of recidivism, that is if they decide to return to their terrorist ways, we will first use the 'zapper' as we call it to shock them and remind them that they need to change their attitude and if necessary shut them down totally."

Capt. Wilcox took over the briefing. "We plan to release all detainees, even those we know will immediately return to the battle field. We intend to track their movements and learn through the CR4M data flow where they are at all times, and who they are talking to. When and if the time is right, we can either shut them down by turning off their autonomic nerve system, or we can dispatch a drone and fire off a hellfire missile to take out not only the one with the chip, but the entire entourage of everyone present."

The Capt. continued, "We have a special gift for the terrorists. We have a person here who is a double agent and we may be able to use his services to deliver a gift that we hope will keep on giving. He serves our interests even though he is a detainee. We will further evaluate his loyalties through expected data flow after we get a CR4M chip into his system. If he proves loyal, as we hope he will, we will send a special gift to the terrorists by way of this person. More on that later. Any questions?"

"OK, if there are no questions we will begin work tomorrow morning at 08:00 hours."

Mike and Maria enjoyed the briefing just as much as if they had been there. They sat in the hammocks on the patio at their townhouse in South Florida reading the text flow from Ari and Kurt's CR4 chips on their cell phones. They were privy to everything said in the Major's office. Mike looked at his sister,

"Hey Sis, this could be dangerous for the world and for the good old USA. What if the project fails somehow? What if the terrorists can't be tracked for some reason? What then?"

Maria responded, "Mike do you think we should keep on doing this stuff? What if dad finds out? How will we explain everything to him, or to Chun Li and the others? This is beginning to get serious. I mean, this could get us in deep trouble if the government finds out we've been following everything they are doing. You read the text flow. The Major said you need a top secret clearance to know anything about the CR4M chip. We don't have any security clearance and we have all the information to make and use the entire system. What if some spies find out what we have?"

Mike, always the one to reassure Maria said, "Stay cool Sis, nothing bad is going to happen. But we don't need to go talking about any of this among our friends."

Mike continued, "By the way Sis, what have you heard from the university about your degree? Do you know when they might award the degree?"

Maria was relieved to change the subject for a while. "All I know is that the President, the Board of Regents, the Dean of Instruction, and the Faculty Senate all have to give their approval before I can receive the degree. The President said it could take a few weeks for all of those people to meet and make a decision. I sure hope they decide in my favor. I would like to know if I can go to work in the field of Bio-Medical Engineering and also if I can start another activity I've always wanted to do."

"What's that Sis?"

"Mike, I've always wanted to learn to fly. You know the company has two good pilots. They both have their instructor's rating and both have always promised me that if dad approves I could take flying lessons."

The sun was just rising over the base at Gitmo as Ari and Kurt enjoyed an early morning swim in the pool behind the BOQ. Following breakfast in the BOQ mess, Cpl. Edmund Harris USMC, gave the two a lift to the detention facility where their work was to begin. They spent the morning teaching interrogators how the CR4M system is designed to work. How with a chip planted in a subject all thoughts and speech can be detected and presented in plain English on the screen of a specially programmed satellite cell phone.

Kurt presented each member of the group of trainees with their own dual satellite phone courtesy of *The Agency*. He explained how to use them to track and differentiate between subjects. For training purposes, three inmates were selected to receive CR4M chips hidden in their noon meal. Soon Kurt's class of trainees would have live subjects from which to learn their innermost thoughts. Several of the interrogators were skeptical of this new system. They dealt with terrorist inmates every day for years at Gitmo and from experience they knew just how devious a Gitmo guest can be.

When the training session resumed at 13:00 hours

everyone in the class was instructed to turn on their satellite phones, sign in with their user ID and password, and to begin scanning for a designated inmate. Several of the young Marines in the class began chuckling.

Corporal Harris laughed aloud, "See Sarge, I told you that guy who calls himself Mahdi was always lying to us. You owe me a beer Sarge, a bet is a bet."

Sgt. Shelton shot back, "OK, you win. I owe you brew. But look what he's thinking as opposed to what he always told us and what I was almost willing to believe. He always insisted that he knows nothing about any terrorist plans for Jihad and that if he were ever released he would return to his family in Egypt and work on a farm in the Nile delta raising vegetables for sale in the Cairo markets. Take a look, his thoughts say otherwise. He is thinking that if he ever gets out of here he will immediately join up with any rag tag bunch killing Americans and be truly happy to do it."

Major Leslie Stratton took over the session at that point. She addressed the group, "We have two kinds of detainees here. We will be able to triage them by the very method you have just witnessed with Mahdi. We will release all of the detainees within the next thirty days. Mahdi fit's the category which we have designated as 'pointers.' We gave them that designation because they will behave like a breed of hunting dog trained to point out game. When the prisoner is released and returns to the fight, we hope to be able to track their CR4M chip to terrorist leaders. We will be able to read their thoughts and pick up conversations with key players in the terror war."

Captain Wilcox added, "We have two ways to deal with a recidivist like Mahdi. If they lead us to a prime target we can use a drone fired missile to take out the leader and anyone who happens to be with him. If a recidivist goes on a solo mission which threatens our people, such as using a suicide vest or car bomb, we will have advance warning through their chip and we can activate the feature which shuts down their autonomic nerve system and kill them quietly before they carry out their murderous intentions."

He continued, "Within the week we should be able to feed the CR4M chips to all of the detainees in this facility. Following that effort we will begin to release all prisoners as directed by the White House."

Ari and Kurt packed their bags and caught a flight from Gitmo to Key West, landing at Boca Chica Naval Air Station. There they enjoyed a short vacation snorkeling and swimming before returning to work at GMH Technology near Miami. While watching TV in a sports bar, they saw a news report. *The President's press secretary announced today that all detainees formerly held at Guantanamo Bay Cuba have now been released. The President wants the nation to know that he has now kept his campaign promise to close Gitmo.*

Douglas Winslow welcomed Frank Fletcher to the White House for a conference with the President's closest advisors.

Douglas began, “The purpose of our meeting this morning is twofold. First we want to report the success of our program to close the Guantanamo Bay Detention Center. The Secretary of Defense reports excellent results from a classified program for tracking and controlling former detainees who are now back in their home countries.”

Winslow continued, “The rate of recidivism has proven to be extremely low given the nature of the program. Out of the one hundred and sixty-five detainees released, only fourteen returned to the fight against us or our allies. Those who rejoined the fight were quickly shut down and are no longer living. We’re tracking several others who are in contact with the leaders of terrorist groups. The system gives us live, real time locations and even gives us the ability to know exactly what they are thinking and discussing. In addition, we have a double agent known as Ahmed who carried a special gift to ISIS. Mr. Fletcher will explain.”

Fletcher began, “As Mr. Winslow told you, *The Agency* provided a special gift to ISIS. It appears from our tracking data that our double agent Ahmed carried out his assignment to the letter. We gave him a large supply of the tiny CR4M chips which he was to feed to as many ISIS leaders as possible. We know from his tracking data that Ahmed volunteered to cook for the leadership and that he mixed a large batch of the chips into a traditional Arab dish called Kabsa. This consists of meat and vegetables served over a bed of rice. He was instructed to mix the chips into the rice after it was cooked and had cooled a bit."

Frank Fletcher continued, "From the tracking data we receive we now have over one hundred ISIS leaders under surveillance with a CR4M chip in their digestive tract. We know exactly where they are and what they are thinking. This intel is filtered and passed on in real time to allied commanders who order air strikes and coordinate ground actions with the Iraqi security forces. For all practical purposes, we are inside the heads of the enemy. For the first time in the history of warfare we know exactly what the enemy is thinking."

Frank Fletcher continued. "The system we have in place is without a doubt one of the best weapons we have to combat terrorism around the world. It has proven its capabilities many times over by preventing attacks rather than reacting to them. The President plans to build upon this success and turn America into a more just and open society. You will learn more about that later."

# CHAPTER 11

## A NEW DIRECTION

Mike Hollister followed his sister's example. Working with Chun Li on some of the rare occasions he was allowed access to the R&D lab he underwent a series of knowledge uploads to his brain. The two were careful to avoid the physiological symptoms Maria experienced which caused nausea, temperature rise, and loss of consciousness. Chun Li insisted on spreading the university curriculum out over four sessions instead of one. By the end of the fourth session Mike had absorbed the equivalent of a Bachelor of Science degree in chemical and nano engineering with a minor in business administration.

Mike made an appointment to see Dr. Emily Landis his academic advisor at the university. When he explained what he had in mind, Dr. Landis pushed back from her desk, gave him a strange look, and said, "Not you too! Your sister made the same request. What is it with the two of you? The President has your sister's request on his desk and I have as yet to receive a response. The chairperson of the faculty senate has the request and I'm getting some blow back from the faculty about giving out degrees without requiring students to actually attend classes."

Mike interjected, "But I thought the university

encouraged students to take advanced placement exams and move as quickly as possible into more advanced studies. What seems to be the objection?"

Dr. Landis responded, "Well..... It's just not been done this way in the past.....that is.....testing out of an entire degree program. The faculty senate and the national association of professors is looking into the problem and there is no consensus. It's causing a great deal of consternation not only at the college and university level, but also among public school teachers unions as well. Nobody has a rational explanation of how the two of you suddenly advanced your educational level. Until we get to the bottom of this I can't promise either you or your sister that you will be allowed to test out of an entire four year degree at this university."

Mike was stunned. He didn't know what to say. He stood up to go, but turned around to face Dr. Landis. "This hurts not only me, but my sister is going to be terribly disappointed when she finds out that all her efforts went for nothing."

When Mike got home he called Maria to the patio to talk. She listened to Mike recount his meeting with Dr. Landis.

"Mike, I know that we both absorbed the entire four year equivalent of our degrees and could easily test out of all courses. If the university will not honor our efforts I have another idea."

"Spill it Sis, what are you thinking?"

"Mike, we have the knowledge and the skills to go into business for ourselves. Let's talk with dad and see what he thinks of an idea. I've been thinking there must be a wide variety of commercial applications for the technology developed at GMH. Maybe you and I can create our own company and produce commercial products and services. What do you say we talk with mom and dad about it?"

"Sis, you come up with some great ideas ....sometimes .... I have to admit."

That evening after dinner Mike and Maria met with their parents. Mike explained the delays and stonewalling in the academic community. Then Maria presented the idea of creating a separate company to produce commercial applications from CR4 technology.

Gordon and Patricia Hollister were not surprised that their kids were always pushing the envelope. During their talks, Gordon agreed with them that they might be able to use some parts of the CR4 technology in commercial applications. He explained that he can license some of the intellectual property to their new company should they decide to go forward with their idea.

Gordon added, "By the way, you may be interested in a new development. The R&D team demonstrated yesterday that it is now possible to read thoughts and upload thoughts without using a chip. The system works in close proximity to a person. It is no longer necessary to always have a chip ingested or inserted into an animal or a person to conduct two-way brain communication. What do you think about that?"

Mike and Maria looked at each other and then at their parents. All four had a broad smile as they contemplated a host of future products and services. What the parents didn't know was that their two teenagers already had the design software of the close proximity system downloaded into their computers and cell phones from the thought channels of the R&D team.

Maria responded, "Dad…that's wonderful. We have an idea for our first commercial product. Mike and I have always been interested in airline safety. Mike and I will write a business plan and get it to you in a day or so. Oh, dad, mom, we love you, and you always listened to our ideas, even at times when you both thought we were just a little nuts."

HCS or Hollister Commercial Services came into being with two very eager young entrepreneurs at the helm. Eighteen year old Mike and seventeen year old Maria Hollister are the beneficiaries of the enormous brain power of GMH Technology's R&D team as well as their own intellectual powers. These characteristics are reinforced by their willingness to work endless hours to make their dreams come true.

Mike and Maria recalled seeing the video of the Nine-Eleven hijackings, the destruction of the World Trade Center, the attack on the Pentagon, and the crash of Flight 93 at Shanksville, Pennsylvania. They remembered how several brave passengers attacked the hijackers on Flight 93 to prevent an attack on the national capitol. They also recalled several instances of pilot or co-pilot suicide which took down airliners. They believe that all of the carnage of the nine-eleven hijackings and the pilot murder-suicide episodes could have been avoided by the application of some simple technology available even at the time of those tragedies.

The first product HCS offered to the airline industry is a complete security system. It consists of a total redesign of the so-called black boxes which record cockpit voices and airplane functions. The HCS system includes a complete video monitoring system of the airplane interior, the cockpit and all passenger areas. An on-board computer collects all video, audio, and aircraft functions, and uploads the data to a cloud server for safe keeping.

The most unique feature is an adaptation of CR4 close proximity technology. Every seat in the airplane, all passenger seats as well as crew seats, are equipped with close proximity cerebral reader sensors. People's thoughts are detected, processed through the computer for negative attitudes and if any are detected, an alert is sent to the entire flight crew and to airline and government security personnel on the ground.

A passenger thinking of harming the airplane or flight crew will automatically have his or her seat belt locked and arm restraints deployed. They will be unable to get out of their seat. If need be the feedback feature to the brain can cause the person to become totally cooperative until the airplane lands and law enforcement personnel come aboard to deal with the situation.

Today Maria will go for a test flight of the new HCS system with two of her dad's company pilots, Emiliano Vargas and Brad Bailey.

Emiliano Vargas is a fifty-six year old Cuban-American commercial pilot who once flew missions for *Hermanos a Rescate* - Brothers to the Rescue. This is a Cuban exile group dedicated to monitoring their fellow countrymen fleeing Castro's island dictatorship on flimsy rafts and crossing the Florida Straits through shark infested waters. Many such journeys end in drownings and shark attacks. Emiliano is known to have once landed a twin engine Cessna Sky Master at dusk on the north shore of Cuba to pick up two defectors from the Cuban intelligence service. The CIA welcomed the newcomers with open arms, but there was no publicity in the mainstream press about the event as well there should not have been. It would have endangered the families of those brave defectors and endangered future rescue flights from those shores.

Brad Bailey is a sixty year old commercial pilot with over twenty-thousand flying hours and has flown everything from crop dusters in the farm fields of South Dade County to the Boeing 747 Jumbo Jet. Brad flew the Douglas DC-10 for National Airlines from Miami International Airport to and from London's Heathrow Airport for a number of years until National merged with Pan American. In the merger shuffle Brad decided it was time to do other things. He opened his own flying service at a local airport. He owns and operates several airplanes and a series of flight simulators to train pilots in all kinds of aircraft.

Brad Bailey and Emiliano Vargas were waiting for Maria in a small café near the flight line at the airport.

Maria greeted them, "Are you fellows ready to make some aviation history?"

Emiliano, always ready for a challenge responded, "Ready and raring to go. Let's get started."

The three boarded an older Boeing 737 which belongs to Brad Bailey. The aircraft is equipped with a test version of the HCS aircraft security system. Brad and Emiliano completed the cockpit check list and started the engines. The ground crew pulled the chocks and the historic project was under way.

Emiliano made the takeoff run. The airplane lifted off and headed west out over the Everglades, that endless grass and water prairie which dominates the South Florida landscape. Maria, thought of her high school friends down there somewhere. Well, she thought, everyone will benefit from this project if we can make it work and sell it to the airline industry.

The idea is that if an incident or accident of any kind occurs, every possible bit of information is captured and safely stored on earth out of reach of hijackers or other criminals. In the case of a crash there will be no need to locate and examine the cockpit recorder or flight recorder to learn the fate of the airplane and its passengers. The HCS flight data recording system captures all of the airplane's vital functions and streams it in real time. All functions of the airplane are relayed to the ground along with its actual flight path as the flight takes place.

For the first time in aviation history all of the thoughts of the three people on board were captured, recorded, analyzed and stored on a ground-based computer along with complete audio and video of every move they made on board. All of this along with all functions of the airplane from engine start to engine shut down.

After an hour-long flight over south Florida and part of the Gulf of Mexico the three technical pioneers returned to the airport. The aircraft went through the familiar groaning and grinding sounds as flaps, landing gear, and leading edge slats activated. The stall warning horn sounded a few seconds before the wheels touched the pavement. This is a common signal that the wings have quit flying and are ready for terra firma. The airplane slowed and made a perfect landing.

Tires screeched on the concrete and emitted a puff of white smoke from the friction of rubber being coaxed from a lazy state to suddenly rolling at just under a hundred miles an hour. Brad, and Emiliano moved the power levers into reverse thrust. They heard the familiar roar of engines ramping up RPM to blow hot exhaust gasses forward around the engine housings slowing the airplane's landing roll.

Maria thanked Emiliano and Brad for a great first flight of the HCS security system. She spent the next several hours with Mike back at the new HCS business location looking at all data from today's test flight. The complete thoughts of the three on board as well as all aircraft performance data were right where they were expected to be on the cloud server. All movements in the cabin and cockpit were captured in bold detail. All sensors for the close proximity readers embedded in the seats were fully functional. Now to sell the system to the airline industry and the Federal Aviation Administration.

Mike brought up a point about their collected data. "Sis, we have way too much personal information in the data base. We need to filter out everything except a passenger's attitude which might endanger a flight. I should re-write our software to give passengers total privacy."

"Not so fast Mike. Maybe we can separate information that effects flight safety from other information and let the system sound any alarm necessary. I admit we need to be careful about personally identifiable information so we don't get into legal problems about privacy issues, but we also might develop spin-off applications from everything the system collects."

Mike gave Maria a quizzical grin, "How's that?"

"Well, for starters do you recall what we learned about how social media collects thoughts and ideas expressed by computer users through their visits to specific websites and then sells that information to advertisers? How that every place people visit on the Internet leaves a tracking cookie in their computer and advertisers tailor their ads to the interests of the individual because of the websites they visit?"

"Yes, go on."

"Well Mike, I've been thinking. Airline passengers are a captive audience just like computer users at home. They spend hours sitting on an airplane. Our security system can collect and analyze their daydreams. You can write a program to sort their thoughts into categories and we could turn it into a survey of likes and dislikes about commercial products and sell the information to advertisers. Better yet, maybe we can find a way to advertise products and services to the passengers while they are flying. What do you think?"

"Whoa Sis, you're getting a little ahead of the game. Are you thinking we should further exploit what we both know about brain wave collection for additional commercial purposes?"

"Of course, dear brother. How about if we first find a way to sell information to advertisers from people's thoughts and then find a way to use the feedback feature to upload ads directly into people's brains while they fly? I don't see anything wrong with that, do you?"

"Well, I have to think about that for a while. It might be possible, maybe we should look into it."

Mike and Maria Hollister reached a decision to totally capitalize on brain wave technology first harnessed in their father's company. Their first big sale of the airline security system was not to U.S. carriers. The domestic airlines all turned down their system as too expensive and not required by the Federal Aviation Administration. HCS hired a Washington lobbyist to try and convince the FAA and the Congress to require the system on all commercial aircraft in the domestic fleet.

While this was going on, HCS made its first big sale of the system to a far eastern airline which had experienced more than one unexplained loss of an airliner in flight. The next big sale came when a Middle Eastern country purchased the system for its entire fleet of luxury jet liners. Several countries insisted that all newly purchased aircraft for their national airlines come equipped with the HCS security system. Ironically, most of those aircraft are manufactured or modified on the same assembly lines where U.S. domestic aircraft originate.

HCS operates the ground based data collection service for all of the airlines using the system. Unknown to any of their customers, HCS sifted all thoughts collected from passengers and flight crew and sold statistical data and personal preferences to commercial advertisers. In addition they streamed ads subtly but directly into the brains of the traveling public.

Mike and Maria Hollister hired many bright young minds to work at HCS. Maria preferred to work alongside their R&D team to develop new ways to use brain wave technology. The team managed to harness the feedback feature of the close proximity system to plant in a person's brain a feeling of wellbeing at having made a specific decision. This was done by using feedback to stimulate the brain and central nervous system to coax the pituitary gland to produce endorphins which are a natural chemical similar to morphine. Just enough but not too much. When this is done a person will be totally happy with a decision such as the purchase of an expensive item.

This application of the feedback feature launched HCS into new territory. Auto dealers around the world purchased the system. It consists of several components. First the showroom is wired with the close proximity brain scanning system. A potential customer enters and their thoughts are collected and analyzed. Positive thoughts about the dealer and their vehicles are fed into a customer's brain. When the purchase is made, and it rarely ever fails, the customer gets a high dose of satisfaction. In all dealerships, there has never been a case of buyer's remorse since the installation of the HCS satisfaction system.

The next market Mike and Maria exploited was the real estate industry. So successful is the HCS system, there is no buyer's remorse reported among buyers of medium and high quality properties, and not even among purchasers of less than desirable desert and swamp lands. The latter often being pushed by high pressure con artists.

The gambling industry was the next big customer for the HCS system. Customers losing large sums of money on the gaming tables of casinos went away with smiles on their faces. They often thanked the croupier for taking their money. It's wonderful what a proper dose of endorphins will do to a person when released by the feedback feature of the close proximity brain wave system.

As might be expected, the gambling industry has a few crooked operators. HCS personnel were offered huge bribes to re-write the software to allow croupiers to read out the thoughts of casino customers playing at the tables. Fortunately the system recorded the illicit offers and relayed them to proper authorities. Evidence supplied by the system helped convict at least a dozen members of one crime family in particular. Others are under surveillance.

HCS sold the feedback system to several theme parks around the world. The emotions of visitors riding roller coasters, log flumes and similar high energy rides are captured and analyzed to help in the design of the next generation of such rides. Park visitors are given a healthy dose of endorphins to reinforce their joy.

Major restaurant chains found the HCS brain feedback system useful at creating repeat customers. No matter what the quality of the dining experience, the customer always went away happy. Endorphins to the rescue even when the food and service may have been subpar.

Mike and Maria harked back to their own experiences with educational advancement through the use of the brain feedback feature. For-profit tech schools and colleges became enthusiastic users of the HCS brain feedback system. While public schools and colleges resisted using brain feedback to advance their students, the privately-owned for-profit schools were all for the feature. A student could graduate in record time. Sometimes an associate's or bachelor's degree could be uploaded in as little as three or four one-hour sessions. The price to the student was reduced by only ten percent from previous tuition levels, but the overhead costs were down by over ninety percent. Profitability soared.

The stock exchange took notice of this outstanding new technology. HCS brain wave technology came into use in almost every aspect of the economy. Mike and Maria were urged to issue an IPO, an Initial Public Offering of stock in the company.

Most pundits projected an initial share price of fifty dollars. When the stock exchange opened, bidding soared past a hundred in the first two minutes, then past five hundred, past a thousand and settled at the end of the day at just over three-thousand dollars a share. The IPO brought in over five billion dollars. Not bad for a couple of teenagers.

# CHAPTER 12

# THE MERGER

The four Hollisters were delighted with the IPO result even though it changed their lives completely. Early in the day TV satellite trucks took up positions around their townhouse. Gordon, Patricia, Mike, and Maria could not go home. They could not get near their townhouse area. The roads were choked with satellite trucks and gawkers. Instead they took refuge aboard a friend's yacht moored in the bay. Sudden wealth and notoriety exacted a terrible cost to their freedom of movement in public places.

The Hollisters remained out of the sight of the general public. Gordon maintained contact with his staff at GMH Tech by way of his secure video cell phone. Mike and Maria did the same with their enterprise at HCS, Inc. The family maneuvered the borrowed yacht down the Intracoastal Waterway to a remote area of the Florida Keys where they anchored out for the next week. Perhaps here they would be spared the prying eyes of the video vultures known as the media.

This interlude gave them a chance to unwind and reconnect as a family. Mike and Maria spent many hours snorkeling in the crystal clear waters of the Florida Keys. Gordon and Patricia spent their time recalling their younger days before Mike and Maria arrived on the scene. They remembered their fishing trips to Black Water Sound. How they slept in the back of their Ford Falcon station wagon in the parking lot at Gilbert's Fish Camp fighting off mosquitoes all night because they couldn't afford a motel room. They laughed about how they fished all day in Boggy Creek getting sun burned just to collect a stringer of pan sized mangrove snapper.

Well, so much for the good old days. Now they must decide how to live their lives with great wealth. Maria brought up the subject while the family watched the sun go down over the water casting its' golden glow on the scene.

"Dad, Mike and I've been thinking about the future. We would like to bounce an idea around with you. What would you say if Mike and I wanted to buy GMH Technology?"

Gordon seemed taken aback by the very notion of selling the company he spent so much of his life building.

"Well….. how would you see my role in the future of the company?"

"Dad, you and mom could retire to a really nice place with a lot of privacy, and you can have as much or as little involvement with GMH as you want."

Gordon thought for a long moment. "You and Mike know how much of my life I've invested in GMH Tech. You know since before you were either one born, it was almost all that I ever knew."

"Dad, we know how you feel about the company and we don't want you to retire unless it is your choice. Mike and I thought you might want to stay on as CEO with a great salary and stock options."

"Well, sweetheart, that's a very generous offer. Let your mom and me think this over and we'll let you two know what we decide."

Patricia chimed in, "Gordon, this is a wonderful idea. Mike and Maria know how hard you've worked to build GMH Tech and they are offering you a permanent stake in the company if you take them up on the offer to sell. Let's think about it. You deserve to be able to retire or work less as you choose."

Gordon hugged his wife and kids, "OK everybody, it's been a long day and we have a lot to think about. Let's get some sleep and talk about this tomorrow."

Dawn broke with a rosy glow on the crystal clear waters surrounding the yacht. Patricia and Gordon were seated on the after deck when Mike and Maria stirred out of their cabins. Coffee was on and the world looked much better than it had in some time, at least in the minds of the Hollister family. Gordon and Patricia admitted that they hadn't slept much during the night thinking about all the possibilities the future holds.

Gordon began, "Well kids, you seem to have made me an offer I don't want to refuse. Your mom and I want to go into semi-retirement and do some brain storming about what life holds for the rest of our years. I would like to have a role to play at GMH Tech. It is my baby and I can't give it up cold turkey. So look for me to be in and out of the office for a time."

Mike and Maria smiled. Mike spoke up, "Dad, mom, you won't regret your decision. Maria and I have talked about what to call the combined company. We will keep the name GMH Technology in honor of dad's work establishing the firm. We'll merge HCS into it as a division of the new company. We also plan to divide the company into three distinct units. One will serve the medical field, another will serve civilian applications, and a third will serve government clients."

Gordon responded, "Sounds like you two have been thinking about this for a while." He grinned. "Looks like you have your ducks all in a row."

Patricia added, "Your father and I have our eye on some Caribbean real estate we saw on TV last night. There is a private island for sale with a lot of features you kids would love. Maybe when the dust settles on the business of purchase and merger, we can all go take a look."

Maria grinned at Mike, "See I told you they were ready to do some relaxed living."

The four Hollisters made arrangements to rent a suite in a well-protected high rise overlooking Biscayne Bay. When they arrived at their new residence all of their personal belongings had already been moved in and arranged by trusted employees of GMH Technology. The townhouse in suburbia was a thing of the past. The family would now be protected by a twenty-four hour doorman backed up by an on-site armed security service.

Legal arrangements were completed to merge the two companies. Mike Hollister took over his dad's former office. Maria returned to her favorite place, working in the R&D lab beside her mentor Chun Li and their friends, Oren Lunsford and David Goldstein.

The sales staff at GMH Technology signed a contract to install the close proximity system for a new client. The pastor of a mega church wanted to use the feedback system to reinforce his sermons. Mike and Maria wondered if this was ethically crossing a line. They reasoned that if car dealers and theme parks can instill happiness in their customers, why not allow this pastor to do the same with his flock.

The installation was one of the largest ever attempted by GMH. It encompassed an auditorium seating well over twenty thousand people. A wireless sensor was placed in the back of each seat including the choir and the seats for the pastor and his staff on the stage at the front of the auditorium. The stage seat sensors were not called for in the contract, but the technicians got carried away and interpreted the words 'each seat' to mean all of the seats in the building.

A computer server was placed in an ante room just behind the senior pastor's office. When a point was made in a sermon, the system uploaded the idea to a person's brain while they occupied any one of the seats in the audience. The computer tracked listener's emotions and adjusted feedback so that the audience would more readily accept what was being presented.

In addition a person's negative thoughts could be recorded for further analysis. This would permit the church staff to single out individuals and call them in for counseling. Counseling sessions would take place in small rooms around the periphery of the auditorium where sensors were also placed.

The church experienced an unprecedented increase in attendance. Members went away with a large dose of endorphins making them very happy. They invited their friends and neighbors promising them a level of happiness previously unattainable from any church service they may ever have experienced in the past. True to the promise, the endorphins flowed freely among the attendees. Happiness reigned supreme. What could possibly be wrong with such a system?

GMH Tech supplied not only the installation of the system, but periodic maintenance as well. During a maintenance visit, Bobby Durand a newly hired GMH technician, downloaded data to analyze later. Included in the data stream were several counseling sessions involving the senior pastor and his staff. What the pastor didn't know was that everything he thought and spoke was captured on the server for the system and in the cloud server as well. Also included in the download was the data stream from many of the pastor's sermons.

During almost every one-on-one counseling session the pastor first prayed with the parishioner and then preyed on the parishioner. The conversation inevitably got around to money.

The pastor appealed to the parishioner to mightily increase his or her financial support for the work of the church.

In many counseling sessions the senior pastor or one of his staff persuaded a church member to actually sell their home or business and donate the entire proceeds to the church. In other sessions some members were persuaded to sign a new will making the pastor their lone beneficiary. It was for the good of their souls they were told. During every one of these conversations, the pastor's own thoughts were revealed. He was thinking, *another sucker fleeced.*

Data from the pastor's sermons revealed that he spoke one thing but was thinking something entirely different. As he preached on heaven and hell he was thinking, *who in their right mind would ever believe this stuff? I only do this week after week because it beats working for a living, and just look at my life style. Man, I live high on the hog with a twenty-million dollar mansion, I have a fleet of luxury cars, a private jet and a bank account in nine figures. Besides that I beat the government out of a huge amount of tax money by scooping cash from the offerings and keeping off-shore bank accounts. This crowd of deluded fools sitting in front of me are just sheep to be shorn. Life just can't get any better.*

Bobby Durand remembered how Mike helped him out when he had a problem back in high school. He appreciated Mike hiring him to work as a technician. Mike had even paid to send Bobby to a technical school where he received a brain upload equivalent to two years of technical education. Now Bobby was a certified electronic and IT technician working for GMH Tech.

Bobby thought about approaching Mike with the information about the pastor's nefarious behavior but decided to act on his own. He downloaded the most incriminating data onto a flash drive and sent it to the local district attorney. The district attorney was appalled at the evidence, but he could not use it alone to obtain an indictment. The DA got a search warrant and seized the hard drives from the church system. From the information on the drives he was able to persuade a grand jury to indict the pastor and his entire staff on charges of operating a criminal enterprise.

The state closed the church, seized the property and put it up for sale with the proceeds to be distributed to law enforcement agencies. The pastor and some of his staff received sentences of ten to twenty years in the state prison. A national organization dedicated to the cause of religious liberty filed an appeal. The higher court upheld the verdicts rendered in the lower court and had no problem with the way the evidence was gathered. This set a legal precedent for the admissibility of brain scan evidence which would have ramifications for the DEA in its war on drug cartels.

The investigation of the mega church drew the attention of law enforcement agencies and prosecutors around the nation. They quickly became interested in brain wave technology.

Many came to GMH Tech to learn all they could about how the systems pioneered there could help fight crime. State legislatures debated the use of brain wave recording as a tool in law enforcement and many law makers agreed to fund purchases of the system.

For the next several months orders flooded in to GMH for the close proximity brain wave system. Contracts were signed to install sensors in police station interrogation rooms across the country. Sheriff's departments and state police all made purchases. Prosecutors contracted to have sensors installed in court houses to insure that witnesses and defendants were telling the whole truth and nothing but the truth. Police cruisers and police officers were equipped with mobile versions enabling law enforcement officers to quickly compare what a detained person was saying with what they were thinking.

Privacy activists and organizations filed hundreds of law suits against the use of the close proximity brain reading technology. Most of the suits were filed against public agencies, but a few were aimed directly at GMH Technology. For a long time to come, the company would tie up several million dollars in legal fees defending these suits.

In Washington the FCC, the Federal Communication Commission, began studying the need to regulate the capture and use of brain waves. After all, these waves, as weak as they are, constitute an electronic transmission. The technology was in its infancy compared to where it would likely progress in the future. The argument against regulation was based on the fact that no person voluntarily transmits their brain waves. They are a natural phenomenon and like electrostatic sources emanating from nature, there would be no way a person could turn them off except by dying, or so it was thought. Even so, the FCC was determined to find a way to regulate the technology.

Gordon Hollister and his wife Patricia received a purchase price for the company of two billion dollars in cash with another billion in stock options to be exercised at the end of five years. In addition Gordon holds the title of CEO for life.

Gordon and Patricia bought the property they visited on a private Caribbean island. The real estate includes a safe harbor for boats large and small, an air strip on top of a plateau, and best of all a fifty room mansion on top of a ridge. Roof-mounted solar collector panels generate all electricity and heat water for baths and laundry. The estate is served by a desalination plant which can supply all the fresh water necessary even for the three swimming pools. The house has a 360 degree view of a dozen other small islands scattered about an emerald sea. One large island can be seen at a distance of about fifteen miles.

Gordon and his wife purchased a Cessna Caravan on floats for island hopping trips, and a private jet for fast trips to the mainland. They hired Emiliano Vargas to be their personal pilot. Emiliano was delighted to get to live once again on a Caribbean Island.

For water craft the Hollisters chose a seventy foot Grand Banks trawler and several smaller boats including jet skis for fun when the kids come to visit. The senior Hollisters seem to be set for a happy Caribbean retirement. They can't imagine anything that could spoil this newfound paradise.

# CHAPTER 13

## A MORE JUST SOCIETY

Douglas Winslow opened the meeting at the White House. In attendance were the President's closest political advisors. "We are here today to build upon the success we enjoyed closing the detention center at Guantanamo Bay, Cuba. I am pleased to reveal to you the administration's proposal to bring about a more fair and just society. The number of inmates in our Federal Prison System is totally out of control and is blatantly unjust. We have the largest percentage of our population in prisons compared with all other industrialized countries. Our system is broken and needs to be fixed."

Winslow continued, "The record of achievement of the Gitmo program is so encouraging, the President now believes we can expand it to solve a major problem here at home. The problem of overcrowding in our Federal Prison System. While doing that we will also save billions in tax dollars to which neither party in congress should object. Mr. Frank Fletcher will explain how the administration intends to go about fixing the system."

Frank Fletcher began. "The President intends to empty the federal prisons. All current inmates and future convicted felons will be controlled by the same technology we used when we released the Guantanamo detainees. There will be some major differences in the way the system works. The technical system we used for the Gitmo release program will not work for the federal prison population simply because the numbers of federal prison inmates is too great. Each former Gitmo detainee currently has a team of live monitors around the clock. The location and behavior of each is watched constantly by a human observer and swift action is taken should any former detainee step out of line."

Fletcher added, "The Federal Bureau of Prisons now houses over two-hundred thousand inmates. Which brings us to the method for control of those who are to be released under the President's proposal. *The Agency* will put in place a computerized monitoring system to track and evaluate each person released from prison. The computer system will screen all thoughts, identify those which are a potential threat to society, and prevent the former inmate from carrying out any criminal act."

Fletcher continued, "*The Agency* has already run a Beta test on the computer software and we have great confidence it will be successful. We believe that eventually we can release one hundred percent of all persons now incarcerated in the federal prison system. These folks can resume a productive life on the outside and we can completely control their thoughts, their behavior, and if need be, prevent them from becoming a recidivist."

Winslow added, "Our biggest hurdle right now is finding a way to carry out this program without a huge battle on Capitol

Hill. The President is so confident that this will work, he considers it a major part of his legacy. He has indicated to me that he will brook no opposition. He promised to veto any bill coming to his desk which gets in the way of closing the federal prisons. A funding battle with congress won't be necessary. *The Agency* has already produced enough CR4M tracking chips in our Maryland Laboratory and has the necessary funds to establish the computer system to monitor all the people to be released. These funds are buried in the budgets of several secret programs which *The Agency* has shelved and will not carry out."

Following the meeting at the White House, the President issued an executive order to effectively close and dismantle the entire federal prison system. He announced his decision to a stunned nation.

"From this time forward the United States of America will be the most just and fair nation on earth. No longer will we be the nation with the largest prison population as a percentage of our total population. From now on," he told the nation, "America will be proud of its justice system." But, he assured the nation, "all inmates will be totally controlled by a new computerized system which will act as a virtual parole agent. No former inmate will be free to harm another human being or to rob or steal from anyone."

A team of computer professionals set up servers in a cavernous site in West Virginia. The location was originally constructed during the height of the cold war to provide shelter to the remnants of government should the worst happen and the nation's capital be incinerated in a nuclear flash.

Software was loaded and tested repeatedly to assure that text flowing from a CR4M chip could be correctly analyzed for negative attitudes and destructive thought patterns. Tests were carried out to determine if the computer could respond by activating shock to the trigeminal nerves in the face of a would-be recidivist. When the engineers were satisfied that the system was ready, the next move was up to the administration.

The presidential press secretary announced the beginning of the bold experiment to release all inmates currently incarcerated by The Federal Bureau of Prisons. The program will began slowly. Those who will be released first will be those whose age and condition mitigates against them returning to a life of crime. The next wave will be those inmates whose sentences are almost complete, and last but not least, the worst of the worst. This would include bank robbers, kidnappers, drug kingpins, and even murderers. So sure is the administration that the CR4M system will work in its new civilian role that the presidential press secretary assured the American people that they have nothing to be concerned about.

Gun control advocates assured the nation that nobody will ever need a gun again for protection of their family or place of business. The nation can now be safely disarmed. They urged Congress to outlaw all ammunition for civilian consumption. Not everyone agreed. Gun rights groups and supporters of the second amendment urged their members to stock up on ammunition and to take courses for concealed carry permits in every state which allows them. They also urged Congress to quickly pass a bill to require uniformity in concealed carry licensing laws in every state.

The prisoner release program seemed to work flawlessly. At first there were no crimes committed by former inmates. New criminals upon conviction were secretly fed a CR4M chip and added to the program. One by one the former federal prisons were placed on the list of surplus properties for sale. Then the unthinkable happened. A crime was committed by a former inmate.

A felon released from Colorado Super Max held up a bank and killed two people with a blast from a sawed off shotgun. The nation was horrified. The program which the president and his spokesmen assured the nation was foolproof seemed to have failed. What could possibly have gone wrong?

Frank Fletcher was called before a closed session of the Homeland Security Committee and grilled for hours on how the virtual prison system is supposed to work and why in at least this one instance it failed. He had no answers. His only response to the committee was, "I'll have to get back to you with an answer to all of your questions."

Mike and Maria Hollister first learned there was a major failure in the new virtual prison system by reading the data flowing from the CR4 chips planted in Ariana MacKenzie and

Kurt Rinehart. They also learned that those two were working at the West Virginia facility. In their conversations at the facility with Frank Fletcher, Ari and Kurt were told that the government's entire computer system was non-functional. The software was inadequate and could not keep up with the whereabouts of the virtual prisoners, nor could it correctly identify negative attitudes.

The reason, Frank Fletcher explained, was the fault of the contractor *The Agency* hired to create the software. The contractor, it turned out, has a track record of defrauding governments, not only in the USA but in several other countries as well. The owner of the company involved is wanted by Interpol, the international police agency, and is believed to be hiding out in a Latin American country under an assumed name. The FBI and other law enforcement agencies are actively seeking him, but haven't found him yet.

Maria looked at Mike, "Should we tell the news media that the whole prison without walls system is not working, and that the country is crawling with unsupervised former inmates?"

"No Sis, how on earth would we explain that we know all this stuff that's going on? The government hasn't told the media yet, so how would we explain our sources?"

Mike Hollister's secretary called him on his private phone line and announced, "Mr. Hollister there is a Mr. Frank Fletcher here to see you, may I send him in?'

Frank Fletcher entered Mike's office even before he was

invited. “Mr. Hollister....” He paused and looked a bit confused. “Mike, what are you doing in your dad’s office? I thought I instructed your dad to keep you and your sister away from company facilities, especially the R&D lab.”

Mike responded, “No doubt you did, but since my sister and I now own the company you will be dealing with us directly. And by the way, Maria works full time in the R&D lab with Chun Li. Perhaps you don’t keep up with business news. GMH Technology is now incorporated and well-funded following a very successful IPO by HCS and its merger with GMH Tech.”

Fletcher seemed flustered. He paused and then continued, “Well then.....Mr. Hollister, *The Agency* has a major crisis and we need outside help. We have a computer problem in a main frame at one of our sites and we need an IT team who knows the CR chip system inside and out to help resolve it.”

Mike responded, “What seems to be the problem?” He tried to keep a straight face and pretended this was the first he’d heard about the fiasco in West Virginia.

Fletcher continued, “The government has released over two-hundred thousand former inmates from the Federal Bureau of Prisons. We thought we could track them and supervise them on the outside using the CR4M chip we developed for the DOD, the Department of Defense. The system worked extremely well with the Gitmo detainees. I can’t go into detail about those results, but suffice it to say the system worked as designed. The difference in the Gitmo release program and the federal prison release program is in the sheer volume of data. We depended upon a computer program to analyze the text flow from the federal prisoners, but the computer program we purchased totally failed to perform as required. How can GMH Technology help us to recover from this disaster? That's why I'm here."

Mike acted surprised. "Mr. Fletcher, am I to understand that there are over two-hundred thousand dangerous felons on the streets totally unsupervised?"

"That's about the size of it. The president is afraid of the political fallout if his opponents learn the scope of the problem."

Mike drew in a deep breath, "Good lord man, you let all those people out on our streets and now you come to me to help rope 'em back in by way of computer software. What on earth was the administration thinking? How could the people in DC base a decision of that magnitude on an unproven computer program after several other major failures in government developed IT programs?"

"Mr. Hollister, we don't have time to second guess the denizens of the district. We need to solve the problem before it becomes known to the whole world. How can you help us?"

Mike responded, "I'll get together with my R&D staff and let you know as soon as I learn something. That's all I can promise."

Mike called a meeting of the R&D team for one o'clock in his office. He laid out the problem to Chun Li, Oren, and David. They were appalled to learn that the government attempted to track so many CR4M chips and use a computer program to filter human thoughts. Chun Li suggested that the team return to the lab and engage in a brain storming session to try and find a solution.

A week later Chun Li and her team reported to Mike Hollister that they had solved the basic problem of keeping track of a high volume of data input. The government software had proven inadequate simply because of sheer volume of data entry. The GMH team overcame the problem with a total rewrite of the government's software program.

Frank Fletcher was delighted with the new software. It performed flawlessly. It proved capable of receiving thoughts transmitted by over two hundred thousand CR4M chips, processing the constant stream of data and making attitude adjustments among the former prison inmates. The administration was relieved that this would not become a political disaster. Could anything else possibly go wrong?

Two months went by and Frank Fletcher paid a second visit to GMH Technology with another problem. One by one the government's computer was losing track of released inmates. The system was failing, but with no apparent explanation. Mike called the R&D team to meet with Mr. Fletcher.

David Goldstein requested samples of the CR4M chips

produced in the government's Maryland lab. Upon examination he found a basic flaw in the composition of the outer shell. While both the government produced chips and the GMH produced chips attached themselves in the human digestive tract and survived everything a human's innards could possibly throw at them, the government lab's chips slowly deteriorated in the presence of alcohol. The Gitmo detainees were all Muslim and did not use alcohol. This, along with the human monitoring program, helped explain the success of that program. The former federal prisoners were free to consume alcohol and that seemed to be the emerging problem of monitoring them using the CR4M tracking system.

Frank Fletcher was once again called before a closed session of the Homeland Security Committee. The committee chairman began, "Mr. Fletcher, when you came before this committee several months ago you promised to have some answers to the problem of recidivism among former federal prisoners who are now roaming the streets of our nation. What information do you have for us today? Remember sir, you are under oath."

Fletcher responded, "Mr. Chairman, *The Agency* first discovered a major problem with the software program. The original software was incapable of processing the sheer volume we demanded of it. We seem to have solved that problem by hiring a private firm in Florida. GMH Technology rewrote the entire software program, installed it on our servers in West

Virginia and now it works flawlessly."

The Chairman interrupted, "Mr. Fletcher, this committee has been informed by the FBI and the DOJ that recidivism among former federal prison inmates is up substantially. To what do you attribute this sharp rise in new criminal activity?"

Fletcher responded, "Mr. Chairman, when the government took over the production of the CR4M chip in our Maryland lab, our engineers missed one major feature when copying the GMH chip outer shell. The GMH design seems to be impervious to alcohol, but not the government designed chip."

The Chairman leaned forward with a scowl, "Do you mean to tell this committee that every time a former federal prisoner has a cocktail or a beer he or she is actually escaping from federal control?"

Fletcher responded, "Unfortunately that is exactly what is happening. The only good thing I can say is that the former inmates are not yet aware of the problem. If they were, they might all go out for a beer. Within a few months, the government program to control former inmates will fail, at least for those persons consuming alcohol. Crime will likely increase exponentially and there is nothing we can do about it."

The Chairman responded, "Mr. Fletcher, the administration's asinine scheme to close all federal prisons has obviously become a colossal failure. You will return to this committee in one week with a solution to this problem or there will be hell to pay for everyone involved including the President. Is that understood sir?"

Fletcher nodded.

The Chairman rapped the gavel, "Thank you Mr. Fletcher, this meeting is adjourned."

Frank Fletcher paid another visit to GMH Tech. "Mr. Hollister, under the contract we have with your firm, *The Agency* has the legal right to any and all developments in the field of brain wave research. That includes the formulation for the outer shell of the CR4 chip. As you are aware our Maryland lab engineers made an error in the design of the outer shell of those chips produced by the government. Tests of your chips and ours revealed that GMH chips are impervious to alcohol, but ours are not."

He continued, "I assume we will have your full cooperation in correcting our error."

Mike responded, "Of course, Mr. Fletcher. It appears that under the terms of our contract with GSA we really have no choice."

Mike called Chun Li on the video intercom and announced that he and Frank Fletcher would meet with the R&D team in the lab.

Chun Li agreed to transfer the design specs of the CR4 chip to the government's Maryland lab. She and her team reiterated to Frank Fletcher that they do not believe that their discovery should be used in any way to torture or kill humans or animals. Fletcher agreed that the government would take full responsibility for any modifications which she and her fellow scientists find objectionable. He assured the R&D team that the government's goal is to control the behavior of paroled felons on the streets of the nation and to prevent harm to innocent people.

Following the visit Frank Fletcher called Douglas Winslow and reported that the government would soon have the correct outer shell for the prison release chips.

Winslow assured Fletcher that if they didn't get it right this time heads would roll. "Frank, the president is extremely embarrassed by the failure of the Maryland lab's chips. We have over two-hundred thousand former federal inmates on the streets and one-by-one they are disappearing from our tracking computer. The only hope we have is to quickly produce the new chips and round up the inmates we can still find using the GPS feature of their current chips. And we need to do that before they imbibe enough alcohol to put us out of business."

# CHAPTER 14

# VENEZUELA

As dawn breaks over the Naval Station at Guantanamo Bay, Cuba, Corporal Edmund Harris, USMC, turns to Sergeant Brett Wilcox. "Hey Sarge, take a look at this."

The two studied the text stream coming from a CR4M chip in an ISIS member in Syria. Sgt. Wilcox responded, "It sure looks like Ahmed did a number on a whole lot of Jihadis when he fed them Kabsa. We've been getting good intelligence from well over a hundred of them so far, but this one is special. Look what he's talking about. It looks like he's giving a briefing to a fairly large group."

"Right Sarge, do you think what he's talking about should be brought to the attention of Major Stratton?"

"I think so corporal, go ahead and patch the data stream to the Major's office. She will see it when she gets her daily on-screen briefing. It certainly looks like the bad guys are planning to come to our neighborhood."

The text stream revealed plans to transport a hundred or more anti-American ISIS terrorists to Venezuela for training, and then to send them across the U.S. southern border to carry out attacks in the continental United States. The plan calls for the Arabs to learn to speak fluent Spanish and to try to blend in with a flood of innocent looking undocumented Latin American migrants.

The Gitmo former detention center staff was now serving as trackers keeping up with the location and activities of all of the former detainees. A number of former occupants had been 'shut down' as the staff euphemistically called it. They posed an immediate threat to Americans and their allies. Their trackers sent signals to their CR4M chip and shut down their autonomic nerves bringing about an immediate and very quiet but unexplained death. The last transmission from their chip was an expression from someone nearby, 'It is the will of Allah.'

Rear Admiral Joseph Bergstrom, USN was in the room when Major Leslie Stratton opened the meeting. Admiral Bergstrom spoke. "We've called the staff together to review a piece of intel which came in this morning. We've known for some time that the Venezuelan President intends to train Middle Eastern terrorists to speak Spanish and blend in with the wave of undocumented immigrants constantly flooding across the southern U.S. border. This morning we received hard evidence of an actual movement to carry out the threat. Major Stratton will fill you in on the problem."

"Thank you Admiral Bergstrom. A number of Middle Eastern men are in Venezuela. We are able to track the locations of some of them from the GPS data coming from the CR4M chips they have in their bodies. We have our old friend Ahmed to thank for that. Some of you remember Ahmed, he was our guest for an extended period. We will continue to monitor the whereabouts of these Jihadis and we have plans to take them out if and when we need to do so. However, there are quite a number of men in that group who do not have a chip. We have a contingency plan for those. I will let Sergeant Wilcox explain."

"As Major Stratton told you there are a number of terrorists who need to have a chip installed. We most likely will not have an opportunity to feed them a chip like we did our former guests. The alternative is to inject them with a CR4M chip. We know they are not going to volunteer for a needle insertion, so we have an alternative in mind. The same firm in South Florida which developed the original CR4 chip has developed a series of autonomous drones no larger than an insect. As a matter of fact they have a real collection of nano machines which appear to be insects of all descriptions.

For our operation we plan to send a team to infiltrate the island where Venezuela trains terrorists. While on the island, the team will release a swarm of nano machine insects which can simulate a bite on a person. Using their proboscis they can inject a CR4M chip deep under the skin. Each nano machine has an additional feature. They can see and hear by way of audio and video which is then transmitted to a satellite and relayed to our monitors right here at Gitmo. These marvelous little creatures will perch on a limb or leaf near the terrorist camp and keep us informed of all movement and sound. Their electrical systems are constantly recharged by sunlight or even by vibrations caused by the wind."

Major Stratton took over the briefing. "For the mission

we have in mind we are sending two people from *The Agency*. A former Marine Corps Major Ariana MacKenzie and her assistant a Mr. Kurt Otto Rinehart. I believe Mr. Rinehart has carried out clandestine operations in foreign parts in the past. These two individuals will be supplied with an abundance of nano insects. Our part in their mission will be to give them transportation to their destination and to pick them up again when their mission is complete. We will give them whatever assistance they require. Any questions?"

"Good, then let's all get back to work watching the data flow from our former guests."

GMH Technology received an order for five hundred nano machines recently developed by the R&D staff and mass produced in the lab under the leadership of David Goldstein. These tiny machines are about the size of the insects they pretend to be.

Each one of the tiny machines has the ability to fly and navigate using a data program which makes them autonomous. They do not need to be radio controlled by an operator but they can be when necessary. They see and hear everything in their vicinity and send data packets via a satellite connection. The information including video and audio can be picked up from the satellite by a specially programmed cell phone capable of either regular or satellite phone transmissions.

For the upcoming mission to Venezuela three hundred of the nano machine insects will be carrying in their proboscis a

CR4M militarized tracking chip capable of spying, torturing, and killing. They are able to inject the chip into a person who will only be aware of the bite as if it were from a natural insect. The site of the injection may itch for a time, but the skin will recover in a day or so. Two hundred others are to be used for audio and video surveillance and do not carry an injectible chip but instead carry a sensor for close proximity two-way brain communication.

Mike Hollister's secretary called him on the video intercom to announce a visit by Ariana MacKenzie and Kurt Rinehart. He welcomed them back to the plant. "Well, what brings you two back to South Florida?" He pretended he had no idea why they had come. He didn't dare let them or anyone else know that he and his sister Maria were still keeping up with these two from the discrete channels in the CR4 chips he fed them right here at GMH Tech.

Ari responded, "Mike it's good to see you again. We heard that your folks retired and that you and your sister are now running things."

Kurt spoke up, "Mike we are here to pick up an order placed by *The Agency* for nano machines. We will only be in town a day or so. How is the order coming along?"

Mike responded, "We have them packaged and ready to go. Some are loaded with the CR4M chips supplied by the government's lab in Maryland. I hope you guys enjoy them. We've had a lot of fun trying out the insects around the plant and around some of the more remote areas of South Florida. I took a dozen of them fishing with me last week-end and had a lot of fun watching them skim over the water driving the fish crazy. The tiny machines are able to recognize when they were in danger of being snatched by a predator. They zoomed away at amazing speeds. I think they will survive a lot of challenges."

Ari responded, "We certainly hope so Mike. We will be testing them in a tropical environment. That's about all we can say. But I'm sure you understand."

Mike smiled, "Of course. We wish you good luck with whatever tests you put them to. Oh, and by the way, could we have some feedback from your field trials? We always appreciate knowing how our products perform."

Ari and Kurt visited the R&D team in the lab, picked up the package of nano machine insects and said their good byes all around. The next stop for these two was Boca Chica Naval Air Station in the Florida Keys. From there they flew directly to the Naval Base at Guantanamo Bay Cuba.

Clandestine operations are nothing new to Ari or Kurt. But this mission called for a different kind of transportation. They boarded a submarine at midnight in the harbor at Gitmo and settled in for a ride to hostile territory. A day later the sub surfaced, again at midnight, about a mile from the shore of a jungle covered island. The ship was clearly within the coastal waters of the sovereign nation of Venezuela. Should the large black ship with no lights be spotted there could be diplomatic repercussions. Ari and Kurt slipped over the side into an inflated raft and paddled toward shore. The submarine slipped quietly beneath the sea. They were on their own.

The night was pitch black. Clouds totally obscured the stars. There was no moon to be seen. Ari and Kurt wore waterproof camouflage clothing, their faces were smeared with jungle green and brown patches of grease paint. Paddling against an outgoing tide and an offshore breeze, it seemed to take forever to reach the island ringed by mangroves on almost all sides. Using night vision goggles they were able to pick out an opening in the tangle of mangrove roots just wide enough to force their small craft through. The opening widened out into what appeared to be a backwater. A few yards further inside and away from the ocean they were able to land on a narrow patch of mud. There they pulled their craft under the protective cover of dense jungle growth. This would be their home for the next forty-eight to seventy-two hours. In whispers they jokingly called this place the Venezuela Hilton.

With dawn came real buzzing insects. Fortunately Ari and Kurt had good protection. Ari removed a small canister and released three nano machines which looked for all the world just like the swarm of tropical pests emerging from the mangroves around this impromptu campsite.

An hour went by before the first signal was received from one of the mechanical insects. A nano dragon fly circled above a large clearing in the middle of the island. From its video stream Ari and Kurt could clearly see a series of huts surrounding one larger structure in the middle of the clearing. A path led from the clearing to the shore on the opposite side of the island from where Ari and Kurt had come ashore. There was a pier there with a large motor launch tied on one side and several smaller boats equipped with outboard motors along the other side. There was a tee head at the end of the pier.

A number of uniformed people were standing in formation on the pier as if awaiting the arrival of someone important. They didn't have long to wait. A very large and luxurious motor yacht slowly inched its way to the tee head. Crew members tossed mooring lines to men on the dock. When the yacht was securely moored, the line of men on the dock snapped to attention and saluted the people disembarking. Ari and Kurt could only wonder who these people were who rated such a military greeting.

The new arrivals along with the greeting party walked from the pier into the clearing and disappeared into the larger structure at the center of the compound. Kurt looked at Ari, "Now?"

She grinned, "Now."

Kurt maneuvered several dozen nano insects at a time into the main building. He settled them onto rafters above the crowd assembled inside. About a hundred men were sitting on coconut frond mats on the ground facing a podium at the front of a single large room.

A man, obviously dressed in military uniform with the rank of colonel on his lapel stepped to the podium and began speaking. "Soldiers of Islam, you are about to graduate and continue Jihad against our common enemy, the great Satan. The United States of America has for decades dominated the economies of Latin America. Yankee Imperialists have sucked the very life's blood of the people of Central and South America. They have intervened repeatedly in our internal affairs, and even now plot to overthrow the Bolivarian Republic of Venezuela as well as the socialist government of our dear brothers in Cuba."

There was a wave of applause. The speaker continued, "You have shown us your courage in training, you have learned our Spanish language, and you have learned to blend yourselves into the fabric of Latin American culture. Soon you will be transported to Mexico where you will easily cross into the USA to begin your mission. Today I present to you your great friend and ally the President of the Bolivarian Republic of Venezuela."

The assembled men all leapt to their feet and gave a huge round of applause. Ari and Kurt couldn't believe what they were watching and hearing. Here was the President of Venezuela attending a graduation ceremony for terrorists. It was now or never. Kurt unleashed the swarm of nano mechanical insects into the crowd. One by one they quietly and softly settled onto the necks and exposed shoulders of everyone present including the President and the Colonel.

Kurt sucked in a deep breath and let it out slowly. "Ari,

do you realize what we have just done? We've inserted a chip into the neck of the President of Venezuela." He laughed. "*The Agency* has him on a short leash now. He's always saying the USA is out to kill him. Well, now *The Agency* could transmit a signal and he would drop dead without a whimper and nobody would even guess what caused it."

The two smiled at each other and gave a high five. Ari grinned, "We now have all of the terrorists 'tagged' with CR4M chips, it's time to break camp and call our ride to take us home." She picked up her satellite phone and made a call through a discrete channel to Gitmo.

The response she got was not what she expected. Their ride, in effect the submarine that brought them to this forsaken island, was not currently available. The skipper was on a rescue mission which would delay their departure for another twenty-four hours. In the meantime they were instructed to lie low and await orders. This was nothing new to these two. They were accustomed to the hurry up and wait so prevalent in government service.

For several hours Ari and Kurt entertained themselves by monitoring the audio and video streaming from the many devices they brought to this place. What they learned was indeed a bonus over and above their mission to tag terrorists for future reference.

Kurt pointed to his cell phone, "Have a look at this. Here is a meeting between the colonel and someone named

Diego Ramos aboard the yacht. They are discussing how the colonel can move tons of cocaine into Puerto Rico for trans-shipment to South Florida. He is bragging about the stupid Yankee drug addicts financing the destruction of the Yankee Imperialists by funneling tons of American money south while the Venezuelan government funnels tons of cocaine north. The nerve of these guys!"

Ari agreed, "We've known about this drug traffic for years, and now we have their own military man confirming it, on the record, in the cloud, and streaming live to the head of *The Agency*. It couldn't get any better." They both laughed.

Ari seemed surprised at what she was seeing on her cell phone screen. "Hey Kurt, one of my dragon flies went astray. According to its GPS coordinates it is not even on this island anymore. It is perched on a bush on an island about 4 miles from here. There is movement nearby. Someone is approaching it. Look at this video stream."

Kurt looked at Ari's screen. "Hey that guy looks like Robinson Crusoe for gosh sakes. He has a long beard like a hermit. Wonder what he is doing on that small island. He doesn't look like a local Indian. None of them grow a beard like that. Maybe he is a fugitive from local justice."

The bearded stranger reached out and picked up the nano dragon fly and held it gently in the palm of his hand. He spoke slowly in plain English as if to address the mechanical insect. "What a beautiful little creature you are. I wish I could fly off this island and go home again. But I'll probably never see home and family. Little dragon fly, do you have a family?"

Ari and Kurt looked at each other wondering who this English speaking stranger could be and why he was in such an isolated place. The bearded man continued, "If only I could get off this wretched place. It's been months, maybe years, I've lost track of time since the rig exploded. Man that was an awful time. Flames everywhere. I got blown into the ocean without a life vest. Had to swim for hours. Got here, and never saw another human since. I wonder if anyone is still looking for me. Probably not. The company probably gave up when they didn't find me, and now.....now....he sighed...nobody knows I'm even alive or even cares to come looking anymore."

Ari remembered reading about an oil rig explosion in Venezuelan coastal waters some time back. Several men were lost and assumed dead. She thought, *could this guy be one of the missing*?

"Kurt, I'm going to do something we've been trained to do. I'm going to use the close proximity brain wave communication feature in the dragon fly he is holding in his hand. I hope this works."

Ari began speaking through the close proximity feature directly to the mind of the ragged stranger. "Sir, what is your name?"

The castaway suddenly sat straight up. "Man, I've been here way too long. I'm hallucinating."

Ari continued, "No, you're not hallucinating. It appears that you are marooned on a small island and wish to be rescued. Is that correct sir?"

The castaway stood bolt upright and dropped the dragon fly. "My God, this thing is talking to me. I'm losing my mind."

Ari shot back, "No sir, you are quite sane. The dragon fly is the key to your rescue. Pick it up again and don't let it get away from you. We can come and find you using the GPS coordinates supplied by the dragon fly. What is your name sir?"

Not having had an intelligent conversation for months, the castaway was hesitant to answer, but finally blurted out, "My name is Roy Durand and I work for an oil company on a drilling rig....that is....I used to work for them, but the rig blew up and I got blown off."

Ari responded, "That's all we need to know at this time. Please, by all means keep the little dragon fly with you. Do not lose it. It provides us a homing signal which will lead us to you. We will pick you up at midnight if the tide and wind cooperate. Do you understand sir?"

By this time Roy Durand would do anything just to be removed from his tropical island prison. He clutched the dragon fly to his chest and whispered to it, "Thanks little guy.....thanks."

# CHAPTER 15

## ISLAND RESCUE

Ari called *The Agency* on a discreet channel to report their plan to move four miles from their current location. Ari and Kurt prepared their gear and loaded the inflatable raft. Daylight and dark each come quickly in the tropics. When the sun set behind the mangrove thicket they launched their raft and paddled through the narrow opening into the sea beyond.

Working together the two were able to make good progress toward their rendezvous with Roy Durand. The sky was clear and many stars shone from horizon to horizon. The moon was not yet up, but would rise in about another hour. Kurt used his cell phone to track the GPS position transmitted from the little dragon fly. This would lead them to the pickup point where they hoped to take Roy Durand off his island prison.

As they neared the half way point between the two islands, a fast boat appeared in the distance. It sped straight toward them. Kurt and Ari flattened themselves in their raft and hoped they would not be seen. The boat passed so close the wake almost swamped them. As it raced by, they could see three men standing in the cockpit. They were relieved when the boat continued on without turning around to investigate their small black raft. Perhaps they had not been seen.

As they neared the shore of their destination the moon rose over the eastern horizon. This would make concealment much more difficult. Even a black object like their raft might be seen in silhouette against the bright golden disk of a rising moon. They began to hear the lapping sound of low-running surf on the island dead ahead.

Kurt took a quick look at his cell phone screen. He spoke in an almost whisper, "Hey Ari, it looks like the dragon fly GPS is about forty yards inland from the beach. Let's land over there to the left, and I'll go look for our passenger."

They stepped onto the sand and pulled the raft half way out of the water. Kurt bounded up a slight incline and disappeared from view. Ari remained with the raft.

Roy Durand was half asleep lying down in a patch of grass. Kurt approached quietly. When Roy saw another human being, he jumped straight to his feet. "Who are you? Why are coming here? Where have you been since the rig blew up?" He continued a string of questions until Kurt put his finger to his lips and urged him to be quiet.

"We can't take time to talk now. I'll answer all your questions later. We just need to get going for now. Don't worry, we are Americans and we've come to take you home."

With that, Roy Durand was satisfied and fell silent. As Kurt started to turn back toward the beach and the raft where Ari was waiting, another voice broke the silence. "Don't move amigos. We've got you covered."

Kurt and Roy watched three figures emerge from the bush coming from the opposite side of the small island. Roy gasped, “I’ve been alone all this time, and suddenly people are all over the place.”

One of the newcomers said, “Shut up old man. We’re not interested in listening to you complain. We’re here on business.”

Kurt asked, “What sort of business?”

The newcomer grinned, “Sometimes narcotics, sometimes people. You name it. We do it.” He broke into derisive laughter. “You two are our latest prize. You are both Americans, we heard you say it. You’re probably worth a good price if you have family with money. Otherwise we turn people like you into human chum and feed the fishes. They have to eat just like the rest of us.” Again he laughed.

The other two men with him held what appeared to be AK-47 Kalashnikov rifles slung over their shoulders. The way they wore the slings made it easy to raise the business end of the weapons and fire a volley. The two armed men did not speak. The one doing all the talking seemed to be the leader.

The leader motioned for Kurt and Roy to move in the direction from which they had come. Roy fell to the ground and began to sob. The leader kicked him in the ribs. “Get up punk and move.”

That was just the distraction Ari needed. She came out of the shadows like a tornado. With a series of Taekwondo kicks she took out the two with the Kalashnikovs. They never knew what hit them. In a split second Kurt took out the leader of the pack with a round house kick. All three of the pirates went down and did not get up. They were out cold.

Ari shouted to Kurt, "Grab their weapons and let's get their boat. It's beached about fifty yards away. I saw it when I circled around to find you.''

Kurt helped Roy to his feet. The three boarded the pirate's fast boat. Ari started the engines and backed it out away from the shoreline. She put it into gear and made a quick circuit around the island to where they left their raft. Kurt jumped into the raft, threw their gear into the fast boat and jumped back aboard their new ride. As they backed away from the shoreline, Kurt fired a volley into their inflatable raft to render it unusable. Now, the pirates could live on the desolate island and only hope for a rescue.

The newly acquired boat was fast. Much faster than paddling the inflatable raft. Now if it just has enough fuel on board they hoped to put some distance between themselves and the Venezuelan coastal islands. The moon was up overhead by now and it was easy to make out objects across the water. This was a dangerous situation as it made them an easy target for any navy patrol craft that might be out looking for just such fast pirate craft.

About a half hour into their run a Venezuelan Navy vessel spotted them and used a spot light to signal them to stop for inspection. They knew their boat was most likely faster than the navy patrol which turned out to be the case. As miles and minutes ticked off the navy patrol boat fell farther and farther astern. It would not be good to summon a pick up from an American submarine in Venezuelan coastal waters. That would be pretty sticky indeed.

Ari throttled back to conserve fuel. The race with the navy vessel was over and they could relax at least for now. Kurt established a contact with their people at Gitmo and arranged a coordinate for transfer to the submarine. Just before daylight they came along side one of the most beautiful sights they had seen in several days, the U.S. Navy sub.

Two sailors jumped aboard the pirate vessel and assisted Roy Durand aboard the sub. Kurt and Ari climbed aboard. The two sailors set explosives in the fast boat and then climbed back aboard the sub. As they left the pirate craft they revved the engine, leaned out and used a boat hook to shove it into gear. The craft roared away. At about five hundred yards, a petty officer standing on the conning tower broadcast a signal detonating the charge the sailors had set. The pirate's fast boat disappeared with a flash and a roar.

Kurt and Ari gave a high five. Kurt said, "Too bad. It was a fine ride while it lasted."

Aboard the sub the skipper had one of the ship's medical corpsman give Roy Durand a total inspection. Roy shed his clothes which were promptly sealed in a plastic disposal bag. He enjoyed his first shower with soap in many months. The corpsman was surprised at Roy's overall condition. He seemed to be moderately well nourished.

When asked what on earth he had been eating all the time he spent marooned, Roy said he caught fiddler crabs and small fish in pools along the shoreline, and ate some wild herbs he found inland along with numerous coconuts. He kept empty coconut shells to use for collecting rain water. He ate all of his food raw having no way to start a fire.

Following a thorough physical exam Roy was given a fresh set of navy dungarees, underwear, socks and shoes. The skipper interviewed a clean and shaven Roy Durand and gathered all the information he could about the man. The skipper took Roy's finger prints and photographed the iris in his right eye. He uploaded these to the FBI. They came back with a positive ID that this man's name is truly Roy Durand and he was an employee of the oil company which lost a rig off the Venezuelan coast. The skipper relayed the news to Roy that the company will be notified and will in turn notify his family that he is alive and will be coming home soon.

Ari and Kurt returned to Gitmo along with Roy Durand their newly liberated friend. The three were given a ride on a Navy aircraft to Boca Chica Naval Air Station near Key West. From there they parted company. Roy Durand was welcomed at Key West by his wife and son Bobby Durand. The three spent a week in a beach front hotel paid for by Mike Hollister.

Kurt and Ari caught a flight out of NAS Boca Chica to NAS Patuxent River near their base of operations in Maryland.

There they tracked many of the CR4M chips they recently planted in terrorists headed for the U.S. southern border.

Data from planted chips flows into a cloud server which is accessed both at Gitmo and in the lab in Maryland. What is not known by federal authorities is that the same data is also tracked at GMH Technology in South Florida by Mike and Maria Hollister.

Ariana MacKenzie is the overall supervisor for the tracking project. She has about two dozen people working for her directly. Kurt Rinehart is second in command. Tracking data shows a steady movement out of Venezuela and into Central America and Mexico. Travel corridors are closely monitored. Many terrorists are seen to be in the flow of humanity aboard 'La bestia,' or the beast, as it is called by those unfortunate human beings who ride on top of the death train coming up from Central America into Northern Mexico.

As the tracking team analyzes the ideas flowing from the brains of those wearing the chips in their bodies, intelligence is passed along to law enforcement in areas which are targeted by the terrorists. In several cases where there was an immediate plan to attack a specific target, law enforcement rounded up a number of American citizens who were identified as part of a specific plot. Those arrested had no idea how authorities came to know the details of their plans.

In more than one case, a terrorist with plans to carry out a mass casualty attack simply died when his autonomic nerves were shut down. His body tumbled to the tracks under the wheels of 'la bestia.' It always appeared to be an accident. The CR4M chip was paying off in cases closed. *The Agency* could not have been happier.

At GMH Tech Mike and Maria were proud to have a part in keeping the nation safe from terrorists domestic and foreign. They were privy to almost everything key people in *The Agency* were doing.

The Drug Enforcement Administration was busy tracking the whereabouts and activities of Diego Ramos from the CR4M chip placed in his body by a nano machine mosquito. It was placed in his person while he visited with the President of Venezuela aboard the presidential yacht docked at the terrorist training island. Government authorities in Venezuela working with Diego Ramos planned to move tons of cocaine into the USA. Everywhere Diego went and all of his contacts were thoroughly tracked and cataloged by the DEA.

Mike and Maria were still tracking and monitoring the movements of Diego's cousin Raul Ramos their old high school classmate. Raul still carried the CR3 chip he ingested at the party at his cousin's mansion near Miami. Mike patched through all of Raul's data to Jack Reynolds at the DEA.

When drug shipments began moving they were intercepted usually at sea or on an airport ramp before they were picked up by Raul's henchmen in the USA. Diego Ramos was not pleased. Again he vowed death to anyone in his organization who was tipping off law enforcement. Little did he know that his own brain was the source of most of the tips to the government.

Jack Reynolds held a meeting with his staff at DEA and discussed the possibility of taking Diego and Raul into custody. They decided not to because these two were valuable links to everyone else in the drug trade. As long as these cousins were free to travel, they would inevitably lead law enforcement directly to cartel participants. It was a little bit like using some of the terrorists in the Middle East as what *The Agency* referred to as 'pointers' those who would point out the rest of the bad actors.

Other bureaucrats in Washington became interested in brain wave monitoring to carry out their missions. Closed hearings were held in several congressional committees to discuss the future of brain wave technology to protect the homeland from all manner of threats foreign or domestic.

Questions were raised in some committee hearings expressing concerns that one company, GMH Technology acting as a monopolist dominated the field of brain wave applications and should be broken up for the good of the economy. Many on the left wanted to act immediately to force GMH Tech to forfeit its exclusive patents. Many on the right maintained that GMH Tech as the developer of brain wave applications was entitled to enjoy its monopoly position until time expired on its patents. The debate raged on with sides gaining or losing ground depending upon the political climate of the day.

The President announced that he would use an Executive Order to end the exclusive rights of GMH Technology under its patents and would do so for the good of the nation and in the name of national security. His spokesman told the media that the Commerce Department would decide which parts of this new technology would be released for other companies to produce and to use. The government would release this technology just as it released GPS technology decades earlier.

Mike Hollister directed his legal department to file suit against the government to protect the company's patents. The case went to Federal District Court and appears stalled in the legal system for some time to come. In the meantime, the President ordered *The Agency* and specifically Frank Fletcher to release as much of the technology as possible to the private sector without jeopardizing national security. Politicians are good at making such decisions. After all, what can possibly go wrong?

# CHAPTER 16

## BUDDING GENIUS

Mike Hollister's secretary called him on the video intercom. "Mr. Hollister, Mr. Bobby Durand is in the outer office, do you have time to see him this morning?"

"Of course Martha, send him in."

Mike rose from his desk to greet Bobby as he entered. "Hey man, what brings you by this morning?"

"Mike, I just want to thank you for all that you have done for me and for my family. And....and...I want to ask a favor."

"What is it? Anything I can do for an old high school friend, I'll be glad to do."

"Mike, you know you arranged for me to upload a two-year electronic education which makes it possible for me to work as a technician here at GMH, but I want to go farther in life. I mean....man it's great to be able to work here, but I just think I could offer more to the human race and to GMH Tech if I could upload an advanced degree in bio-medical research. What do you think? You think it might be possible?"

"Bobby, consider it done. I will talk with Chun Li and the R&D team and let you know as soon as I get their answer."

"Thanks Mike, you won't regret it. I promise you."

"Bobby, in high school all the guys teased you about being a nerd, but I knew from the beginning that you have a truly great talent and interest in science, and being a nerd is a truly positive thing in my book. So, yes, let's increase your nerd capacity. It just may pay great dividends to the human race." They both laughed. Bobby thanked Mike, shook his hand and left the office.

Chun Li and the R&D team programmed the equivalent of a doctoral degree in bio-medical research into one of the lab's computers and prepared a room for Bobby to undergo up to a dozen uploading sessions to his brain. They learned with Maria that loading information into memory housed in the hippocampus too rapidly can cause problems. Chun Li didn't want to repeat that mistake.

Bobby Durand became Doctor Durand in the space of twelve weeks. He followed up with advanced information uploads spread over a number of months giving him the equivalent of several years of research on the many areas of the human brain and their specialized functions. His progress was phenomenal. Bobby Durand joined the R&D team at GMH Technology working alongside the brilliant young scientists Li, Lunsford, and Goldstein.

Bobby studied the roles of the amygdala, the part of the brain which reacts to fear and the frontal cortex which maintains calm in an individual. The team wrote a computer algorithm which when applied through the feedback feature of the CR4 chip could be used by the military, by first responders, and by athletes or anyone else for that matter to balance the role of fear and calm thereby making it possible to function successfully while facing situations of great stress.

The R&D team's next development was a method for sorting out memories and permanently removing bad memories leaving only good and productive memories in the human brain when desired. This technique was first put to use at a Veterans Administration Hospital in a psych ward treating the worst of the worst cases of PTSD, or post-traumatic stress disorder. The results were so encouraging that the GMH Technology method for treatment was adopted system wide, and in hundreds of psychological practices around the world. The entire R&D team including Bobby Durand was nominated for a Nobel Prize.

Mike and Maria Hollister recalled that Bobby Durand was suicidal at one point in his young life. They remembered they tricked several friends into ingesting a CR3 chip during a pool party at the town house community. They learned of his situation at the high school, and how he had been molested and was strongly considering killing himself. Mike recalled that he had to lie to Bobby about talking in his sleep in order not to reveal how he found out what was going on in his life at that time.

Mike turned to Maria, "Do you suppose it would be alright now to reveal how we found out about the abuse?"

"No Mike, let it go. Just be glad for Bobby and the whole human race that we played the prank with the CR3 chips at the party. We don't want everybody to find out how devious we both were as kids." She chuckled.

"You're right Sis, we've been very lucky up until now that hardly anybody knows how we learned so much about so many people. And how we are still keeping up with a bunch of federal authorities even now."

"Wow, Mike, I hadn't thought about that in a while. What if somebody finds out how many federal employees we are still tracking with our encrypted cell phone channels?"

"You're right. We could be in a lot of hot water. Let's hope nobody ever discovers what we've done and what we're still doing."

Doctor Bobby Durand moved on to research the motor cortex of the human brain. He and the R&D team wrote a computer algorithm which they applied in a series of experiments uploading motor skills normally learned through years of practice and repetition.

Maria Hollister volunteered to test the system. Since her experience in the high school band, Maria had always wanted to learn to play a range of instruments. For several months the R&D team uploaded the ability to play keyboard instruments including piano and organ. Maria excelled at both instruments. She gave a concert of classical piano compositions for the enjoyment of the entire staff of GMH Tech. All agreed this was a remarkable feat for a young woman with very little previous musical experience.

Maria turned next to her desire to learn to fly. Working

with the R&D team she was able to upload all of the required ground school and flight training required by the FAA. She did this first for a private pilot's license and then for an instrument rating and a commercial pilot's license. Last but not least she uploaded all ground school and flight requirements for an Air Transport Pilot rating. Maria proved her expertise to the FAA inspector by taking her flight exam in the company's Boeing 737. To the inspector's amazement Maria passed all written and practical exams. Once again the CR4 system proved that not only information but also motor skills can be uploaded to the human brain.

GMH Technology began marketing these newly developed methods for motor skill instruction. Airlines and the armed forces became early adopters. This new method cut costs and training time to produce new pilots by over ninety percent.

The teacher's unions and university faculties strongly opposed these new methods. Dozens of lawsuits were filed to stop the company from spreading this new technology. The company and the unions will be in the courts for decades and spend tons of money to fight theses legal battles.

Bobby Durand turned his attention to another area of the human brain, pain control. The body can produce natural opioids or pain reducing chemicals which attach to receptors in the brain and reduce the sensation of pain. Bobby, working with the R&D team, developed a computer algorithm which when uploaded using the feedback capability of the CR4 system trains the brain to instruct the body to produce its own chemicals to block pain. The development included instructions to the brain to produce only enough at any one time to avoid dependence and the risk of developing chronic pain from overuse of these natural pain defenses.

As soon as the development was released for commercial use, the pharmaceutical industry filed a series of lawsuits to block its implementation. Again, GMH Technology found itself immersed in a new round of court battles over a process which could conceivably benefit the human race.

Bobby Durand turned his and the R&D team's attention to yet another possible use for technology involving the human brain. The human eye is like a camera. The retina catches the image coming through the lens. It then transit's the image through the optic nerve to the brain. The brain stores the image and can recall it upon demand. The team believes that if the CR4 chips can read a person's thoughts and transmit them to a cell phone application then why not optical information as well.

The result of their investigations and lab experiments was a new version of the cerebral readout chip, the CR5. The latest chip can actually see the world through another person's eyes. The person with the CR5 chip in their body will literally become a walking, talking video camera transmitting digital video and audio to a dedicated and encrypted cell phone in the hands of someone of whom the chip bearer is totally unaware.

Needless to say, this latest development was kept well-guarded for a time. It was not reported to *The Agency* right away. Mike and Maria debated long and hard about letting anyone know about the CR5 chip outside the R&D staff.

Oren Lunsford developed a new and improved satellite cell phone application for use with the new CR5 chip. The chip uses a discreet encrypted channel and scrambled data packet system to monitor the CR5 chip. A person or animal with the chip in their body can be monitored from anywhere on earth using a dedicated satellite phone. This makes it possible to keep track of the activities of almost anyone anywhere anytime.

To test the system in a live situation David Goldstein suggested to Mike that GMH consider approaching Mossad, the Israeli intelligence service. After pondering the possibility, Mike agreed. David made arrangements to fly directly to Tel Aviv in the guise of a tourist.

Arrival at Ben Gurion Airport was uneventful. David cleared customs and immigration and took a taxi to his hotel. His travel arrangements were no different than those of the average American tourist visiting Israel. What was different was an after-dinner meeting with agents of Mossad. David was taken in a closed panel van to an undisclosed location where he met with the chief of state security. There the two reached an agreement to insert CR5 chips into several feral donkeys which would be turned loose to wander into Gaza and into the West Bank.

On the second day of the test the donkeys wandered

unmolested and uncorraled along the main streets of Gaza city and into Hebron. Mossad agents monitoring their progress received high definition audio and video data through the satellite phone system.

Soon about two dozen feral donkeys wandered about in Palestinian areas. They served as mobile observation posts feeding back audio and video to Mossad from where ever they wandered. Mossad officials were impressed and asked, “Can we insert the CR5 chip into an animal or human using the nano machines which mimic insects?”

David was quick to assure them, “Yes, the CR5 chip is even smaller than its predecessors and will easily fit into the proboscis of most of the nano machine insects available from GMH Technology.”

The Israeli government placed an order for an undisclosed number and variety of nano machine insects and CR5 chips to accompany them. When David returned to Miami he handed the order to Mike Hollister. Mike was more than pleased with the size of the order. GMH Technology filled the order within a week and delivered the materials to a member of the Israeli Embassy. They were transported to Israel by a specially chartered jet and were escorted by several members of Mossad.

Soon Qom, Natanz, Isfahan, and several other Iranian nuclear sites as well as the streets of Tehran experienced an invasion of what appeared to be biting flies and mosquitos.

Nobody seemed to notice anything unusual as this type of insect was common in Iran at this season of the year. For several weeks technicians and scientists working in the Iranian nuclear facilities experienced an above average number of stinging bites. They simply scratched their welts and went about the business of developing nuclear materials.

What the Iranians did not know was that Mossad agents sitting in a bunker in Israel were listening to everything they said, and seeing in high definition everything they were looking at. Nothing in the history of espionage had ever been this effective.

Maria and Mike Hollister were proud of their role in helping monitor the Iranian nuclear threat to the world. Israeli operatives used the feedback feature of the CR5 chip to plant instructions for sabotage in the brains of Iranian nuclear technicians. Many Iranians did the previously unthinkable. They shut down centrifuges thinking that instructions to do so were issued by their superiors. This was a hundred times better than the Stuxnet worm released earlier by computer hackers against the Iranian nuclear program.

In addition to Iran, Mossad spread nano insects into every corner of the West Bank and Gaza. There wasn't a plot hatched by Hezbollah or Hamas that the Israelis didn't know about. Rocket launches from Gaza were largely stopped before they could materialize. The locations of smuggling tunnels from the Egyptian side of the Gaza border were known and the tunnels destroyed quickly. Suicide bombers from the West Bank were stopped before they could strike. Bobby Durand's discoveries were contributing to the security of Israel.

Mike and Maria were not sure how to approach *The Agency* in their own country. They had been bullied into turning over technology in the past with mixed results. Their own government had fumbled badly in the release of federal prisoners. The government was still trying to round up former federal prison inmates with mixed results. Many very bad actors were still out on the nation's streets.

It was inevitable that *The Agency* would find out about the new CR5 chip. *Agency* spies in Israel got wind of it about four months after Mossad began using the technology.

Frank Fletcher came storming into Mike Hollister's office. He was fuming mad. Martha Wilson couldn't stop him. He blew right past her.

Frank pounded on Mike's desk. "What the hell do you mean selling the CR5 chip to Israel and you didn't even tell us you had it? *The Agency* has the rights to any and all security technology developed by this firm. You better read your contract Mr. Hollister."

Mike responded, "Mr. Fletcher, we are well aware of our contract with GSA, but nowhere in it does it require us to report immediately new developments prior to conducting field trials. That is what we did with the Israelis. These were field trials. You wouldn't want to buy something that hasn't been thoroughly tested would you?" He smiled.

Frank Fletcher was still standing in front of Mike's desk. "Dammit Hollister, you better transfer this technology to our Maryland lab within the hour or....or....." He stopped.

"Or what, Mr. Fletcher?"

"Or we'll close this place down and seize all of your intellectual property. I'll call on the DOJ to have you and your entire staff arrested for espionage....or cooperating with the enemy....or..." He sputtered.

"Mr. Fletcher, calm down and let's come to an understanding about which intellectual property is covered by our contract. Otherwise we are getting nowhere."

Mike called Martha Wilson and asked her to send someone for a tray with coffee and pastries. When they arrived he and Frank Fletcher settled down for a discussion over coffee. They agreed that *The Agency* would receive the design specifications for the CR5 chip to be produced in the Maryland lab. Mike cautioned Frank that the last time the government produced a chip they got the outer shell wrong, and he reminded him that the administration is still trying to recover from the prison release disaster.

Frank Fletcher prepared to fly back to Maryland with the complete specifications for the CR5 tracking chip as well as its cell phone applications in his tablet computer. While changing planes in Atlanta his tablet computer disappeared.

# CHAPTER 17

# LOST AND FOUND

Frank Fletcher lost no time in calling investigators from *The Agency* to assist in trying to locate his tablet computer. The data contained in the lost tablet computer was encrypted, but nevertheless any word of its loss would create a political fire storm. The administration was still reeling under the weight of the failed prison release program. Tens of thousands of convicted felons were free to roam the nation and commit mayhem. The administration could not stand another public relations disaster.

Frank and his fellow agents scanned video surveillance recordings from the time of the computer's disappearance. They were able to see what appeared to be a poorly-dressed man pick up the tablet and slide it under an overcoat carried on his arm. The suspect exited the airport to the parking area and departed in an older model small car. The license plate was visible. When the agents ran the number through the department of motor vehicles the plate did not match the vehicle.

Frank Fletcher attempted to locate the stolen tablet computer through an anti-theft application in the computer's firmware. It would only be possible when the computer is turned on and booted up. While the computer is off the firmware ID feature would not be able to respond to a search query. *So much for that approach*, he thought. *Now what can we do?*

Frank and his fellow agents gave the Atlanta Metropolitan police agencies all the information they had about the man and the small car with the unmatched license number. The police in a suburb reported that the license plate had been stolen only a day earlier in their area. Fortunately there was a surveillance recording of the parking lot from which the license had been taken.

The lot from which the license plate disappeared was that of a used car dealership. The individual appearing in the airport surveillance recordings turned out to be a part time maintenance roustabout working for the used car lot. When questioned, he admitted taking the tablet computer and pawning it to get money to buy drugs.

Frank Fletcher along with several federal, state, and local law enforcement people visited the local pawn shop. They presented the pawn ticket and redeemed the computer. *Now*, thought Frank, *it is over. I have the complete CR5 system design back in my hands and safely on its way to Maryland.*

Frank Fletcher thanked all those who assisted him in recovering from his own failure to properly watch over a sensitive piece of national security. He caught a flight out of Atlanta and arrived just after midnight at Reagan Washington National Airport. Exhausted he returned to his apartment and fell into a deep sleep.

Waking just before noon, Frank took a cab to *The Agency* to report on his trip to South Florida and his acquisition of the latest brain wave monitoring system incorporated in the CR5 chip with all of its attendant hardware and software. He was roundly congratulated in having brought *The Agency* at least up to the level of Mossad's ability to keep track of everything in a potential enemy's brain as well as everything in an enemy's field of vision.

The next afternoon Frank Fletcher took his tablet computer to the Maryland Lab. Here he was to give the newly acquired design data to the engineering team headed by Myles Burwell.

Myles eagerly accepted the tablet computer. He turned it on and watched it boot up. When he looked for the folder containing the files for the CR5 system it was not found.

"What is this piece of junk you just handed me?" he shouted at Frank. "There is nothing here even resembling the files you described. So what are you trying to pull?"

Frank Fletcher turned pale. "They have to be in there. I loaded all the data files myself. I know they're there."

Myles shot back, "OK, so show them to me!"

Frank Fletcher began searching for the CR5 files to no avail. "So, maybe the system just isn't finding the folder. I know it's in there. It's in the miniature SD card. Here, let's turn it off, and I'll pull the SD card and we will try it on another computer."

Frank waited until the tablet computer was off, and slid the cover from the slot for the mini-SD card. "Holy crap, there's nothing in the slot. The SD card is missing. It had the entire CR5 system design on it and it's not here."

Frank Fletcher thought for a moment. "I'll bet that SOB at the pawn shop took the SD card out of the computer. I didn't even have the foresight to check it before I left the shop. Now what are we going to do?"

Myles Burwell responded, "You better figure it out before the administration learns of your mistake and blames *The Agency* for another disaster. The president is still smarting over our screw up of the prison release program. God alone knows where that SD card may be by now."

Frank Fletcher summoned Ari MacKenzie and Kurt Rinehart to a hastily called meeting. "Ari, you and Kurt are being reassigned." He recalled the loss of the computer and the subsequent loss of the SD card. "We need to find and retrieve that SD card before someone figures out what they have. It is vital to our national defense that the CR5 system be militarized and deployed just like we did with the CR4 system."

Ari asked, "Frank, didn't you have the foresight to upload the encrypted files to *The Agency's* discrete cloud storage facility? Why did you take such a risk as to travel on public transportation with everything in a tablet computer? What on earth were you thinking?"

Frank shrugged, "I feel so stupid. I wasn't thinking! But too late for recriminations right now. We must get that SD card before it falls into the wrong hands."

Ari and Kurt packed and took a red-eye flight to Atlanta. In the pale light of early morning they drove out of the airport in a rental SUV and headed straight to the pawn shop where Frank's computer had been retrieved earlier. They walked in and asked for the owner.

A slightly built older man appeared from an office in the rear of the establishment. Ari presented her federal ID and said, "We are here to get some information about a tablet computer that you recently held and released to its owner in the company of several police officers. Do you remember the incident?"

"Why yes, how could I forget? The place was crawling with police and plain clothes types. So what is it that you want with me now? I released the computer. Isn't that the end of it.?"

Ari responded, "Not quite sir, we would like to ask if you or anyone in your establishment can recall if someone took a miniature SD card out of the machine?"

"Why yes. I always take the SD cards out of pawned computers. I have a box full of them in the back of the store. Periodically a hobbyist comes by and I sell him all that I have. Why do you ask?"

Kurt intervened, "Well sir, do you have the SD card that came out of the machine in question?"

"No, just yesterday the fellow who buys them came in and I sold him the whole lot."

Ari looked at Kurt and then back to the owner. "Sir, it

is vital that we meet this hobbyist. Do you have his address?"

"Actually I do. Let me get it for you."

The owner stepped back into his office and returned with a business card in hand. "Here is his card with his home address and phone number. I hope this will help."

Ari thanked the owner. She and Kurt returned to their rental car and programmed the hobbyist's address into the car's GPS. A few minutes later they were pulling into the driveway of a run-down older apartment complex on Atlanta's north side.

Kurt knocked on the door. He and Ari waited for an answer. Nothing. He knocked again with a bit more emphasis in the blows he landed on the old wooden door. Still nothing. About that time an elderly lady walked up the hallway.

"What can I do for you folks?" She asked, speaking with a decidedly English accent.

Ari turned and spoke, "We are looking for a gentleman who lives at this address. Do you know him?"

"Why yes," she replied, "he's my son. Why would you be looking for him? I hope he's not in some kind of trouble."

Ari responded, "We just need to speak with him about his computer hobby. Do you know where we can find him?"

"He isn't here. He left for London this morning. He's going to see his aunt, my sister, who lives there."

Kurt asked, "May we have your sister's address? It is urgent that we interview your son about his computer hobby."

"Well, my gracious, I can't imagine why anyone would

want to interview my son about his hobby. But if you insist, please come inside and I will get my sister's address for you."

Kurt and Ari shot each other a glance. They were both thinking, *well at least this is one step closer to the SD card if it even still exists.*

Ari and Kurt took a flight to London from Atlanta. They arrived at Heathrow Airport just after seven the next morning. With an address in hand, they took the London Underground to Southfields Station and walked the few blocks to a series of row houses.

Kurt rang the bell. A lady answered the door. Kurt spoke, "Good morning, my name is Kurt Rinehart, and this is Ariana MacKenzie. I believe you are Helen Scarborough, is that correct?"

"Why yes. Yes it is correct. What brings you young people here?"

Ari responded, "We would like to talk with your nephew Thomas Scarborough. Is he here?"

"Yes, I'll call him. Won't you please come in? Would you like some tea?"

"No thank you, we just had breakfast."

A gentleman about forty years old emerged from the rear of the house. "Good morning, I'm Thomas Scarborough. What can I do for you? My aunt tells me you want to speak with me."

Kurt responded, "Yes, your mother in Atlanta told us you would be here. We are interested in your computer hobby. It seems you collect SD cards from pawn shops in Atlanta. We are also interested in collecting SD cards. Do you have some you want to sell?"

Thomas looked at Kurt and Ari with an air of suspicion. "What on earth gave you the idea that I want to sell my collection of SD cards?"

Ari spoke up, "Just a hunch. Is there some reason you would not be amenable to selling your entire collection?"

Thomas responded, "Well, there must be something very important on one or more of my SD cards or you wouldn't come all the way from the states to inquire about them, now would you?"

Kurt, never the patient one began to get a bit testy, "Look Thomas, let's not play games. Either you want to sell what you have or you don't. But in this case I can assure you that you definitely want to sell."

Thomas paused, "Well, sir you seem mighty anxious to acquire my SD card collection. Do you have any idea how many I have? Or what the collection may be worth?"

Ari interjected, "Sir we are only interested in one card out of your entire collection, but we are willing to buy them all just to make sure we get the one we need. It is a proprietary bit of software and we need to return it to its rightful owner. You see, the computer it came out of was stolen and pawned. That is where you obtained the SD card and we aren't interested in why you have such a fetish, but believe me sir, we won't be leaving without that one SD card." She gave Thomas a look that convinced him she was serious.

"Wait here and I will bring the box of SD cards and you can look through them for the one you want."

Thomas returned and dumped about a hundred miniature SD cards on the dining table. "Can you identify the one you want?"

Ari smiled, "Sir, it will be difficult and time consuming to pick out a single SD card from that pile and be certain we have the right one. How about if we just buy the entire pile and call it even? Name your price."

Thomas thought for a moment, "Well, the two of you are so terribly eager to own this pile of SD cards so it seems to me that the price should be rather high, wouldn't you agree?"

Kurt was fuming mad, "Now look here, we didn't come all the way to the UK to be fleeced by some two-bit hobbyist."

Thomas just smiled. "Well call me what you will, the price will be two-hundred thousand pounds sterling. Not a penny less."

Ari urged Kurt to calm down. "Thomas, we will have to get approval to pay that much, but it may be possible."

"Kurt, step outside, call *The Agency* and arrange the payment."

She turned back to Thomas Scarborough. "Just out of curiosity, why do you collect SD cards from other people's computers?"

"Well, you just never know what you might find. Take today for instance. Who knew that two Americans would show up on my aunt's doorstep wanting to buy one card in particular and then offer to buy the whole kit and caboodle? One just never knows."

Ari continued her inquiry, "Well Thomas, have you sold many cards to other buyers?"

"Now that you mention it, yes I have. I usually examine the data on the cards I collect and then decide who might be interested in owning them. That way I enhance my chances of making a good sale."

"So Thomas, who are your best customers?"

He thought for a moment, "That's hard to say, sometimes software companies looking for a competitor's developments. Sometimes government agencies here and abroad looking for clues to what other governments are doing. Almost anything you can name."

This struck a chord with Ari. She thought, *that is exactly why we are trying to retrieve what Frank Fletcher let get loose in a world of digital espionage. If only Frank hadn't been so absolutely careless with something as powerful as the CR5 system design. Kurt and I could be fishing somewhere, but now we are fishing for an elusive SD card in the land of fish and chips. The problem is not that The Agency can't weaponize and produce the CR5 system by getting backup data from GMH Tech. It is that this one SD card is loose and god forbid that it may have been copied or shared with any of the worst of the worst actors in this very violent world.*

Kurt returned from making a satellite phone call to *The Agency* to arrange payment to Thomas Scarborough. He wasn't smiling. "Ari, we have a problem. The boss says we will not pay that much or any amount to retrieve one single SD card. So what are we going to do now?"

Ari turned to Thomas Scarborough. "Sir, we are not able to pay what you ask. Would it be possible for us to examine the SD cards on the table and decide which one we are looking for if it is in the pile and then make another offer?"

Thomas shot back, "No, not at all. I think I'll just keep the entire collection and look for other customers. You have given me the idea that there may be one card among all of these that has a very high value. I don't have any idea what it has on it, but it may appeal to others more than it does to you."

Ari responded, "Sir, don't be so hasty. If you fail to make a deal with us it may become very dangerous for you to retain the card we are looking for. So here is my final offer. Kurt and I will look for the card on the table. If we identify it, we will walk out of here with it. If you refuse, you could have a serious problem. Do you understand me sir?"

Thomas was taken aback. "Well, since you put it that way, go ahead and examine the pile. After all, what is one card among so many. I think I might be able to live without just one."

Kurt gave him a look. "Good thinking sir, good thinking."

For the next two hours Kurt and Ari handled the entire pile of miniature SD cards spread out on the table. They used a small scanner to probe each and every card for its data files and folders. When they finished the entire pile they looked at each other in stunned silence.

Ari spoke, "Kurt, it isn't here. The card from Frank's tablet simply isn't in this pile."

Kurt shot a glance toward Thomas. "OK sport, what are you trying to pull on us? The card we are looking for isn't here. Have you sold or disposed of any cards since you arrived in the UK?"

Thomas responded, "Well, actually yes. I sold one in particular to a gentleman who came yesterday and scanned the pile like you two have just done. He seemed very pleased with his find and paid a decent price for it."

Ari asked, "May we meet the person who bought that card? Can you arrange it? It is of the utmost importance."

Thomas hesitated before he spoke, "Well….he might not be so eager to meet the two of you."

Kurt almost lost it. "Look Thomas, we are not going to play games. Either you are going to arrange a meeting with this customer of yours or we are going to involve Scotland Yard in your situation and it won't be pleasant. Do you understand me sir."

Thomas responded, "Well, the two of you were willing to pay my price for my collection. I guess I can take a chance that I can arrange for you to meet one of my best customers. Let me make a phone call."

Thomas stepped into the hallway and picked up a phone. He was only gone for a few minutes. When he returned he gave Ari and Kurt a slip of paper. On it he had written: *Meet in the Undercroft at St. Paul's following Even Song this evening. I will be wearing a tan cardigan and standing next to the Duke of Wellington's tomb.*

# CHAPTER 18

# LONDON

Ari and Kurt took the train from Southfields into town. The train passed the Battersea Power Station and entered the London Underground just beyond the bridge over the River Thames. Ari and Kurt exited the train at Victoria Station. They were both in the mood for a good meal since it was already mid-afternoon. As they turned onto Vauxhall Bridge Road just a block from Victoria Station they found the *New Maple Grill and Trattoria del Fungo*.

Kurt chuckled, “What a name for a restaurant.”

Ari responded, “Right now I don’t care what they call it, let’s drop in and have lunch.”

Following a great Italian meal the two spent some time riding around on top of a London double deck sight-seeing bus. They ended their tour at the Museum of London and walked the few blocks to St. Paul’s Cathedral well in time for Even Song.

To make sure they knew where to rendezvous with the stranger they descended into the Undercroft and found the sarcophagus of the Duke of Wellington. Here also was the tomb of Admiral Lord Nelson, one of the most famous of British naval heroes. They enjoyed the statuary in the Undercroft featuring some of the more notable people from British History. They stood for a time before the statue of Viscount Adam Duncan, the British admiral who defeated the Dutch fleet at Camperdown in

1797. Ari was especially interested in this monument. She told Kurt that her grandmother was a Duncan and traced the family lineage directly back to Admiral Viscount Duncan the tallest man in the British Navy up to that time.

Kurt and Ari returned to the main floor of the Cathedral and took seats in the Nave. The robed choir consisting of boys and young men entered right on time at five o'clock. When the musical program of Even Song ended Ari and Kurt descended once again into the Undercroft. There they stood silently beside the Wellington sarcophagus. Within a matter of minutes a man wearing a tan cardigan sweater entered and stood silently beside them.

At first no one spoke. Ari broke the silence. "Are you a tourist?"

"No," the man responded. "But it would seem the two of you are American tourists. Am I right?"

"Not exactly," Ari responded. "We are in London on business."

"What sort of business?"

"We collect antiques."

"Oh, I see, and what sort of antiques?"

Kurt butted in. "Oh for heaven's sake let's cut to the chase. We are supposed to meet you here. We don't know why you wanted to meet in such a place, but here we are. So how do you fit into the computer business?"

The man responded, "My name is Ian Paxton and I

believe we have something in common."

Kurt responded, "OK Ian, what do we have in common? Spill it."

"I believe we are both interested in the same technology. I would like you to come with me and take a ride to meet my associate who has the same interest. How about it?"

Ari spoke up. "Perhaps that will be possible. But first, Mr. Paxton, you need to allow me to take a photo of the iris in your right eye. Is that agreeable?"

"Yes, I suppose you want to run my identity through *The Agency*. I certainly don't blame you for taking precautions. I would have done the same if I were invited to accompany a total stranger."

Ari zoomed her cell phone camera in for a close-up of Ian Paxton's iris. She uploaded the photo to a computer in Maryland. The answer came back within a minute and a half. The individual is a Mr. Ian Paxton, an agent of MI5, the British equivalent of Homeland Security in the USA.

Ari and Kurt followed Ian up to street level and out of the Cathedral past the Queen Anne Statue onto Ludgate Hill Road. Ian motioned to the driver of a van parked nearby. A panel van pulled to the curb. Ian motioned Kurt and Ari to get in.

The three sat in the rear of the van. There were curtains over the back windows and a curtain behind the driver cutting off their view of the road ahead. There were no side windows.

Kurt spoke, "So Ian, just where are we going?"

"We are going to a location where we can discuss business. My superior is aware of your presence in the UK and the purpose of your being here. Sometimes we work very closely with *The Agency* in the USA. However under your current administration our connections with *The Agency* have become…shall we say….a bit more distant. We intend to rectify that situation."

"Just how do you intend to rectify ….as you put it…..the situation? Kurt asked.

"You will learn that and answers to your other questions when we meet my superior."

The ride did not last long. The driver took the M-4 motorway out of the heart of London to West Drayton where the journey ended in an alley behind a row of office buildings. Ian motioned for Kurt and Ari to follow him through a door leading into a long hallway. At the end of the hall they stepped into a large windowless office. A man who appeared to be in his sixties was seated, but rose to greet them as they entered.

"Good evening Ms. MacKenzie and Mr. Rinehart I believe. I am Aden Harper and I am delighted to meet the two of you. I've heard a lot about you. I very much enjoyed learning of your Venezuelan adventure."

"OK, so you seem to know a lot about us," interjected Kurt, "So why are we here and what is it you want from us?"

"You have been thoroughly vetted by MI5 and found to

be free of…shall we say….security defects and you are reliable. The UK has a number of domestic security risks just as most modern civilized nations have."

Ari spoke up, "We agree that both of our nations have domestic security risks, but how does this involve the two of us?"

Aden continued, "We sought to purchase certain technology from a company in the USA and our request was turned down by your administration in Washington. The UK has always been a reliable ally and partner in many wars in the past, and currently we regard ourselves as an ally and partner in the war against ISIS and radical Islam. But unfortunately that is obviously not how your administration sees us at the moment. So we pursued another course of action.

The theft of Frank Fletcher's tablet computer was no random crime. Our agent Thomas Scarborough works in the Atlanta area…shall we say…acquiring intelligence through a seemingly innocent hobby. The Atlanta area is home to a number of defense contractors whose employees sometimes behave carelessly with their laptops, tablets, and smart phones. Thomas hired the thief to target Frank Fletcher. We follow Mr. Fletcher's every move and know his whereabouts by pinging his cell phone. We will be even more accurate with our tracking program when we obtain the CR5 system."

"Sir we are security agents and technical people," said Ari, "but we aren't political. So I don't quite understand how we can help the UK to obtain the technology you seek."

Aden continued, "We learned from Mossad that Israel recently purchased the CR5 system directly from GMH Technology and that they are putting it to good use against the nuclear program in Iran as well as Hezbollah and Hamas on their borders. We would like to have the same capability to combat radical Jihadists in the UK and overseas. It is a shame that your administration is refusing to allow us to purchase the technology directly from the USA. However, we are in possession of the miniature SD card containing the entire design for the system. Our only problem is that the data is encrypted. What we would like the two of you to do is to persuade someone in the USA to release the encryption key to us so we can employ the technology against our domestic terrorists."

"Sir," Ari interjected, "that is asking us to become politically involved with decisions made by our administration, and that is not part of our job description."

Aden looked at the two thoughtfully for a moment. "Well, in the absence of your cooperation we will be forced to take time to break the encryption code and open the data files without the permission of the American administration. That will take longer and will leave the UK in danger of domestic terrorism for a longer time than we feel we have. But if that is your attitude, so be it. You may very well become our guests for an extended period unless we get the cooperation of someone in your country."

At the offices of GMH Technology Mike and Maria Hollister, using discreet channels, monitored the entire journey and all of the conversations of Kurt and Ari from the tracking chips which were still active in these two.

Maria turned to her brother, "Mike, I don't like the sound of what Aden just told Ari and Kurt. He said that they may become guests of MI5 for an extended period. It sounds like they are going to be held against their will."

Mike responded, "You're right. It does sound like a threat. Should we get involved in their situation?"

"I think so Mike. What I don't understand is why the administration objects to our selling the CR5 system to the British. After all, the British are our allies."

Mike responded, "Sis, ever since we sold the system to Mossad in Israel the administration has been angry with us and has insisted on approving any and all sales in the future. But put that aside for a moment. I think we need to see what we can do for Ari and Kurt. They're our friends and are in a bit of trouble right now. How should we go about it?"

"Mike, what if we released the encryption key to MI5 and nobody finds out?"

"Sis, we could be in a lot of hot water if *The Agency* finds out we did it, but that is probably the fastest way to resolve the plight of Kurt and Ari. Besides, I want the British to have the system and use it the way Aden described to counter their domestic terrorists."

Ari's cell phone rang. She looked toward Aden as if to say, "Shall I answer it?"

Aden Harper motioned for her to answer the call, but cautioned her to put it on speaker so all in the room could listen.

"Hello."

"Hello Ari, this is Mike Hollister. How are you and Kurt?"

"Very well thank you. How are you and Maria?"

"We're fine. I understand you and Kurt were sent to find a mini SD card which became lost in transit. Is that right?"

"Well, Mike, I'm not at liberty to talk about something like that."

"Ari, don't ask me any questions about how I know your situation, but if you let me speak to Aden Harper, perhaps I can work something out."

Ari and Kurt looked at each other and at Aden and Ian with shocked expressions. Ari handed her cell phone to Aden Harper.

"Hello, this is Aden. How did you know my name, and how the deuce did you know I was with Ari and Kurt?"

Mike responded, "Mr. Harper, it is part of my job to know where to find key people from time to time and this is just one of those times. I understand that the UK tried to buy the CR5 technology but were refused permission by our current administration. It seems you are quite adamant about owning our technology. Am I correct in this assumption?"

Mike continued, "Mr. Harper, how would it be if the UK were selected for a field trial of the CR5 technology? I think we can arrange something like that if it meets with your approval."

Aden responded, "How do you suggest getting it approved for export?"

"Don't worry about that sir. We have our ways."

"Mr. Hollister, I will accept your proposal and your friends will be free to leave the UK just as soon as we have the CR5 design specs. How does that sound?"

"Mr. Harper, you will have the encryption key in a few minutes. Please open a discreet channel to the MI5 cloud server and standby."

Aden Harper watched the monitor on his desktop computer as Mike uploaded the encryption key to unlock the data files on the miniature SD card. That stray card which was so carelessly lost by Frank Fletcher in the Atlanta air terminal. When the upload was complete, Mike spoke again to Aden Harper.

"It is our desire at GMH Technology to spread our knowledge throughout the free world. By the way Mr. Harper, we expect to be paid for our intellectual property, is that understood?"

"Mike, you can be sure of it. I will submit a purchase order as soon as you forward an invoice to me personally. It is good to do business with someone who knows how to cut through the bureaucratic maze and get things done."

"Mr. Harper it appears that you and MI5 know a bit about how to get what you want. But I must say I find your methods a bit heavy handed. No offense meant. I understand the pressure you must be under to combat radical Jihadism in the UK."

"Thank you Mike. Your friends will be returned to Heathrow for a flight home. Ian and our driver will take them to the airport which is only a matter of minutes from our current location."

Ari and Kurt came storming into Mike Hollister's office at GMH Technology. They both demanded to know how Mike knew where they were and who they were with.

Mike wasn't quite sure how to respond.

"Can I get you two some coffee and something to go with it?"

"No Mike, we didn't come for coffee, we demand to know how you knew our whereabouts and who we were with. Not that we didn't appreciate your intervention. So, did you inject the two of us with tracking chips like we did the Venezuelans?"

Mike rocked back in his chair and smiled. "Do you two remember when Frank Fletcher demanded access to the CR4 technology so *The Agency* could modify it and use it as a weapon system? When Myles and Dennis came to the lab to study the system and when you all went away to Maryland to the government lab there? Well, I confess, I didn't trust the government to get it right, so I fed all of you a CR4 tracking chip. It would seem that the little chip is embedded somewhere in your body and can be monitored wherever you go via a discreet channel on my modified satellite phone."

Mike continued, "Maria and I followed your Venezuelan adventure hour-by-hour and vicariously enjoyed every minute of it. The same when you went to Atlanta to pull the chestnuts out of the fire for Frank Fletcher's blunder. Then we watched your London journey with great interest and that's how we knew you were being detained by MI5. It looked like you might be held against your will and we didn't want that to happen."

"Mike, Kurt and I should be furious with you for invading our privacy this way, but in view of the technical trends of the day we should have expected something like this. We both appreciate your intervention with Aden Harper. He was adamant about obtaining the CR5 system and we probably would have been held incognito without your help. So in that regard we both thank you, but we still feel that our persons have been in some way violated."

Mike responded, "The very nature of this technology is changing the way we all feel about privacy issues. Maria and I have talked about it and we agree that nobody knows exactly where it will lead. The world is changing rapidly for better or for worse. We can only hope that our technology will make the world a better place to live and not the opposite."

British scientists modified the CR5 system. They were able to combine it with features from the close proximity brain wave detection system already in wide use among the world's major airlines. The close proximity system allows a computer to monitor a person for negative attitudes without a tracking chip involved. It could only do so within about one to two meters or about three to six feet. The British modification extends the range out to about ten to twenty meters or thirty to sixty feet from the sensor. This gives British authorities the ability to read and monitor people's thoughts without the necessity of using a chip inserted into the person being monitored.

The UK already has a system of video cameras monitoring their streets and public spaces. The new system was named Intermediate Proximity CR5 and has been installed in every public video camera in the UK. A series of computers at monitoring stations can now filter the thoughts and the conversations of people as they go about their daily routines. If a computer or an operator at a monitoring station has a reason to suspect a person of an illegal attitude, the operator can record everything the person thinks, says, or even sees. The system even reads the output of the person's optic nerves.

Should the need arise, the monitor can send a signal to the person shocking their trigeminal nerves and thereby causing great pain and suffering. Scotland Yard, MI5, and MI6 assured Parliament that the latter method will only be used in the most extenuating circumstances. The monitoring computer can also shut down the autonomic nerve system and cause immediate death. Again, Parliament was assured that this might only occur in the most extreme case as Britain does not have a legal death penalty. The issue remains under review in closed sessions of the intelligence committee in the House of Commons. Even so, the system is already in wide-spread use throughout the UK.

In the USA, Mike and Maria were delighted to receive feedback from MI5 about the range extension of the Intermediate Proximity System. GMH Technology incorporated this improvement in their airline security applications. The greater reach of this new system sold well to the Transportation Security Administration. It was installed in all major airline terminals in the USA. Many other countries also purchased the system.

Banks and jewelry stores were quick to adapt the Intermediate Range Sensors to read the attitudes of people entering their establishments. Many other retail stores and businesses which are regularly targeted by criminals installed the system. This development helped mitigate many of the dangers brought about from the government's poorly thought out prison release program.

One-by-one criminals were slowly rounded up and re-incarcerated. The Federal Bureau of Prisons spent an inordinate sum of tax money to re-purchase and rebuild prisons.

Many prisons had been sold as surplus property and had been dismantled. Instead of saving the tax payers money as the administration originally planned, the program turned out to cost many times more than if the prisons had never been closed. Additional costs were incurred rounding up and trying recidivists in the courts.

The administration still maintains that the original move to close the prisons was the right thing to do in order to create a more just and open society. The laws of inertia apply to most government programs. Once set in motion they tend to stay in motion.

## CHAPTER 19

## CARIBBEAN HOLIDAY

Mike Hollister received a call in his office on his video phone. “Hi dad, it’s good of you to call. What’s on your mind?”

“Mike, your mom and I would like to invite you to come to the island for some much deserved R&R. Maria is planning to come down and she’s invited several of your high school friends. How about it son?”

“Dad, I’d love to take some time off in paradise. I’ll be there. Count on it.”

Mike called Emiliano Vargas and Brad Bailey to schedule a flight from Opa-Locka Executive Airport to Hollister Island, the Caribbean private island estate recently purchased by Gordon and Patricia Hollister. *It should be a fun outing*, he thought, *a time to get away from bureaucracy and government entanglements*. Since there would be a large number of people Mike decided they should use the company’s Boeing 737. The airplane was new and equipped with the latest GMH Tech in-flight security system.

A loud and boisterous bunch of partiers assembled at the flight line to board the aircraft. Maria was chattering away with Beverly Talbot, Alicia Byers, Cassie Phelps, and Rhonda Barrett. Mike found himself surrounded by Alex Gardner, Chuck Bentley, Lyle Weaver, and Bobby Durand. Everyone talked at the same time but they all seemed to be catching up on what each had been doing recently.

In addition to the high school crew, Mike also invited the whiz kids, Oren, David, and Chun Li as well as his secretary Martha Wilson. The plant would just have to do without these key people for a week or so. Crystal clear Caribbean waters beckoned. Two of their favorite dogs were also on board. Martha Wilson's Scout, a German shepherd, and Oren Lunsford's Murphy, a brown Lab. Both dogs had the latest CR5 chips inserted in their shoulders.

The private island airstrip measured just under one mile in length. More than enough room to land and take off for the Boeing 737. The flight to the island was smooth and uneventful. The partiers landed at nine in the morning and were met by Gordon and Patricia Hollister along with several of their island employees. Baggage was tossed into a panel van and people were transported in several SUV's from the airfield to the house on top of the ridge. The Hollister's house guests were given a traditional island welcome by a calypso steel band hired for the occasion. Everyone agreed the scenery from the roof top veranda was totally stunning. Today the sea was bluer than ever with low running surf, and a slight tropical breeze.

Gordon and Patricia were eager to visit with Mike and Maria, but had to share their time with all of the invited guests. The younger Hollisters agreed that there would be no talk of business on this occasion. That can wait until they return to the rat race. Unfortunately, such was not to be the case as events would soon demonstrate.

Lunch was served on the huge patio in the shade of the main house. Most of the guests were eager to explore the island and perhaps to go for a swim in the ocean. The entire island was surrounded on all sides by a fabulous coral sand beach. Even the boat harbor had a great swimming beach on two sides.

Gordon gave his guests a briefing about where to find recreational equipment such as water skis, snorkel and scuba gear, and jet skis. Mike and Maria's friends agreed this was a truly remarkable place. They couldn't wait to hit the water.

Murphy and Scout were allowed to roam the island to their heart's content. The guests were amazed as they observed the thoughts of the two dogs on Mike and Maria's cell phones. The dogs seemed to get along very well in spite of Murphy's previous territorial jealousy expressed one day at GMH Technology. The day when the CR concept first revealed that it is possible to read an animal's or a person's thoughts from their brain waves.

The young people spent several hours water skiing behind jet skis. At the end of the day they returned to the house exhausted, a bit sun burned but laughing and happy. Everyone showered and changed for dinner. A fabulous meal was served under the stars on the rooftop veranda. From here one could see the lights of boats passing between some of the islands in the distance. Large and small water craft passed in a constant procession day and night in this tropical paradise.

People broke into small groups and huddled over drinks late into the night. All of their high school friends by this time were aware that one could advance their education by uploading to the human brain. They were amazed that Maria, Mike, and Bobby Durand had advanced so far in such a short time. Mike explained that if they wanted to advance themselves they would have to do it outside the mainstream of the educational establishment. He told them about the stone walling treatment he and Maria experienced at the university level.

Later in the evening Bobby Durand talked with Mike and asked him if he would explain the opportunities for advancement to his dad Roy Durand. He told Mike that his dad was working only part time and was not willing to go back to work on off-shore oil rigs. Perhaps it would be possible for Roy Durand to become a technician or engineer by undergoing a brain upload. Mike agreed that when they returned to South Florida he would encourage Roy to consider the possibility.

Around one in the morning Mike's cell phone sounded a chime indicating some brain wave activity from the dogs. The text translation read, "We don't like these guys. We don't think they are friends. We're going to watch them and if they make a wrong move we'll take them down."

Mike sat upright and continued watching the text flow from the two dogs. They were watching someone walking on the beach on the opposite side of the island from the estate. Fortunately, whoever it is on the beach is nowhere near the airstrip or the house.

Mike became somewhat concerned. If the dogs don't like someone, they are probably not to be trusted. He learned at an early age that a dog is a good judge of a person's character. *Well*, he wondered, *should he wake his dad and alert him to the presence of people on the island who may be a threat?*

Mike switched his cell phone from text scrolling to receive live real time video output from Murphy's optic nerves. It appeared that Murphy and Scout were sitting quietly on a tall grassy dune about thirty or forty yards from a small skiff with its bow on the sandy beach. Two men were just pushing the skiff back into the water as Mike began viewing. The men and the skiff disappeared into the darkness very quickly.

After a hearty breakfast Mike took his dad to one side and asked him about security on the island. Gordon told his son that they have a fairly good security system in place with motion sensors at key locations. The airstrip, the hangar, the boat docks and harbor as well as the main house and out buildings are all well protected by sensors and video cameras.

Mike suggested that he and his dad review the security layout during the day and see if it needs anything added. He told his dad about the dog's text flow and video output during the night. Gordon couldn't imagine who it might have been landing on the most remote beach on the opposite side of the island from the harbor and airstrip. He wondered if it might have been some of his employees who went for a night time boat ride.

Mike insisted that if the dogs didn't like the people, it was very likely some unsavory characters. He suggested that they test this theory by watching the text flow from the dogs during the day as they interacted with the island employees. The dogs seemed to approve of all of the employees indicating that the people they saw the night before were not people who belong on Hollister Island.

Mike invited his high school friends to take a hike clear around the island to see the lay of the land. He and his buddies set off with the dogs for the long trek. They started on the back side of the island away from the main part of the estate. After about an hour's walk they came to a place on the shore where it appeared that a boat had been pulled up onto the sand. There were human foot prints in the sand indicating more than one visitor. The dogs barked and sniffed the entire area. It certainly appeared that they had been here earlier. Mike noticed the dogs had indeed been here. Their paw prints were on the scene from their earlier visit. He knew also from their GPS output that this is where they were when their text flow indicated they were viewing someone they didn't like.

Returning to the house in time for lunch with their guests, Mike and his friends were famished. The hike had been rather long. After lunch Mike spoke quietly to his dad and told him about finding signs of someone landing on the island in the night. Gordon wasn't too surprised at the news and informed

Mike that unfortunately the island is directly in the path of narcotics traffickers and human smugglers. About the only thing he could think of to counter such traffic would be to hire a private army to constantly patrol the beaches and the estate.

Mike had a better idea. He suggested to his dad that GMH Technology install the British-designed intermediate range CR5 system with video cameras and CR5 sensors at intervals around the entire perimeter of the island. Gordon was intrigued by the prospect. They previously agreed not to talk business, but after all, this was for the good of everyone on the island.

Mike said he would have his engineering staff custom design a solar-powered video and WiFi system fed by CR5 brain wave and optic nerve sensors. Placed at proper intervals, the video scanners will see and the sensors will detect the brain waves of any person or animal, and transmit the data to a central computer at the main house. Negative thoughts will be filtered and if detected an alarm will be triggered. The system will then transmit everything in the field of vision of those who are being monitored.

Gordon Hollister never ceased to be amazed at the things his son and daughter could come up with. He readily agreed to the project. Mike assured him that the job would get top priority. Mike made a call to the plant on his satellite phone and set things in motion. His engineers told him they would be able to complete the project before the end of the week.

Two days later another plane arrived at the airfield. A crew of installers unloaded all of the materials for the intermediate range CR5 system and began placing sensors. At the end of the day the system was complete. The family and their house guests gathered around for a demonstration. With a ninety-inch plasma TV monitor turned on they began scanning all sensors.

"Wow, would you look at that?" shouted Alex, "right there on the beach is about a dozen, no, more like a hundred Kemp's Ridley Sea Turtles. They're coming ashore. Wow, what a sight."

Everyone was glued to the monitor. For the next two hours wave after wave of sea turtles came ashore and burrowed nests into the sands and laid their eggs.

Mike said, "Well, at least the island is being invaded by friendly creatures. Let's hope it will always be this way."

The family and their guests stayed up watching the turtles until after midnight. Finally Mike said, "Well, I'm going to hit the sack. Is anyone else with me?"

Cassie Phelps cast a glance in Mike's direction. He caught this gesture out of the corner of his eye. *Well*, he thought, *I hope she didn't take my remark the wrong way.*

The house was quiet. Everyone seemed to be settled in their rooms for the night. Mike was sound asleep. The door to his room opened slowly. In the pale light of the moon a young woman slipped quietly into the room and stood beside Mike.

She stood motionless for what seemed like an eternity staring down at his shirtless sleeping form. Cassie Phelps wanted more than anything to slip into bed with Mike. She had wanted this ever since their early high school days.

Dawn broke over the crystal sea surrounding the Hollister's tropical paradise. Mike woke early and slipped into his swim suit for a dip in the main pool next to the mansion. Maria came out a few minutes later and joined him. The two swam several laps around the perimeter of the pool finally stopping in the shallow end. They stepped out and grabbed their towels to dry off.

"Mike, there is something you need to know."

"What's that Sis?"

"This morning I was scanning in my cell phone and came across something I hadn't realized was available. Do you remember when Cassie Phelps and Alicia Byers and I worked to set up the banquet at the home of Diego Ramos?"

"Yes, what about it?

"Well, it appears that Alicia and Cassie both ingested the tracking chips I took to the banquet. I didn't realize it until now. I reviewed Cassie Phelps data from last night."

"And?"

"Well, Mike, Cassie Phelps entered your room last night well after midnight."

"Sis, you're kidding. Right?"

"No Mike, I'm serious. She has a thing for you. She

was thinking seriously about slipping into bed with you. She made a very revealing decision while standing beside you. She thought it over and decided that if she made the move on you, she would lose any future chance to have you respect her enough to want to go out with her."

"Wow Sis that was close. I'm just glad she let her better judgment take over. I wouldn't want to have to fight her off." He grinned. "I'm not sure I could have." He laughed.

"Mike! Don't talk like that. You know good and well you wouldn't fall prey to the wiles of Cassie Phelps."

"Well Sis, the guys at school all talked about how they would like to score with a hottie like Cassie, but as far as I know no one ever did."

"OK Mike, let's forget this for now and go to breakfast. The rest of the crew is probably already up and hungry for chow."

Following breakfast the four Hollisters took a walk down to the beach from the mansion. Mike expressed concern that the island has been visited by unknown people during the night on more than one occasion. Mike suggested that the family review recorded video from the new security system to see if there were any recent visitors. They sat down on the seawall at the harbor's edge. Mike took out his modified satellite cell phone and began shuffling through the previous night's recordings.

"Hey guys, look at this!"

Mike held the phone where the other three could see it. In the same spot where the dogs had recorded their dislike for someone a few nights earlier, three men appeared to drag a skiff half way out of the water. The three set to work robbing the nests of the Kemp's Ridley Sea Turtles. Their thoughts revealed that they intended to sell the collected turtle eggs on the black market. Turtles and their eggs are protected by law, but are vulnerable to scavengers both animal and human. It appeared that the turtle eggs on Hollister Island were as endangered as any in the Caribbean.

Mike called the Island Wildlife Management office in St. Thomas and reported the theft. The next evening three wildlife officers were on patrol just off Hollister Island when the poachers returned. Gordon Hollister, his family, and all of their guests watched on the big screen as the poachers came ashore and began pillaging turtle nests. Mike reported their exact location, their every move, and even what they were talking about among themselves. Within minutes three wildlife officers stormed ashore and at gun point ordered the poachers onto the ground. They were quickly shackled, taken aboard the patrol craft and whisked away.

"Did you see that one guy's expression as the officers pointed their guns at him?" Mike shouted.

"Hey that was great," exclaimed Maria.

"Our technology has all sorts of uses," added Oren, "and it was the dogs who first tipped us off about undesirable people coming ashore. Gotta love it, just gotta love it." He reached over and patted Murphy on the head. Murphy looked at Oren. The dog's data stream read, "Any time pal, anytime."

When the turtle poaching episode came to an end, Mike began shuffling through other recordings from the sensors around the island. He whistled aloud, "Take a look at this would you?"

He pointed to a bottle nosed dolphin in the boat harbor. The sensors were clearly picking up the thoughts of the beautiful mammal. She was speaking to her calf nearby and urging the calf to follow her example. Mom was showing her calf how to work with the dolphin pod to surround schools of fish in the harbor basin. The pod methodically moved in a tighter and tighter circle to cut off escape and assure a good meal for all.

Mike thought, *the intermediate range sensors are picking up the thoughts and the sights seen by this wonderful animal. It's all flowing into the computer and being displayed on the screen. What if we could implant CR5 chips in dolphins and follow them farther a field? We could advance science by another great leap.*

Chun Li and Mike were thinking the same thing. *Would this be a new development coming out of GMH Technology?*

The island holiday came to an end with Mike and Maria and the whole crew returning to the airfield for the flight back to Florida. There was hugging and laughter all around as Gordon and Patricia thanked everyone for coming and urged them to all come again soon.

On the return flight Mike and Maria sat and talked with their high school friends about their future plans. They urged them all to consider uploading as much knowledge to their brains as they desired. Maria assured them that if they performed the brain uploads at a reasonable pace, the process was actually safe. Each person made a list of the skills and knowledge they desired. Maria and Chun Li promised each that they would set up appointments and perform the uploads at the R&D lab as soon as everyone was ready.

Brad Bailey made the final approach to Opa-Locka Executive Airport. The GMH Tech Boeing 737 touched down and taxied to the parking area. A truly great holiday came to an end with everyone back in town and ready to return to work with renewed inspiration.

Mike Hollister called Roy Durand and made an appointment for him to come to GMH Technology for a visit and some brainstorming about his future. Roy was delighted to get the call.

Mike greeted Roy in the reception area and invited him to step into his office. "Roy, I'm glad you could come by this morning. Bobby tells me that you might be interested in making a career change."

Roy responded, "Absolutely Mr. Hollister. I worked most of my adult life on oil rigs including several offshore rigs. The last one I was on blew up and changed my life totally. I will not go back to that industry if I have to do part-time grunt work the rest of my life."

"Can't say I blame you Roy. Please call me Mike. I would like to introduce you to a new concept of education and training. We've developed a method for uploading the equivalent of many years of formal education in just a few sessions in our lab. Would you be interested in trying this out?"

"Anything....absolutely anything to move into a new career path Mr. Hollister....uh...Mike. Whatever you suggest, I'm willing to try."

"Well then Roy, take some time to decide what new career path you would like to pursue and we will set it in motion for you. How does that sound?"

"Mike...this is the best thing that has happened to me since Ari and Kurt rescued me from that tiny bug-infested island. I'll start looking at careers and let you know in a day or two. Oh, by the way, would this process of uploading to the human brain that you describe be available to teach...or upload...a language other than your own...I mean like if a person speaks one language but needs to learn a different language....like a person needs to learn English?"

"I don't see why not Roy. I'll talk with the R&D staff and let you know when you decide on your new career path. How's that sound?"

"Mr. Hollister...uh...Mike....it will really make a difference in the life of my family. My wife is from Costa Rica and speaks very little English. She tried several times taking courses in English as a Second Language, but for some reason the methods just didn't work for her."

"Consider it done Roy. GMH Technology has a great track record of brain uploads in some very heavy subject areas. I think we can adapt the system for language learners."

Chun Li and the R&D staff set up a series of appointments to upload knowledge to quite a list of people. First came Roy Durand who selected Electrical Engineering and IT as his new career path. In five sessions Roy passed all exams showing he possessed the equivalent of a master's degree. Next came Alex Gardner, one of Mike's high school friends who uploaded a master's degree in nano technology. Cassie Phelps uploaded a master's degree in banking and international finance. Beverly Talbot chose a master's degree in Economics and International Business. Alicia Byers became an Attorney. Rhonda Barrett uploaded a master's degree in chemical engineering. Chuck Bentley and Lyle Weaver both became IT engineers. Roy Durand's wife became the first person to master English as a second language using the GMH brain upload method.

Mike and Maria Hollister held a special graduation ceremony and party to celebrate the accomplishments of this new breed of brain upload scholars. Each passed a rigorous series of tests in their chosen field. GMH Technology hired most of the new graduates.

# CHAPTER 20

## TALK TO THE ANIMALS

Martha Wilson paged Mike on the video intercom. "Mr. Hollister, there is a naval officer here to see you. He is waiting in the reception area. Do you have time to see him this morning?"

"Of course Martha, please send him in."

"Good morning Mr. Hollister, I am Rear Admiral Joseph Bergstrom. I am the new commander of the Navy's Marine Mammal Program. Perhaps you have heard of it."

"Yes, admiral. I have heard of it."

"Mr. Hollister, we recently learned that your company's R&D team developed a method for directly reading a dolphin's thoughts and even getting a readout from their visual cortex. Is this true?"

"Yes…yes it is true. I first witnessed the phenomenon while vacationing at my parent's home in the Caribbean. I was amazed to say the least. I never cease to be amazed at how my R&D team constantly moves ahead in brain wave research. So…how can I help you this morning?"

"Mr. Hollister, the Navy would like to offer your company a contract to assist us in the utilization of dolphins and sea lions in the service of the country. The military uses highly trained dogs to sniff out explosives on land and we use dolphins and sea lions to locate and reveal the presence of underwater mines which endanger shipping."

Mike asked, "Are these animals harmed in anyway?"

"Mr. Hollister, we go to great lengths to protect the animal members of the armed forces. But as you well know, there are always dangers to people and animals in civilian as well as military roles. We do the best we know how to make sure our military animals are protected."

"Well, Admiral, how can GMH Technology participate with the Navy in your program?"

"We would like to have members of your R&D team come to our facility and train our staff in the use of the CR5 system with all of its components. We would like to start soon in this endeavor."

"Admiral Bergstrom, send us your contract and let us have a look at it. I can't imagine any impediments to our participating in the Navy's Marine Mammal Program."

"I'm glad you are willing to entertain our contract. I have it right here in my briefcase."

Mike smiled, "Well, I should have expected that our Navy would be ready to move quickly. I will forward this to my legal department and we will give you a response within forty-eight hours."

"Thank you Mr. Hollister, I'll be going for now. We look forward to a profitable working relationship with your company."

When the Admiral departed, Mike leaned back in his

chair with his hands behind his head thinking, *there doesn't seem to be any end to the possibilities for brain wave detection, decryption, and utilization. And to think it all started with Oren Lunsford's dog Murphy. Then there was the party where Maria and I tricked our friends into ingesting CR3 chips. Wow where that went! It could have really gone badly, but thank goodness, here we are in a very profitable industry. We have so many patents we can't count them all. Profits are through the roof, and our company's stock is keeping the market fueled on Wall Street and in exchanges around the globe.*

At the morning conference with his R&D team Mike brought up the subject of the Navy contract.

"Yesterday Rear Admiral Joseph Bergstrom came to my office with a contract for us to participate with the Navy in their Marine Mammal Program. They want us to supply our hardware and software and send one or more of you to their facility to train their staff. What they want to do is to extend the use of dolphins and sea lions in underwater search missions. I believe we all witnessed dolphin thought and even dolphin visual cortex output while we were at my folk's place in the Caribbean."

David Goldstein spoke up. "If this means getting to hang out near the beach somewhere I'm in."

Oren added, "I want to go with David. I could use some time near the ocean again."

Chun Li laughed, "You two are just like a couple of

teenage surfers. You can't stay away from the waves can you?"

Mike said, "Well, if I send you guys to work with the Navy for a while who will work with Chun Li in the lab?"

Chun Li answered, "Not to worry Mike, Maria and I will hold the fort while these two go off to play with dolphins. Rhonda Barrett, Alex Gardner, Chuck Bentley, and Bobby Durand are totally capable members of the R&D staff. We have a full house of great young scientists thanks to the knowledge upload capability of the CR system."

David and Oren quickly reminded everyone in the room that they learned the hard way, the old fashioned way, hitting the books, pulling all night sessions in a library with stacks of books. Much of this effort, they added, took place when information was contained in the form of ink on paper and before the advent of total electronic presentations via smart boards, lap tops, tablet computers and cell phones.

Maria chuckled, "Well, now you guys are showing your age. Those methods were so....shall we say....last century."

Everyone laughed.

Mike looked at Oren and David. "I'll send you two to work with the Navy, but only on the condition that you don't get so enamored of the California surf that you forget to come back to Florida at the end of the contract."

While working with the Navy's Marine Mammal Program Oren and David discovered a major problem using the CR5 system with underwater creatures. On land or in the air data packets were easily transmitted between the CR5 chip and a satellite phone application. Chips inserted into the body of a dolphin or sea lion tended to lose their efficiency the deeper the creature swam below the ocean surface. All contact was entirely lost below ten fathoms or about sixty feet of depth. This rendered the chips useless at greater depths.

David and Oren returned to GMH Technology to work out a totally new design for the chip's internal electronics, its outer shell, and to design ways to stay in contact from the surface to a chip at great depth. While working with Oran and David, Alex Gardner discovered a way for the CR5 system to communicate between people aboard ships and dolphins deep under the sea.

Alex designed a small receiver-transmitter to be housed in a streamlined fiberglass shell and attached to the outer hull of a vessel. GMH Technology produced several prototypes and tested them in the waters between Florida and the Bahamas where the depths reach over four hundred fathoms or around two-thousand four-hundred feet.

Between these three young scientists they were able to offer the Navy a totally new product line. The system would now be called the N5 designating it as unique to the needs of the Navy. Two months later Oren and David returned to the Navy's facility in San Diego to field test the newly redesigned system off the coast of Baja California.

Rear Admiral Joseph Bergstrom gave the order to cast

off aboard the research vessel USS Sturgeon Bay. The ship departed its home port of San Diego for sea trials of the newly developed N5 system. The admiral, along with Oren and David, monitored two bottle nose dolphins carried aboard in a salt water tank in the hold of the ship. The dolphins, Ralph and Oscar, were veterans of earlier dolphin research conducted by the Navy prior to the advent of the N5 system. These two carry the new chip in their bodies.

A sailor on the bridge picked up the UHF radio mike and reported the Sturgeon Bay's course and position to the Mexican Coast Guard as they entered Mexican territorial waters off Baja California. Arriving at Coronado Canyon, an undersea canyon which ranges from just under one hundred to over five hundred fathoms, the crew carefully released the dolphins for the first test series.

The dolphins swam about the ship for a time. Their data output was very clear. As they swam below the ship their visual cortex output clearly showed every detail of the ship's hull, its dual propellers, its steering gear, and even a few barnacles and scratches.

Admiral Bergstrom smiled. "If we can get images that clear at greater depths this system will give the Navy a totally new tool to keep the nation safe."

David Goldstein uploaded a set of instructions to the dolphins. They were to dive along the walls of Coronado Canyon and descend slowly giving the researchers aboard the

Sturgeon Bay a look at the scenery on the way down.

At about ten minutes into the dive, Admiral Bergstrom said, "Stop the dive. Hold the dolphins right there. Instruct them to turn back to the canyon wall just behind them. There.....that's got it. What have we here?"

Clearly visible on the wide screen was the marine-encrusted shape of an airplane. As the dolphins moved in closer the view screen revealed a Grumman F4F Wildcat fighter in a vertical position just below a ledge. Admiral Bergstrom was quiet for a long moment. "That is the type of aircraft my grandfather Ensign George Bergstrom was flying out of North Island Naval Air Station in 1943 when he disappeared without a trace. We need to arrange to bring this airplane to the surface for further identification.

The Sturgeon Bay carried aboard a robotic submersible craft with many capabilities. One of its talents was that of carefully attaching all kinds of retrieving gear to underwater objects.

The dolphins completed their scheduled list of duties and returned to the ship. All features of the N5 system had proven to work as designed. GPS location was tracked even at great depths. Total two-way communication was clear between humans and dolphins. The research crew completed all of their tasks with no problems. Admiral Bergstrom suggested that if the system was to serve the navy in remote areas where a ship was not likely to remain on patrol an alternate communication link would be needed to stay in touch with deployed marine mammals. Oren and David took note of the admiral's suggestion.

The Sturgeon Bay continued on station above the newly discovered airplane in Coronado Canyon. By late afternoon the dripping wreckage of a World War II fighter plane was hoisted onto the ship's after deck. The cockpit canopy was still closed and totally covered by silt and sea creatures.

The Sturgeon Bay docked in San Diego after midnight. The airplane remained aboard until a crew from NAS North Island came aboard to remove it. Once in a hangar at the Air Station the old fighter plane began to give up its decades old secrets. Salvagers carefully removed silt and barnacles from the engine and airframe. Comparing the engine serial number of the wreck to the serial number on the list of missing aircraft revealed that this was indeed the airplane flown by George Bergstrom on the fateful flight into oblivion in 1943. On his last radio contact Ensign Bergstrom reported that he was flying into a rainstorm somewhere off the California coast. He was not sure of his position. Nothing else was ever heard from the young pilot.

When the canopy was finally opened, the skeletal remains of a person were found to be intact and still strapped into the seat. It was obvious that the aircraft hit the water and sank quickly taking this intrepid young aviator to a watery grave. DNA testing confirmed the identity of the pilot. Finally the

Bergstrom family found the answer to the decades-old mystery and were able to attend a military funeral laying to rest a young naval officer and pilot.

David and Oren returned to GMH Technology with the Navy's requirements for communicating with dolphins without a ship present. To solve the problem, Lyle Weaver and Alex Gardner designed a small buoy which could be dropped from a ship or an airplane. The buoy contains a two-way link between a dolphin with a chip and a satellite in space. Once again the satellite phone system was called upon to link people and chip wearers anywhere on the earth, and now even beneath the sea.

# CHAPTER 21

## THE BLIND SEE AND THE LAME WALK

With the navy contract satisfied, the R&D team turned their attention to a totally different problem, but one which the CR5 chip seemed destined to play a part. Bobby Durand working with Chun Li and Maria Hollister began testing a product to help blind people. They reasoned that if the visual cortex can be read, why not collect the vision from a sighted person and upload it to the brain of a blind person.

Once again Oren's dog Murphy was called upon to play a part. With the CR5 chip worn by Murphy the R&D team easily viewed what the dog was seeing. By feeding the visual information from the dog's eyes through the CR5 upload feature they were able to place the dog's view directly into the visual cortex in the brain of a blind person.

The R&D team was ecstatic, not to mention the ecstasy of the first blind person to receive the system. From this development Mike and Maria decided to produce and distribute the system at cost and without taking a profit from any part of the system. GMH Technology licensed the visual system components of the CR5 to any company around the world willing to manufacture and distribute it on a non-profit basis.

Bobby Durand and Chun Li suggested a further development. They immediately set to work designing a visual system that does not require an animal participant. They reasoned that not everyone on the planet is fortunate enough to be able to have a seeing-eye dog or other service animal. Using a CCD or Charge Coupled Device, which is what a cell phone or other digital camera uses to capture an image, the team designed a pair of glasses to be worn by a blind person. The glasses frame contains the close proximity features of the CR5 system. The CCD literally sees the image and the CR5 upload feature transfers it to the blind person's visual cortex. This way the blind person using the special glasses sees exactly what a sighted person sees.

This device is also offered by GMH Tech as a non-profit item and is licensed to any other company willing to make it available on the same basis. The two developments together got the attention of the Nobel Prize committee.

Gordon and Patricia Hollister came to GMH Technology for a visit. The two along with their offspring Mike and Maria entertained the R&D team at a private dinner party at the Hollister high rise overlooking Biscayne Bay. There they recalled the many developments of the past and wondered what the future may yet hold for humanity.

During dinner Maria suggested the creation of a non-profit institute. It's purpose would be to harness technology for the betterment of humanity. She recalled the recent development of sight for the blind.

Gordon and Patricia were eager to hear more. Maria

continued, “I think GMH Technology might assign a number of patents for use by the institute. Perhaps Chun Li, Bobby Durand, and I could work as a team at the institute. What does everyone think about the idea?”

Gordon smiled across the table at his daughter. “I think that is a great idea. Your mom and I will talk over our possible contribution. What do you think Mike?”

Mike grinned, “Not a bad idea coming from my younger sister. I will get together with our chief financial officer and figure out what the company can do to support the institute. What shall we name it?”

Chun Li spoke up. “Perhaps it should be called the Hollister Institute for the Advancement of Science in the Interest of Public Health.”

“Not a bad choice, but a bit long.” Gordon responded. “I like the idea. Keep us posted on getting it going Mike. I’m sure with the accumulated profits of the firm and the resources your mom and I have accumulated from investments we can make it work.”

As the people around the table rose from their seats, Patricia gave Mike and Maria a big hug. She turned and did the same to all the other guests. “I’m so proud of all of you. You’ve become one big family to Gordon and me. Please stay in touch by video phone, and feel free to come to the island anytime for rest and relaxation. I know you all get wound up in your work, but just remember, you need to unwind sometimes. The latch string is always out for our GMH family. You don't need a reservation at our place. Mi casa Su casa."

Following the morning staff meeting Mike paged his Chief Financial Officer Cassie Phelps and his Legal Department Director Alicia Byers. He invited them to his office to discuss the formation of the Hollister Institute. The three went over a number of issues deciding how much of the company's cash and stock should be given to the institute, and how financial resources should be controlled and managed. In addition Alicia Byers took on the task of writing the legal documents and filing them with various taxing authorities at the state and national level.

When the three concluded their talk about the new institute, Mike asked Cassie to stay to go over the company's most recent financial reports. Cassie moved to Mike's side of the desk. She propped her tablet computer up so both could see the screen. The two of them reviewed a series of spread sheets containing company financial performance information for the previous quarter and the previous year. Cassie was reluctant to end the session as she always enjoyed being near Mike. Today was no different.

Mike enjoyed the hour as well. He wasn't sure what was happening to him, but he thought, *back in high school all the guys wanted to spend time this close to Cassie Phelps, and here I am able to call her into my office and enjoy her company. The guys would be envious to say the least. Get hold of yourself*

*Mike, keep the relationship all business. Don't give in to youthful memories no matter how far from reality they might take you. Just don't do it. Keep it all business. At least for now.*

***The Hollister Institute for the Advancement of Science in the Interest of Public Health*** became a reality. Its initial endowment was a total of eighteen billion dollars. A tidy sum indeed. A third of the fund was in the form of cash from company profits, another third was donated by Gordon and Patricia in the form of accumulated income from their personal investments, and a third came in the form of preferred stock in GMH Technology.

Chun Li was named director of the institute's research staff and in turn she named Maria Hollister as her deputy director. Bobby Durand was hired by the institute to be a key member of the R&D staff there.

At the Institute's first staff meeting Bobby Durand brought up an idea for a major project using modifications to the CR5 system. He suggested that the system might be used to restore memory to people who suffer from amnesia, dementia or even short term memory loss.

Maria asked, "How do you propose to do this?"

Bobby responded, "We know that we can upload thoughts to the human brain and even give instructions to animals. Perhaps we might be able to first collect memory from healthy people and store it in a cloud computer for safe keeping.

Then if the person loses long-term memory, upload their own memory back to the person while keeping a copy on the cloud server for future reference. What do you think?"

Chun Li smiled. "Well....we've seen and done a lot of other things previously thought impossible, perhaps we should give it a try."

While working on the theory of memory restoration, Maria made a discovery. She recalled that most people at any age tend to lose track of what they were thinking when they leave one location and go to another such as walking into the next room.

Maria and Bobby created a pendant to be worn on a lanyard from the neck, or to be worn as a bracelet. The pendant was small and simple and can be made available at a very low cost. The pendant collects immediate thoughts, stores them, and when a person appears puzzled about why they arrived at a new location, the pendant immediately uploads all previous thoughts to the person's brain thus restoring the reason for going to the next room or changing their location.

The pendant was so popular that four million were produced and sold at cost within the first month. Users even reported that the pendant detects any degree of confusion about the past few minutes and restores previous thoughts even when the person remains in the same location. This proved extremely popular with teenagers when trying to recall what their parents had just asked them to do. It also proved useful to other absent minded people.

Memory restoration became a major project. Healthy volunteers came to the lab and uploaded all of their personal memories to the cloud server. This created a bank from which a person might recover all or part of lost memories. To make memory banking easier, the institute created a web site through which people can create their own free accounts and save memories for future retrieval.

A group of psychiatrists from five nations came to the institute and performed experiments using perfectly healthy lab animals. The psychiatrists first copied the animal's memories onto the cloud server. Following the collection, they artificially induced amnesia into the animal's brains.

The animals were allowed to remain in this memory loss state for a full month. When tested at the end of the month they all revealed complete amnesia. Memory was then uploaded from the cloud server back into the animal's brains. Total success was achieved except for one major mistake. A lab assistant got two of the animals mixed up and uploaded the opposite animal's memory thereby totally reversing their personalities. Each became the other.

*Now that could be a real problem if it occurs with humans,* thought Chun Li. It became readily apparent that in spite of people's best efforts mistakes in the application of science can occur and the long-term impact of those mistakes is not predictable.

Since the lab animals were of the same species and were actually siblings from the same litter, it was thought best to just let this mistake go and not worry any more about it. But the implications of shifting memory between subjects are totally unknown and fraught with peril if used for nefarious purposes.

Somehow word got out about the experimental use of animals at the Hollister Institute. Animal rights organizations quickly took up the cause. Protesters appeared outside the institute on a daily basis. The crowd grew from a handful to a few dozen. When TV crews set up vans and began broadcasting to the world, suddenly the number of protesters swelled into the hundreds and then into the thousands.

Things got nasty. Rocks were hurled at the cars of staff and lab workers coming to the institute. Windshields were shattered. Chun Li and the entire staff were under siege. Things could go from bad to worse.

Maria made a suggestion. She asked, "Do you recall the British modification to the CR5 sensors extending their range out to about sixty feet? Why don't we deploy those sensors around the perimeter of the institute and see what we learn from the rioter's brains? How about it?"

Chun Li and the others agreed. Security personnel spent a few hours during the night quietly installing intermediate range CR5M sensors. When completed the institute's external walls were well protected. Chun Li and Maria watched the thoughts of the rioters on screen and quickly identified the riot leaders.

Maria looked at the others, “Shall we upload an attitude adjustment to these people?” They all agreed.

Maria uploaded a new attitude into each of the riot’s key leaders, an attitude of acceptance toward everything the institute stood for. One riot leader picked up a bull horn and told his followers that perhaps they were all mistaken about harm to the lab animals and maybe it would be best to stop the demonstrations. Maybe it would be best to try to understand what Hollister Institute was trying to accomplish. The street mob looked astonished at this, but many followed the leader back to their cars and drove away.

A few people stood around looking dumb founded. Maria homed in one at a time on these individuals and uploaded the same attitude adjustment message she applied to the riot leaders. One by one each previously agitated person walked away from the scene. The trouble was over, at least at present.

Chun Li and Bobby Durand smiled and gave Maria a high five. Bobby observed, “All’s well that ends well.”

Chun Li suggested a project for which she is personally well qualified and in which she has a personal interest. She previously worked on brain controlled prostheses at NRI, the Neurological Research Institute at Guangzhou, China. She has a cousin who was severely injured in a mining accident in China and who is currently being treated in a private hospital near San Francisco. Chun Li thought, *he would make a perfect subject for this project.*

Maria called Emiliano Vargas and asked, “How would you and Brad Bailey like to fly with me to San Francisco to pick up a special passenger?”

“When do you want to go?”

“In a couple of days. We need to arrange for the transfer of a medical patient.”

“No problem. We’ll be ready. Which airplane do you want to take?”

“Let’s take the Boeing 737. It has everything we’ll need.”

“Brad and I will be ready when you are. Just give us a call. I’ll have the ground crew pre-flight the airplane tomorrow morning.”

“Thanks, I know we can count on you guys.”

Chun Li called the private hospital and arranged for the transfer of her cousin Chun Wei to Florida for further treatment. What the California doctors did not know was that the Hollister Institute planned a complete makeover for this patient.

The round trip to San Francisco was uneventful. Maria piloted the Boeing around any threatening weather and made smooth landings at both ends of the trip. Brad and Emiliano took turns serving as co-pilot. Medical personnel accompanied the patient all the way from California to his destination at the Hollister Institute.

When Chun Wei arrived at the institute he was moved

into a suite prepared especially for his comfort and reconstruction. Maria, Bobby, and Chun Li were not quite prepared to see a human being with so much physical and mental damage. Chun Wei was blind, was missing both arms, both legs, and had no memory. The accident which robbed him so thoroughly left a person with no expectation of anything like a normal life.

The first challenge for the institute's R&D staff was to restore sight and memory to the patient. Sight was no great problem. Chun Wei was fitted with a pair of glasses with the combination CCD and CR5 technology which 'sees' and uploads sight to the wearer.

Next came memory restoration. This was not an easy task. There was no previously recorded memory to retrieve. Chun Li held a video conference with colleagues at NRI in China. They agreed to find the closest relatives of Chun Wei. Using the brain wave readout from the CR5 system, they gathered family memories surrounding the life of Chun Wei. These were uploaded via satellite connection to Hollister Institute and placed in the cloud server.

As the days passed, Chun Li and her associates slowly uploaded these family memories into the brain of Chun Wei. The patient began to speak in short sentences revealing that he was indeed absorbing family memories. He recalled his childhood, his adolescent years, and his years working in the mines. All of this was in Chinese, but the R&D staff was able to communicate via two-way brain waves using the CR5 technology.

To make things easier for both the patient and local medical personnel Chun Li uploaded a Basic English course into the brain of her cousin. Within a few days Chun Wei was speaking perfect English with his nursing staff. Once again the brain upload procedure performed flawlessly.

The next phase of reconstruction involved the creation of powered robotic prostheses to replace Chu Wei's missing limbs. For this, Chun Li and her staff turned to GMH Technology for help. Alex Gardner and Lyle Weaver came to work with Bobby Durand at the institute. Together they manufactured artificial limbs. These composite arms and legs were powered by electrical impulses however small from the body of the wearer. The wearer's own brain controlled every movement of arms and legs, fingers and toes.

Chun Wei was ecstatic at being able to get out of bed and move about on his own. It took just three weeks for him to gain full mental control of his new appendages. He was able to dress himself, eat with western utensils and even eat with chopsticks. The latter talent gave Chun Li and the others the greatest thrill. Chop sticks require delicate finger dexterity. This ability indicated a high degree of success with the newly designed appendages. The team of engineers and technicians were elated. There were some minor drawbacks at first. The first set of artificial fingers did not activate cell phone touch screens.

A slight change in the chemical makeup and a softening of the fingers took care of that problem.

Psychiatrists working with the R&D team asked Chu Wei for permission to conduct a further experiment in brain upload technology. Having come so far, he was delighted to be the subject of one more trial. The team uploaded a set of memories which he would not have collected in his normal life. They planted memories of having attended a number of sporting and cultural events.

Chun Wei was suddenly able to converse about ball games and concerts he had never even heard of, let alone attended. This was all the psychiatric team wanted to know. The question was resolved. Is it possible to plant false memories? The answer was an unqualified yes. Everyone wondered, what impact could this have for the future of humanity?

## CHAPTER 22

## FIGHTING TERRORISTS

Martha Wilson paged Mike on the video intercom. "Mr. Hollister, there is a Mr. Ian Paxton in the reception area. Do you have time to see him this morning?"

"Of course Martha, please send him in."

The door opened and Ian Paxton stepped into Mike's office. "Mr. Hollister, I am certain you remember me from an earlier introduction."

Mike grinned. "Yes of course. You and....I believe a Mr. Aden Harper.... were holding a couple of my friends in London."

"That's correct sir. We were impressed with your business acumen and that's why I'm here this morning. Her Majesty's government has a contract with the Nigerian government to furnish aid in their fight against Boko Haram. I'm sure you have heard of them."

"Of course. Anyone watching the news from Africa knows about the atrocities committed by that rag tag bunch of thugs."

"Right. We have a proposal and we believe that your firm has the technical expertise to create a new kind of weapon. Would you be interested?"

Mike, never one to turn aside a challenge, asked, "What sort of new weapon do you have in mind?"

"Boko Haram operates in many different environments. These include swamp, jungle, and desert. We know about your nano insects which are copied from nature. We need nano insects which mimic the natural environment and which can operate either by receiving signals from a controller via satellite or can operate with implanted instincts of their own."

"That sounds like some we already have in our inventory."

Ian continued, "We would like to add a totally new feature and we are convinced that your R&D team is up to the task."

"And what might this new feature be?"

"We think it is possible to include an on-board computer in a CR5M chip with an algorithm which can sort out good versus evil thoughts. We plan to load the new CR5M chip into the proboscis of each insect and proceed to implant these into terrorists where ever we find them."

Mike leaned back in his chair. "Now you're taking us into new territory and I like that. I hadn't quite thought about an independent thinking chip. I'll bet we can do it."

"Thank you Mr. Hollister. How soon can you produce a prototype?"

"I'm not sure, but I will get right on it."

"I'm staying in town. Here is my address and cell phone. Please ring me up as soon as you have something to show me."

Mike thanked Ian for coming to GMH with her Majesty's project. When Ian departed, Mike went immediately to the R&D lab. He found Alex Gardner and Lyle Weaver busy writing computer code.

"Sorry to interrupt you two, but something has come up which may challenge your expertise. I hope we can do this."

Alex responded, "What is it Mike?"

Mike laid it out for them. As the three pondered the problem, Alex suggested that since Boko Haram is holding a number of kidnap victims who are likely innocent of any evil thoughts, perhaps the best approach would be to create a chip with some added features. These would include Ian Paxton's suggested algorithm which would discriminate between good and bad intentions. Part of the problem would be to create software which can distinguish between hatred and fear. If a person harbors a certain kind of hatred they will be identified as the bad guy. If a person is constantly fearful of mal treatment, they will be isolated as a victim and spared any consequences.

For the next several hours Alex and Lyle wrote computer code for a new breed of autonomous chips. Chips which will have no need to contact a computer to filter attitudes, but will filter attitudes directly on scene. These new chips will act as free-standing independent thinking computers.

When that problem was resolved, Alex grinned at Lyle. "Guess what we get to do now?"

Lyle looked puzzled for a moment and then broke into a

wide grin. "We get to zap bad guys. We get to do it via computer code while sitting right here in South Florida." They both broke into laughter. "Man this is getting to be better than any computer game we ever played."

The prototype chip contained computer code which first determined if a person was good or bad. If the filter determined the person was a terrorist the chip will shut down their autonomic nervous system bringing about instant death. The chip will act as judge, jury, and executioner.

Mike and Lyle added a feature which Ian Paxton had not requested, but which they thought would be a humane thing to add. Contained in the chip's internal software was a brain upload to an innocent wearer encouraging them to take heart and make plans to escape. It even included a GPS tracking system and map directions to take the wearer to safe territory. The rescue feature was programmed to constantly upload to the wearer's brain the route to freedom and encouragement to keep on trying.

An order was placed by Her Majesty's government for thousands of nano insects. Each insect carried the new CR5M chip in their proboscis. Each insect had been thoroughly tested and found to be ready for this new mission.

A week after Ian Paxton flew from Miami to Abuja, Nigeria, Mike began scanning output from a CR5 chip he tricked Ian into ingesting while they dined together in the GMH plant cafeteria. Using his Sino Dragon cell phone Mike watched and heard all the action live in real time on an encrypted channel. He watched through output from Ian Paxton's visual cortex as the MI5 agent boarded a Nigerian Army helicopter for a flight into territory controlled by Boko Haram terrorists.

The helicopter landed in a clearing near a burned out village. The remains of a school, a church, and several small commercial buildings were still smoldering. From all appearances this place had been recently visited by the terrorists. Many dead were still on the ground.

The Nigerian colonel in charge of the helicopter mission called in reinforcements to secure the area and to bury the dead. It was here that Ian released the first wave of nano insects. The little machines flew high and set off in the direction of the border with Cameroon. Somewhere just short of the border they caught up with a large group of people moving slowly on foot. The swarm of nano insects descended and set to work inserting the new CR5M chips into the necks, backs, and even buttocks of anyone in their path.

Mike was able to track the output from some of the freshly planted chips. *Wow*, he thought, *those little guys did a job on that crowd.* The first chip returned thoughts of terror. A young girl was thinking about how she might escape. She was thinking of running away as soon as it becomes dark. Mike remembered how Alex and Lyle wrote into the software encouragement to do just that. In a few moments, the young girl's thoughts revealed that she was suddenly optimistic about her chances to get away when night falls in a few hours. The software was working.

A second chip revealed that it was planted in one of the young men who kidnapped the people of the burned out village. His thoughts revealed that he was forced to enlist in the terrorist gang by threats against his family. His mind was not that of a true terrorist. He wanted to escape and not be forced to take part in atrocities like today's raid and kidnapping.

A third chip revealed the mindset of a true terrorist. He was a true believer in the movement. The true meaning of the words Boko Haram is up for debate but most media reporters translate it as "Western Education is a Sin." Most who know the Hausa language dispute the meaning, but no matter, this guy wearing a CR5M chip at the base of his neck is a true terrorist by any definition. As Mike watched and listened the young man continued scratching at the fresh nano insect bite. Mike wondered if the CR5M would kill as it was designed to do. He didn't have long to wait.

With Mike watching through the terrorists own eyes, he saw the ground come up and meet his face. He hit hard as he went down. Mike heard the staccato burst of a dozen rounds fired when the terrorist's finger tightened on the trigger of his Kalashnikov. Bullets sprayed the group directly in front of this dying man. Seven more terrorists fell writhing with fatal wounds from the AK-47 fusillade.

Mike scanned back to the visual output of the young girl.

She was witness to this sudden turn of events. He watched in fascination through her eyes as she scanned the scene. Other terrorists scattered in all directions shouting that the Nigerian troops had caught up with them. They did not realize that it was their dying comrade who accidentally fired the fatal shots.

Kidnap victims began running in the direction of the burned out village. Terrorists were falling like flies. Evidently their CR5M chips were shutting down their autonomic nervous systems as they formed hateful thoughts toward their intended slaves. Mike thought once again, *man Karma really does bite. These guys got what they deserve.*

About a week after the success of the new chips in Nigeria Mike received a visitor from France. Mr. Bertrand Broussard came with a contract from the French government to purchase the new CR5M chip and a host of nano insects to deliver them. He explained that France has a special relationship with Cameroon and Chad as well as Algeria. In order to fight Al Qaeda and ISIS elements in all three areas France proposes to follow the example set by the British assistance program in Nigeria.

Mike was pleased to share what he already knew about the success of the British and the Nigerians working together against Boko Haram. He suggested that if the French effort works as well in the other areas of Africa, terrorists would have few if any places to operate.

GMH Technology was becoming quite an element in the

war on terrorists around the globe. Following France's successes in their areas of influence in Africa, Mike received another large order for nano insects loaded with CR5M chips. These were to be used in Metropolitan France. French security forces distributed the nano machines in areas known to harbor terrorists in every major city in the nation. Terrorist attacks became a thing of the past. Many radicalized young men died quietly from apparently unexplained causes. Not even the local coroners could explain the phenomenon.

Sweden, Norway Denmark, Britain, Belgium, Spain, the Netherlands, and Italy all experienced the same phenomenon. Many radicalized young men and a few young women simply died without any previously observed health issues. All was quiet in Western Europe. No more talk of Jihad was heard in public places.

Frank Fletcher directed *The Agency's* Maryland lab to begin production of the autonomous CR5M chip for use in the USA. The government lab made a few modifications to the chips internal software code in order to speed up production. The Maryland lab turned out tens of thousands of the chips and nano machine insects to implant them. Myles Burwell and Dennis Cottrell stockpiled the chips and the mechanical insects in a vault in *The Agency's* West Virginia facility.

The first release took place in a Somali neighborhood in Minnesota. Reports circulated among Federal Agencies that several young Somali men and even a few women attempted to travel abroad to join ISIS in Syria. Dennis Cottrell traveled to Minnesota and released a dozen nano insects outside a community center frequented by young Somalis.

For a few days nothing happened. At the end of the first week of the release two young Somali men died without explanation. The local coroner was stumped. They seemed to be in perfect health. Myles Burwell scanned the computer output from their chips and discovered that these two young men had harbored thoughts of killing people outside their religious community. Their thoughts recorded on the mainframe computer in West Virginia revealed an unimaginable depth of hatred toward people who practiced other religions. This seemed to validate the necessity for deploying the government's CR5M chip over a wider area in the USA.

A limited number of nano insects were released in Northern Virginia in the vicinity of a Mosque rumored to have some radical attendees. Three days after the release a young man died without explanation. Myles Burwell pulled up his data flow from the mainframe computer in West Virginia. He was shocked to see that the young man was not a terrorist. Just before he died, he expressed hatred against a vending machine which robbed him of his money.

Myles called Frank Fletcher and shared the information with him. It appeared that *The Agency* programmers missed key elements in the computer software when they modified the algorithm for filtering human thought. All of the government's chips in circulation were potential killers of innocent people. The nano insects were out there and their chips had a mind of their own. They could decide who lives and who dies. The problem now was to locate and neutralize all remaining nano insects before they kill other innocent civilians. Not an easy task to say the least.

Frank Fletcher ordered the immediate destruction of all nano insects still in storage in West Virginia. What else could go wrong for a program with such noble intent?

Frank made a quick trip to Miami. He came storming into Mike Hollister's office without the courtesy of calling ahead or stopping by Martha Wilson's desk. He threw himself down in a chair in front of Mike and explained the predicament *The Agency* was in. He demanded to know how to corral dozens of nano insects the whereabouts of which nobody actually knows.

Mike wasted no time. He assembled the R&D team and laid out the problem. David Goldstein explained that every nano machine has a unique code. If any nano insects are in circulation they can be tracked and located by their GPS function and identified one by one. When found, each individual nano insect can be shut down or destroyed.

Frank Fletcher gasped. "Why didn't we know this?"

David responded, "Because you were in too big a hurry to produce the insects and chips and didn't ask all of the right questions. *The Agency* has always been too eager to score big without adequate information."

Frank shouted, "Well, get busy, find and shut down all stray nano insects in the Continental USA. Get on it man. Innocent people may be dying."

David and Oren began a scan for nano insects. They found none still in the wild. It seems all nano insects have injected a CR5M chip into a person or an animal. About a dozen were in Minnesota and a half dozen were in Virginia. Fortunately there were no more innocent victims. As a matter of fact there were no more victims. All of the CR5M chips were discovered in the bodies of animals.

A polar bear in the Washington DC zoo received one and several dogs and cats and a raccoon in Minneapolis were host to the remaining missing chips. Since animals are incapable of hatred, there were no more human casualties.

Mike thought, *too bad people are capable of hatred, even hatred which leads to their own destruction. It's sad that people can't be a little more like the animals.*

# CHAPTER 23

## SMART CARS SMART HIGHWAYS

Roy Durand went to work on a project which was something new for the GMH Technology. He became the lead design engineer for a smart highway to be built connecting a west coast container port with a Midwest freight terminal. Eighteen wheelers will travel across the western half of the continent with no driver aboard. East bound trucks will be controlled by a master computer in the container port in San Pedro, California. They will be loaded with cargo containers lowered from ships onto flatbed trailers. West bound trucks will be controlled by a master computer at the freight terminal near Kansas City, Kansas. Trucks and some smart cars will travel over two-thousand miles in either direction totally untouched by human hands.

The smart highway has lanes set aside solely for automated trucks. Drivers in cars and lighter vehicles will also travel on the smart road. Their vehicles will be controlled by signals from wires buried in the roadway. Drivers will enter the highway and automatically relinquish control of their vehicles. The master computer will set speeds and keep vehicles separated. Drivers will only be able to select an on and an off ramp. Drivers will be awakened and notified when they are approaching their destination.

Bobby Durand suggested to the R&D team that they

consider developing another application for highway safety which will include all vehicles, not just those traveling the new smart road system. DOT, the Department of Transportation adopted the idea and required all new vehicles to be equipped with the CR5 close proximity system and for all vehicles to be so equipped within one year.

The system will do several things for drivers and the safety of the traveling public. It filters the thoughts of all drivers while they are in transit. Any negative thoughts such as road rage will alert the computer and it will intervene when necessary. Drivers are also monitored for alertness and possible impairment.

The most unique feature is attitude adjustment. If a driver becomes irritated or angry the CR5 system will upload a new attitude into their brain, one of equanimity. In addition all insurance and licensing requirements of vehicle and driver are known to the master computer. Vehicles are tracked by GPS and their speeds adjusted to traffic and highway conditions. DOT was so impressed with beta testing that they ordered all vehicles in the USA to be equipped with the CR5 close proximity system.

DOT exercised its rights under the blanket contract with GMH Tech to take possession of, develop and deploy, systems developed by the company. The Department assigned Myles Burwell and Dennis Cottrell to develop and implement the software at the West Virginia computer center. The government hired private contractors to write the computer code which will control virtually all vehicular traffic in the United States.

Several foreign countries hired GMH Technology to install the same system in their vehicles but with one main difference. GMH programmers wrote the computer code for those projects. The first to launch the system nation-wide was a Latin American country which previously had a terrible record for traffic crashes. When the GMH system went into effect traffic accidents were reduced by over ninety percent. Most noticeable was a sharp reduction in road-rage incidents. Previously road-rage accounted for almost half of all vehicular crashes in that country. With the GMH system in place, road-rage crashes fell to near zero. The attitude adjustment feature really works.

The DOT launch date fell many months behind schedule. Myles Burwell was called to testify before a committee of the congress. During questioning he revealed that the same private contractor who provided the computer software for the prison release program was once again in charge of an expensive government program. Cost overruns ballooned the price to the taxpayers and delays were interminable. The chairman of the Transportation Committee was furious.

"Mr. Burwell, am I to understand that the same company that this government hired to roll out that disastrous prison boondoggle is now in charge of our much touted traffic control system?"

Myles responded, "Mr. Chairman that is correct."

"Mr. Burwell, how could that happen? Can you explain to this committee and to the American people who are watching everything we do on Capitol Hill, as well they should be, why this government continues to make so many dunderheaded decisions?"

"Mr. Chairman, I cannot explain the decision. It was made by someone in the DOT. We were told that the company they hired had made substantial changes to their personnel. We were also told that the company has a new owner and CEO. The former owner is now in a South American prison serving a long sentence for fraud."

"Mr. Burwell, are you aware of any political connections between the current owner and anyone in the administration?"

Myles hesitated. He cast a glance around the room.

"Mr. Burwell, I addressed a question to you. Do you have an answer sir?"

"Mr. Chairman I am unaware of any political connection between the current administration and our software contractor."

"Mr. Burwell, I would remind you that you are under oath and stand to be charged with lying to Congress if you do not tell the truth in these hearings. Do you understand sir?"

"Yes....I uh....understand."

"Well, then tell this committee if you have any knowledge of political favors or connections with the current software provider for the highway control project of which you are the manager."

"Mr. Chairman....I uh.....would like to discontinue all further questioning and stand on my rights under the Fifth Amendment not to testify."

"Very well Mr. Burwell, I can see that we will not learn the truth from you. You are dismissed. These proceedings stand adjourned."

Myles Burwell and Douglas Winslow exited the hearing room and went directly to the parking garage where they entered Douglas' Mercedes. Winslow spoke, "It's a good thing you took the Fifth Burwell. The administration will not be pleased if you let Congress find out about a few political favors and some rather large donations to the President's campaign coming from the current contractor."

Myles responded, "Doug, you're going to have to shield me from any more of these hearings. I just manage the project, I don't know nor do I care how the decision was made to hire our current software contractor."

"Myles, you stay cool. Leave the committee to me. I'll put pressure on several committee members in our party. These are members the party owns lock stock and barrel. They will do what I tell them to keep the committee off balance and away from the facts. As the saying goes, the administration knows where the bodies are buried. That is a metaphor of course, nobody is missing....at least not yet." Winslow laughed derisively.

He added, "By the way, DOT hired your lab to produce the close proximity sensors for installation in all of the nation's vehicles. How is that coming along?"

Myles responded, "We have almost enough for the entire fleet of American vehicles ready to go. My assistant Dennis Cottrell is in charge of production and distribution. Do you want to talk with him? I can get him on my cell phone."

"No, I'll leave all that technical stuff up to the two of you. Just don't screw it up. The President will not be pleased. You do understand there could be ramifications beyond your wildest imagination."

Myles Burwell returned to the West Virginia computer center. Testing was under way for the introduction of the most sweeping changes in how people travel the nation's highways. Dennis Cottrell told his colleague, "We are almost ready for Beta testing. Do you want me to announce a date and place?"

"Are you absolutely certain that the software is ready?"

"As far as we can tell, it's a go."

"Did you test the system for its ability to handle analyses for a high volume of queries? That's what brought down the prison release program. We better be absolutely certain this time that we get it right."

"Relax. I've got it covered. There will be no glitches." Cottrell assured him.

All went well for several months following the rollout of

the traffic control system. Vehicles moved smoothly along the nation's Interstate Highway System and all major secondary roads. To everyone's surprise including Myles Burwell and his team in West Virginia nothing seemed to be amiss. Everyone in DOT hoped it would continue this way.

When the nation's first automated smart road opened, trucks moved with ease and safety between the container port on the west coast and the freight terminal near Kansas City. Driverless trucks formed a virtual conveyor belt moving at seventy-five miles per hour in their dedicated lanes. Valuable cargoes moved with ease. Trucking companies sharply reduced their payrolls and increased their profitability with no need for human drivers. Fuel stops were automated as well. Trucks rolled into fuel depots and robotic pumps refilled diesel tanks in record times. All safety checks were made and trucks returned to the roadway to rejoin traffic.

Energy Department officials became interested in using the smart road to move shipments of radioactive materials. Without drivers they would no longer have to provide hazardous duty pay. Cost of shipping everything from medical isotopes to spent fuel rods to nuclear bomb materials would be sharply reduced.

An eighteen wheeler bearing the letters DOE and the universal nuclear danger symbols was jockeyed into position for the start of the first nuclear shipment to the west coast using the smart highway. The big rig rolled along without incident for the first hundred or so miles. A large black pickup truck maneuvered alongside the big rig. Two men dressed in all black and wearing ski masks, jumped from the bed of the pickup onto the moving eighteen wheeler.

With a large caliber hand gun one of the men blew out the glass on the driver's side door, then opened the door and the two climbed into the cab. One of the men turned off the automated system guiding the truck and took over manually. The second hijacker disconnected all monitoring equipment including the GPS and the close proximity system. At the next off ramp the nuclear cargo hauler disappeared into the night.

The government's smart highway management system in the super computer in West Virginia failed to sound an alarm. The software was designed to track and adjust the movements of trucks in both directions via the terminal computers at each end of the line. Their departures and arrivals were scheduled, but the possibility that a vehicle's tracking system would suddenly stop working and a truck would simply disappear had not been considered by the government's software contractor.

Frank Fletcher's phone rang in his Washington office.

"Frank, this is Doug Winslow, the administration has a huge problem and you need to solve it before the media finds out about it."

"What's up Doug?"

"Frank, a load of nuclear material disappeared last night somewhere in Kansas. The West Virginia computer center only became aware of it when the truck failed to make a fuel stop in New Mexico. For some reason the computer didn't sound a warning when the truck left the smart highway. We're looking into the glitch, but that doesn't help us find the missing nuclear material. This stuff is hot. It could be used to make dirty bombs and wipe out whole cities."

"Doug, we have to find and retrieve that material. I'll get right on it."

"Thanks Frank, the administration is counting on *The Agency* to get the job done."

Frank Fletcher lost no time. He assembled a group headed by Ari Mackenzie and Kurt Rinehart. These two were given the task to bring to a safe close a so-far unannounced critical safety problem for the USA, not to mention a thorny political problem for the administration.

Ari briefed her team. "If the truck is anywhere in the open it won't be hard to spot from the air. It has large letters DOE painted in yellow on top of the trailer and cab. It also has the universal three bladed radioactive symbols in several places on the top and sides of the trailer and the cab. We will begin with an air search starting at its last known location. We will fly a search grid from there in the four cardinal directions. Hopefully we can find the truck in the open before the cargo disappears."

Kurt took over the briefing and assigned teams to fly together, some in fixed wing aircraft and others in helicopters.

People in Central Kansas were told by the media that these were simply routine military exercises. For two weeks there was no sign of the truck.

Ari recalled that GMH Technology had sold and installed all of the existing close proximity systems in state, county, and local police vehicles. The system allows police officers to read the thoughts of anyone taken into custody and held even briefly in a patrol vehicle or a station holding cell.

Ari and Kurt began canvassing all police agencies for any possible clues which might be gained from brain scans. At each agency they ran a rapid data scan filtering all thoughts which were found on local computer servers. At one small town sheriff's office they seemed to hit pay dirt.

The recorded thoughts and conversation between a deputy and a local woman named Gracie Norman revealed that Gracie had seen something peculiar on the night the truck disappeared. Gracie had been stopped for a missing headlight on her pickup. The deputy gave her a warning ticket and told her to get it fixed. Gracie's thoughts while she sat in the patrol car indicated that she may have witnessed a hijacking. She hadn't told the deputy about it, but her thoughts were captured in the deputy's close proximity recorder.

Ari and Kurt paid a visit to the small town diner where Gracie worked. A slight woman in her forties stood behind the lunch counter. Seeing the two enter the establishment, she quickly wiped her hands on her grease-stained apron and turned to face the newcomers.

“What can I get you folks?”

Ari opened the conversation, “Hi, are your Gracie Norman?”

She grinned. “That depends on who wants to know?”

“I’m Ariana MacKenzie and this is Kurt Rinehart. We are looking for a Ms. Gracie Norman to ask a few questions about a truck hijacking which took place on the new smart highway a couple of weeks ago.”

“Well, why would anybody think I had anything to do with a hijacked truck? I don’t know a thing about it, so you folks can be on your way.”

Kurt interjected, “Relax Gracie, we don’t think you had anything to do with the hijacking, just that you may have seen or heard something which could help us find the missing truck.”

A calmer Gracie responded, “Well, in that case I’ll tell you what I saw. By the way, are you folks from the insurance company?”

Ari responded, “You might say that. We just want the rightful owners to have their property returned.”

Two men entered and took seats at the far end of the lunch counter. They ordered the lunch special with iced tea. Gracie took their order, served them their tea and then returned to the conversation with Kurt and Ari.

“Well the night you speak of I was driving on the new smart road and I saw something very strange. Some guys were standing up in the bed of a pickup truck. Everybody knows that is not only dangerous, but it is also against the law in Kansas. The truck pulled alongside a big rig and in my rearview mirror it looked like those two idiots in the back of the pickup jumped onto that big rig. The rig sped up and passed me and a little way ahead it turned off at an exit ramp. I thought that was strange because the driverless trucks are supposed to stay in their lane and are supposed to stay at the same speed all the time."

Ari smiled, "Gracie, can you tell us which exit ramp the truck took?"

"No, I don't actually remember. I was preoccupied and can't really remember."

There was a stir at the other end of the counter. The two men who ordered lunch didn't seem to have any appetite. They rose from their seats, dropped a twenty dollar bill between their unfinished plates and hurried out the door to the parking lot.

Kurt asked, "Gracie, do you have the required CR5 close proximity system in your truck?"

"Well, yes I do. I was forced to install it when the law took effect. I can't imagine why we need some of these fool things the government comes up with, but yes, I spent a month's tips to have it installed. Those politicians in Washington don't have any appreciation for how hard it is for some of us folks out here in the heartland to afford to comply with all the insane laws they pass. If they had to work as hard as we do they might appreciate common folks like me."

Ari asked, "Would you mind if I take a look at your pickup? Is it the red one I see parked just outside the rear door?"

"Well, I don't know why anyone would want to look at my little truck. There isn't anything special about it. It's ten years old and got a few scratches here and there. But if it will make you happy, go ahead. Take a look."

Ari excused herself from the conversation and left the restaurant for a few minutes. When she returned she thanked Gracie for the information and motioned for Kurt to leave. Kurt pulled his wallet out and pressed a hundred dollar bill into Gracie's hand."

"What's this for? Mister, you didn't even have lunch, why the big tip?"

"Gracie, we both appreciate you. You will never know just how much."

Back in their rented SUV Ari told Kurt that when she left the restaurant and stepped outside she ran a rapid scan of Gracie's CR5 sensor recorder in her pickup. What she found were Gracie's subconscious musings recorded in the CR5 monitoring sensors backup memory. Gracie's optical observations revealed the license number of the hijacker's pickup and the location of the off ramp where the hijacked DOE truck left the smart highway.

Kurt smiled, "Gracie's observations were retained in the CR5 system even when they were not retained in her brain's prefrontal cortex. So it is possible that the CR5 system can be accessed to restore memory which may be temporarily forgotten. We should tell Chun Li and Maria about this phenomenon in case they haven't already discovered it for themselves.

Ari smiled, "We will share this with them later. Right now we need to find a load of nuclear material that has gone astray. Thanks to Gracie we now have a lead."

# CHAPTER 24

# STRAY NUKES

Ari's cell phone sounded an incoming call.

"Hello."

"Ari, this is Maria Hollister. Sorry to bother you in the midst of your search for the missing truck, but there is something you need to know."

"What's that Maria?"

"Our company, GMH Technology, sold RFID tracking chips to the NNSA, the National Nuclear Security Administration. Each individual nuclear container should be tagged with one of those chips. You can access them through our cloud server with a discrete code. Shall I upload the code to you?"

"Absolutely. But why weren't we told by the DOE about the existence of these tracking chips? It makes no sense."

"I don't know Ari, but you may be able to find the hijacked load by tracking the GPS location of the individual containers. I'm not sure if the DOE had the foresight to tag the truck itself with one of our chips, but if they did, then you can find the rig by its individual ID. Good luck and good hunting."

"Maria, I suppose you and Mike are tracking the two of us just as you did when we were held by MI5 in London. We're grateful to you for your assistance in that situation, and in this one as well. Thanks. We'll keep you apprised of our progress."

She laughed, "On second thought we won't need to will we? You and Mike are watching us wherever we go."

Maria chuckled, "That's about it. We love sharing your adventures, and hope you both stay safe. Call on us if you need us. We are always here to help."

Frank Fletcher received an encrypted text message from Ariana MacKenzie. Find out why we were not told that NNSA purchased and may have used RFID chips to identify and track each nuclear container. Need the info ASAP.

A return text informed Ari that Department of Transportation officials were so eager to prove that the smart highway could safely move nuclear shipments across the country that they did not communicate with the DOE and its internal agency the NNSA to learn how the materials could be tracked. The NNSA was kept in the dark about the missing shipment. Lack of coordination between federal agencies was once again exposing the nation to security risks.

Frank Fletcher informed Douglas Winslow of the current situation. Winslow and the administration were not pleased to say the least. Winslow told Frank that someone has to take the fall for this screw up, and it would not be someone on the political side, but more likely someone in the bureaucracy. Perhaps even Frank himself.

Kurt drove slowly along a Kansas secondary road as Ari began tracking the individual RFID chips attached to the missing nuclear containers.

"I've got a fix on a place about fourteen miles from here. Turn left at the next intersection and follow a county road for three miles and then stop."

"Slow down Kurt, we are coming to the turn. Make a left onto that gravel road ahead."

Kurt turned down a dusty gravel path just wide enough for an eighteen wheeler and not much more. On either side of the road wheat fields extended to the horizon. A brisk Kansas breeze moved the wheat stalks like ocean waves. About a mile ahead lay a cluster of buildings including a large barn with a corrugated metal roof. Kurt slowed the SUV to a crawl.

"Do you think our hijacked eighteener may be in that barn?"

Ari responded, "A good place to hide a truck. Look at the height and width of that door."

No one was in sight. Kurt slowly pulled the SUV to a stop in front of the barn. An ancient dwelling house sat about fifty yards away. Parked beside it was a black pickup truck with a license matching the one seen by Gracie Norman on the night of the hijacking.

"Looks like we've found the pickup. Let's go see if the big rig is in the barn."

Kurt and Ari exited the SUV and approached the barn.

A voice called out from behind them. "What brings you folks out this way?"

Kurt and Ari turned to face a man holding a pump

shotgun pointed directly toward them.

Ari answered. “We are antique vehicle collectors and sometimes we find some really great old cars and trucks in barns like this one. Didn’t mean to trespass. We thought the house was unoccupied by its appearance. We should have knocked and asked permission to look around before we approached your barn.”

“Well there ain’t no antiques on this place. You might just as well get back in your vehicle and go back the way you came.” He lowered the shotgun slightly. “Didn’t mean to frighten you folks, but we’ve had a lot of thievery goin’ on around here. People stealing farm machinery and such. City people think they can grab some stuff, sell it and buy drugs. Been goin’ on for some time and we’re tired of it. Hope you understand.”

Ari responded, “Certainly sir, no problem.” She handed him a false business card. “If you have any neighbors who might have some antique vehicles they want to sell, have them give us a call. We always appreciate good leads. Well, we’ll be on our way sir. Sorry to cause you any worry about theft. Have a great day.”

On the way back to the main road, Kurt said, “Did you recognize that guy? He was one of the two men we saw in the diner when we were talking with Gracie. You are a smooth operator. I probably would’ve tried to disarm that guy and force him to open the barn. We know darn well that eighteen wheeler is in that building. We are getting returns from the RFID chips on the nuclear containers. At least it appears from most of them."

Ari responded, "Most of them. That's true, and that is something to be very concerned about. We didn't get returns from all of them. We are going to have to get inside that barn and inventory the entire load. Let's stop here. We have other ways to get inside that building."

Kurt pulled off the road into the edge of a wheat field about a mile from the farmstead. Ari pulled a canister from the console. "There is more than one way to do reconnaissance." She pulled the lid off the canister and released a host of nano machines including mosquitoes and dragon flies.

As they watched the afternoon sun drift toward the horizon, Ari manipulated the nano machine insects to the farmstead. Luckily the Kansas breeze was blowing in the right direction. She sent dozens of mechanical insects into the barn through a high level open window. There on their cell phone screen sat the hijacked truck replete with its markings DOE and the nuclear danger symbols.

Kurt said, "No wonder the dude met us with a shotgun. He couldn't afford to have us go inside the barn and see that truck. Well, now we know where the truck is hidden, but what of the nuclear containers? How many of them can we track?"

Ari responded, "Not enough of them. Out of the twenty four that were shipped, there are only twenty one still in the truck. I'm going to send some nano mosquitoes into the house along with some other insects and see if I can plant a CR5M chip into either or both of those hijackers."

For the next twenty minutes Ari and Kurt controlled a swarm of little mechanical creatures around the house to find any openings. A man opened the kitchen door and stood on the rear step for a long moment. That is all it took. A swarm of little nano creatures winged their way inside above the man's head. He swatted at them but to no avail. They were just too fast and maneuvered around his flailing hand.

Within minutes Ari maneuvered mosquitoes onto the necks of the two hijackers. CR5M chips were quickly inserted into their flesh. Kurt opened a discreet channel to each hijacker and began monitoring their thoughts and recorded everything within their field of vision. Kurt and Ari gave each other a high five.

The hijackers were talking about their motive for taking the truck and its cargo. They revealed that they were hired by a union organizer to disrupt the use of driverless trucks on the smart highway. They chose a nuclear load to make a point. They wanted to show the nation that driverless trucks could not be trusted to safely deliver any cargo, let alone one so dangerous to public safety. In their discussion they revealed that they had sold three containers to some guys from Minneapolis. They had no idea what the people could possibly want with nuclear stuff, but what difference did it make? After all they raked in a bonus from their crime over and above what the union organizer paid them.

Ari and Kurt sent an encrypted message to Frank Fletcher. Within an hour sixteen helicopters descended on the farmstead. A swat team blasted the hijackers through the CR5M chips ability to induce a taser-like shock to both sides of the face. Their trigeminal nerves incapacitated the two almost instantly. The swat team entered the farmhouse unopposed. People from NNSA took control of the hijacked truck and removed it from the premises. At least most of the load and the truck were now back in government hands. But where were the three containers sold to the people from Minnesota?

Ari and Kurt, working with a team from NNSA began a search for the missing containers. Using discrete channels by way of a geosynchronous satellite they discovered that the missing containers had gone in three directions. One was in Colorado, another in Illinois, and a third one was in the borough of Queens in New York. Teams from the NNSA quickly fanned out to those locations.

The container in Queens was quickly located and retrieved. It had not been unsealed and the RFID chip was still attached. Several Somali young men were taken into custody. Upon questioning it was learned that they were but one team of terrorists bent upon creating a dirty bomb. It was their mission to contaminate the New York metropolitan area. Their scheme was not very far along when it was detected and broken up, but nevertheless it had been set in motion.

Another NNSA team located an RFID tracking chip in a field outside Chicago. No container was anywhere to be found. Evidently whoever had the container realized that this little chip on the side was not to be trusted. The NNSA team retrieved the chip and identified it as coming from one of the missing containers.

Maria and Mike busied themselves scanning all possible news stories from the regions where the two containers were still missing. They came up with several stories of interest. In Illinois a highway construction site lost an unknown quantity of blasting caps and blasting powder. A shed was broken open the previous night by burglars who seemed only interested in explosives. A storage locker at O'Hare International Airport was pillaged. About a dozen weather balloons were taken along with helium canisters. Authorities could not explain who on earth would want to steal weather balloons and helium unless it was a teenage prank. A hobby shop suffered the loss of a number of model radio control systems. And last but not least a forty-two foot motor yacht was stolen from a Chicago marina on Lake Michigan.

Mike called Ari's cell phone and relayed this information to her. They agreed that if someone wanted to destroy an American city with a dirty bomb, these were certainly some of the ingredients needed. If these items were not retrieved quickly, Chicago might very well suffer horrendous casualties from a WMD, a weapon of mass destruction, and become completely uninhabitable.

Putting this information together, the Coast Guard concentrated on finding the stolen motor yacht. A few hours into the search, three young Somali men were apprehended aboard the stolen boat just east of Chicago. They had in their possession the missing nuclear material strapped together with blasting powder, blasting caps and a radio receiver to ignite the explosives. An explosion would pulverize and spread the nuclear load into the wind. When caught they were just beginning to inflate the first of the stolen weather balloons, one of four they intended to use to take the load aloft over Lake Michigan upwind from the Windy City.

The stolen motor yacht was isolated for decontamination as were the three Somali terrorists when taken into custody. The three would-be terrorists were already showing signs of radiation sickness. The Coast Guardsmen and their vessel were isolated for their own safety. Chicago escaped a horrible fate. Mike and Maria Hollister were proud of their part in putting this puzzle together.

Two of the three missing nuclear containers were now accounted for. Where was the third? Its RFID tracking chip placed it in the Denver area. Just as in the Chicago plot, the tracking chip was found without the container. It lay in the grass alongside Interstate 70 just east of the suburban city of Aurora, Colorado.

Once again, Mike and Maria set to work searching for news of unusual thefts of materials to make a dirty bomb. Evidently the Somali terrorists were using a similar method of operation. A road construction site in Kansas lost a quantity of explosives and blasting caps. There was no sign of any theft of model radio control devices, weather balloons, or helium containers. It appeared that the terrorists had a slightly different approach in mind.

Federal authorities put out the word about two Somali terrorist plots and encouraged all local and state police to be on the lookout for any sign of Somali men in unusual situations. The Denver Police were called to Denver General Hospital to interview a Somali man who came to the Emergency Department with what appeared to be serious radiological burns over his hands and face. The man was isolated in the radiological department in a shielded room. It was obvious that he was in dire straits. He was crying and sobbing when the police arrived.

A police lieutenant donned lead shielded clothing and entered the room. The young Somali man said his name was Muhammad Yasin and that his older brother forced him to get involved in what turned out to be a very dangerous and deadly plot. He told the police interrogator that they constructed two dirty bombs. He begged to be cured from is burns. He said that the location of the bombs were hidden in rocky outcroppings in Clear Creek Canyon, and Bear Creek Canyon west of Denver.

The bombs were to be exploded by cell phone calls when Chinook Winds were expected to begin in a day or two. The Chinook Winds would spread deadly radiation to most of the Denver Metro area.

Ari and Kurt flew to Denver landing at Denver International Airport. They got a rental SUV and headed straight to the hospital where Muhammad was being held in isolation. His brother was still not in custody. Their primary concern at the moment was that the Chinook Winds might begin soon. There was no time to lose. Ari talked a nurse into giving Muhammad a shot with syringe loaded with a CR5M chip. It worked. Muhammad's thoughts revealed the exact location of the two dirty bombs as well as the motel on East Colfax Avenue where his brother was staying.

A swat team arrested Abdul Yasin at a cheap motel in Aurora. He too was suffering from radiological burns about his hands and face. The swat team seized a dozen cell phones along with receipts for their purchase from a local big box store. The receipts were dated just one day prior to the raid.

Now to find and defuse the dirty bombs. Fortunately the CR5M chip inserted into Muhammad did its duty revealing the exact location of the two bombs. Nuclear cleanup crews with hazmat gear found the bombs exactly where Muhammad's thought stream revealed them to be. Once again GMH Technology played a major role in preventing the death of millions and preventing three of the nation's major cities from becoming uninhabitable wastelands.

Kurt and Ari paid a visit to GMH Technology to thank Mike and Maria for their role in stopping this near disaster. They shared a private dinner at the Hollister high rise residence overlooking Biscayne Bay. These four were bonding like brothers and sisters. They wondered, what else could possibly threaten the human race. They hoped that technology would be used for the good of mankind and not for destructive purposes.

## CHAPTER 25

## REACHING OUT

Oren and David were unusually quiet at the beginning of the morning conference with Mike Hollister. Mike was a bit puzzled by their demeanor.

"What's with you guys this morning? You both look so serious."

Oren answered, "Mike we've just learned that a Swedish scientist discovered a method to detect brain waves from great distances. From much greater distances than any we or the British ever imagined possible."

David added, "The guy's name is Lars Lundquist and he has a private laboratory near Uppsala, Sweden.

"Are Chun Li and Maria aware of this development?"

"I don't know Mike. We just learned about it this morning. How do you think this will impact our work?"

Mike responded, "I'm not sure, but I suppose I ought to find out how far this fellow has progressed."

When the meeting ended, Mike returned to his office and established a video call to Lars Lundquist."

"Mr. Lundquist, please allow me to introduce myself. I am Mike Hollister owner of GMH Technology in the USA. How are you this afternoon? I hope I'm not disturbing your dinner hour."

"No Mr. Hollister, we haven't started dinner yet. How

are you? I have heard of you from many sources. I am honored to receive your call. What can I do for you?"

"Mr. Lundquist we may be able to work together on some research projects of mutual interest. I can't discuss them on a non-secure video call. May I come and visit you at your location?"

"Of course Mr. Hollister. I would be delighted to meet you and show you some of the things we no doubt have in common."

"Mr. Lundquist, how would it be if I come to visit two days from now?"

"Delightful Mr. Hollister. Delightful I'm sure. Please come for a visit. When you arrive at the airport in Stockholm someone from our lab will meet you there. I look forward to your visit."

Mike lost no time arranging the trip to Sweden. He called Maria at the Institute.

"Sis, how would you like to make your first overseas flight? I need to go to Stockholm with a few of our people from the company."

Maria was quick to respond. "Great Mike. When do you want to go?"

"Day after tomorrow if you can arrange it."

"OK, I'll give Brad and Emiliano a call and ask them if they would like to come along for the ride." She chuckled as she knew she would need these veteran pilots for their expertise.

Both had flown international routes for years. This would be Maria's first ever flight overseas. She eagerly looked forward to the experience.

Mike assembled a group of his most trusted business and technical people from GMH Technology for the journey to Sweden. He chose David and Oren to represent the technical side of the company, and Alicia Byers, Beverly Talbot, and Cassie Phelps to represent the business side.

Mike had in mind to either purchase the Swedish lab or hire its most advanced researchers or to form an international partnership. For this effort he would need his best business, financial and technical personnel.

The group assembled at Opa-Locka Executive Airport early on the morning of departure. They boarded the company's brand new Boeing 737. It was configured as an executive airplane. The interior was not at all like an airliner. It features private dressing rooms with sleeping facilities and their own lavatories. In the open areas there are work stations, and plush sofas and seats.

Maria taxied the aircraft from the parking area to the end of the active runway. The tower gave clearance for immediate takeoff. She advanced the power levers and the group were airborne in a matter of seconds. She pointed the aircraft out over the Atlantic and set up a course directly to Newfoundland.

Weather was good all the way to St. John's, Newfoundland. There they took on fuel for the trans-Atlantic flight directly to Stockholm, Sweden. Maria, Emiliano, and Brad took turns flying from the left seat as PIC or pilot in command. Maria was adding hours to her log book as PIC on her first international flight.

Maria handled radio traffic reporting to controllers as they passed just south of Reykjavik Iceland on a course which would soon take them over Norway and into Swedish airspace. She again handled the radio reporting to Norwegian controllers at a flight control center near Oslo.

Upon approach to Stockholm's Arlanda Airport, Maria concentrated on flying and left the radio traffic to Brad Bailey. A brisk wind was blowing from the south. She passed the airport to the south, flew a left downwind leg and touched down on runway one-nine left. The control tower voice crackled in the overhead speaker.

"Boeing 737 turn right at the first convenient taxiway and proceed to the designated parking area for business aircraft. Contact ground control on one-two-one point seven. Good day."

With the new Boeing's engines in reverse thrust it was easy for Maria to make the first high-speed exit off the active runway. She taxied the aircraft to a parking area set aside for private jets.

It didn't take long to meet someone from the Swedish lab. Lars Lundquist himself approached and shook hands all around. He led the GMH group to a large van waiting on the other side of the hangar. From the airport at Arlanda they took the E4 Motorway and headed north. Lars turned to the right off the E4 onto highway 77 and proceeded several miles into a beautiful forested region.

At the end of a dirt lane Lars stopped the van in front of a row of older cabins. A lady emerged from one of the bungalows. Lars introduced his wife Lisa Lundquist who shook hands all around. Lisa took the ladies aside and showed them to their cabin. Lars took the men to another cabin. Each cabin was sparsely equipped with bunk beds, a small bathroom and kitchen along one wall. It was obvious that this place had once been a tourist haven for city people from Stockholm and Uppsala. Now it was a private property used by a couple bent on discovering some of the great secrets of science.

When everyone was settled in, Lisa invited the group to dinner in the crowded little cottage she and her husband refurbished and which they now call home. They proudly showed before and after photos recalling the work they put in to turn a rundown tourist lodge into a combination home and science lab.

Lars took Mike, Oren, and David to a shed behind his home. Here he showed them his science lab. He told them that his experiments up to now had been quite successful in reading human brain waves at a great distance.

David asked, "Just how great a distance have you achieved?"

Without hesitation Lars responded, "Hundreds, even

thousands of miles."

Mike, David, and Oren fell into stunned silence. They looked at one another and back to Lars. Mike spoke, "Sir, with all due respect, can you show us proof?"

Lars turned to a panel of instruments arrayed along the back wall of his lab. "Here," he said, "I will turn on the array, and we will see what is coming in right now. I have an antenna array on a tower a few feet behind this building. I have been able to receive brain waves from several different countries."

A flat panel lit up. Lars adjusted the intensity of the display. What appeared on screen astounded the GMH group. The output was in Russian and appeared to be from the brain of someone in charge of a factory in the vicinity of St. Petersburg in the north of Russia. A conversation was taking place with a subordinate about some missing items from the factory. As they followed the conversation the factory supervisor became more and more agitated. He finally told the subordinate that he would be placed under arrest if he showed up at the plant again.

Mike was skeptical. He questioned Lars. "How do we know that this is not just a recording you made to impress visitors?"

Lars responded. "You have every right to question the technology. I find it hard to believe myself. What I have not yet succeeded in doing is to pick out an individual and tune in solely on that one person. I seem to pick up brain waves at random, much like tuning around the radio spectrum and finding different stations."

Oren spoke up. "What we need to do to make this discovery serve a good purpose is to be able to pick and choose which person we want to tune in."

David added, "I believe Oren and I might be able to write a computer algorithm which could make that possible."

Lars responded, "Now that is what would refine my discovery and make it practical. Do you really think you could do that?"

"No promises Mr. Lundquist, but we can always try. Give us a few hours or a day or two and we will see what we can come up with."

Lars conducted the group back to his small cottage. There they gathered and shared conversation over beverages far into the night.

When daylight came David and Oren were up early. They worked around the clock writing and re-writing computer code. Finally at the end of the second day they called Lars and Mike together.

David began, "It appears that brain waves from each individual have distinctive characteristics. Perhaps we can think of it as a kind of cerebral DNA. We spent time downloading previously recorded brain output from the GMH cloud server and this characteristic seems to stand out. Oren has come up with a possible way to capture and identify specific individual's brain wave output. I'll let him explain."

"We believe that we can use data compression when capturing brain waves from a great distance. We can run compressed data packets through a filter and identify the individuals from whom they are received. We also found that using Lars' receiver we can pick up and record tens of thousands of individuals. With data compression we believe we will be able to pick up and differentiate whole populations."

David took up the explanation again. "What this suggests is that whole populations may be contacted by way of a modification of our CR5 system with its ability to see and hear. We also may be able to upload information into huge numbers of people at the same time. We can likely do this using data compression and microwave radio propagation as a conduit. Can you imagine what this could lead to? We could teach whole populations new skills. We could plant what amounts to an education into the brains of millions of people at the same time. This is truly revolutionary."

Lars was astounded at these suggestions. He said, "I had no idea what my discovery might offer to the human race, but I am thrilled at the prospect. Perhaps this could lead to world peace in a way in which mankind has never known it. We can only hope."

Mike urged everyone to keep this discovery totally secret. He suggested to Lars and Lisa that tomorrow they could enter into discussions for a business arrangement.

Mike decided to go for a walk along a forest trail leading

down to a nearby lake. He liked to be alone at times to think more clearly. When he arrived at the edge of the lake he found Maria, Alicia, Beverly, and Cassie standing on the shore watching the moon come up on the opposite side casting a golden glow across the water.

They talked for a while about nothing in particular. They just shared their feelings about this pristine place, the beauty of the scene and their recent trans-Atlantic flight. The young ladies started back toward the cabins.

Mike thought he was alone. He was surprised to see that Cassie Phelps remained behind and was standing almost beside him. They made small talk for a time and then fell silent. Mike moved closer to Cassie and had the urge to put his arm around her shoulders. He had felt this way many times before, but always avoided the temptation. Tonight was different. Here he was with one of the most popular girls from his high school days. He had to admit to himself that this was a rare opportunity to make a move if he was ever going to.

He recalled Cassie's thoughts from the time at Hollister Island. He wondered if she still felt the way she seemed to when she stood looking at his sleeping form. Mike inched closer. He put out his arm and rested it on Cassie's shoulders.

"It's kind of chilly out here at night, even in the summer time."

Cassie responded, "As a matter of fact Mike it is. But that could change."

Mike instantly recognized a golden opportunity. He turned slowly toward Cassie looking directly into her upturned face. He thought, *it's now or never Mike, get it on or forget it."*

Mike did not hesitate. He kissed Cassie on the lips and held her firmly in his arms. She did not resist but folded herself into his caress.

The next morning Mike met with Lars and his business staff. Cassie was all business along with Alicia and Beverly. It was as if nothing had transpired between Mike and Cassie the evening before. They both knew that an office romance could have unforeseen repercussions.

GMH Technology agreed to pay for the rights to use the patents already owned by Lars Lundquist. They also agreed to buy his property and to hire Lars and incorporate his lab into GMH holdings as a Swedish subsidiary.

On the return flight from Stockholm to Opa-Locka, David, Oren, and Mike shared their thoughts about what this new technology might mean for the good of humanity. They also realize that it can be used for nefarious purposes. They expressed optimism about the future and pledged to try and steer technology in a positive direction.

In time we will all come to know the full impact of brain wave technology. This is the beginning, not the end of our long voyage of discovery.

**END OF THIS EPISODE**

## About the Author

Carroll Williams is a retired college professor. He began his working career selling newspapers on the streets of Ft. Lauderdale, Florida at the age of eight. In his teen years he baled hay on a farm, worked in grocery stores, washed dishes in a restaurant, unloaded fishing boats on the Miami River, and worked in maintenance at a Miami Beach hotel. Carroll has been a salesman at a Ford dealership, an aircraft mechanic, aircraft electrician, and electronic flight control technician. He earned his bachelor's degree in history at the University of Miami, and his master's degree in history at the University of Denver.

Carroll is a veteran of the United States Air Force. During the Korean War, he worked on the flight line on the B-29 bomber in Strategic Air Command and later maintained an F-86D fighter interceptor in Air Defense Command. Carroll and his wife Mary worked in the Aerospace industry for the Boeing Company early in their marriage. Mary was a flight test data transcriber for the Boeing 707 airliner project. The 707 was the world's first commercially successful jetliner. Carroll worked in electronics first at Boeing on the early models of the B-52 bomber, and later for Convair Division of General Dynamics on the B-58 bomber program.

At various times in his twenty-nine year teaching career

Carroll taught American History, Western Civilization, Modern Russian History, Aerospace History, and History of the Republic of Mexico. He purchased one of the first IBM personal computers and taught himself computer programming. He used this skill to enhance his teaching by writing and selling educational software. Carroll followed his teaching career working as a computer systems analyst for the Georgia Department of Family and Children's Services serving twenty-three counties across South Georgia.

Carroll and his wife Mary have traveled extensively throughout North America, and Europe. They traveled in a VW camper on the highways and byways of forty-nine states, Canada, Alaska, and throughout Mexico as far south as the Isthmus of Tehuantepec. Over the years, they visited seventeen countries concentrating on getting to know the people and their customs.

Email: authorcarrollwilliams@gmail.com

This book is available in print from:

CreateSpace.com and Amazon.com

and for Kindle and E-Readers from Amazon.com

Made in the USA
San Bernardino, CA
29 April 2018